# Broken
# Dolls

## by
## L. T. Bartiromo

I

ISBN: 978-0-578-13008-8

# Broken Dolls

Broken Dolls website is:
http://www.MagicWavesMedia.com

The author is available for book club discussions and interviews.
The author, L. T. Bartiromo, may be emailed at:
MagicWavesMedia@gmail.com

Printed by lulu.com

# Dedication

"Broken Dolls" is dedicated to all the abused Men, Women, & Children, and those who help them.

A message from the author!

"Broken Dolls" is a departure from my previous books. Where my "Confidant Trilogy" was a collection of romance books that could be read by men or women, "Broken Dolls" begins as a mystery and ends as a tale of a marriage gone horribly wrong.

This is a book independent of the "Confidant Trilogy," but I used characters from that line of stories to populate "Broken Dolls." I was never quite satisfied with the way I wrapped up Xian's fate and Dagmar was intriguing but I could not explore her more in my last book. "Broken Dolls" gave me a way to grow and expand these two underutilized characters.

While "Broken Dolls" stands on it's own, reading the "Confidant Trilogy" gives a more complete view of the background of almost all the characters in this book. I recommend reading that series first, or go to it if you are interested in any of the characters in "Broken Dolls."

Either way, thank-you for buying this book! I hope you have as much fun reading it as I had writing it. I also hope you write me about this, or any of my books, at MagicWavesMedia@gmail.com.


L. T. Bartiromo

# Contents:

"I've Lost the Use of my
Heart,
        but I'm...
                Still Alive..."

*"Soldier of Love"*
from the album
*"Soldier of Love"*
by Sade

x

# *Chapter One*

# Assignment

Her Porsche convertible was seven years old but looked new as it tore its way through highway traffic. The pilot of the well-maintained vehicle was late for an important meeting at her practice. The longish, pixie style cut, danced on her head until she found her exit and slowed to a glide. Woman and machine worked in smooth concert to arrive at the psychiatric practice of Kane & Teasdale. Scooping up her shoulder bag and travel portfolio, the woman left her car and entered the office. Even though she was rushed, the African-American lady looked beautiful, relaxed, and composed as she walked to the reception desk.

"Good morning, Doctor Lamont," the twenty year old Hispanic receptionist greeted.

"Good morning, Harmony. Are the witches in the conference room?"

"You're the last to arrive."

Handing her travel portfolio to Harmony, the doctor said, "Here are my receipts and my report is on the thumb drive."

"I'll post everything on the server. Coffee, Doctor Lamont?"

"Thanks. Dark and sweet."

Feeling she was being watched, the doctor turned. A good-looking and familiar man in the waiting area stood up. The thirty-five year old heartthrob had brown hair, brown eyes, and a winning, boyish smile. "Hi, Dagmar."

"Hey, Rich!" Dagmar Lamont said as she returned the smile. "Long time no see. How are your wife and daughter?"

"They're doing fine."

"And how's my future husband, George?"

Rich clarified, "You mean my eighteen month old son?"

"If he stays as sweet as he is… I'll wait for him. I'd love to chat but I'm late for a meeting with some important client."

"I know. I'm the 'important client'."

"You? The most stable guy in the world? Now I'm interested! I'd better get in the conference room before they boil me in oil. See you in a few minutes."

The beautiful doctor walked into the large meeting room and was greeted by stares from her colleagues. In the first chair, looking tired, was her best friend Anabelle Loomis. Next to Anabelle, first day back from maternity leave, was Jane Teasdale. Beside Jane was a stern-looking Candace Kane. Keeping an eye on everyone from the corner of the room was their office manager, Suzy Cohen.

"You're late!" Candace snapped.

"My flight was delayed," Dagmar said brushing off the question and then turning to Jane. "Welcome back to work Sexy Mama! How's the baby?"

Smiling broadly Jane said, "He's a little dream come true."

"And how are YOU?"

"I'm good. First day back at work. I miss Nicky junior already."

Dagmar looked at Anabelle. "You okay?"

"Tired," was her only response.

The receptionist walked into the room and handed Dagmar her coffee. As she was leaving, Candace said to Harmony, "Send in the client, that is, if Doctor Lamont can get her ass in a seat."

Dagmar sat beside her boss and with pseudo exuberance said, "I missed you so much this weekend!"

The door opened and Rich Sedgwick entered. The handsome man walked to the conference table and stood in front of the four doctors. "Ladies, I want to get right down to business. To different degrees, you all know my wife. What some of you don't know is that she is one of several very… special sisters. The oldest sister, Xian, has just gotten a divorce from a businessman in Japan. She came back to the Connecticut yesterday and she's staying with us… but there's something wrong with her. Where the other sisters are energetic, 'type-A' personalities, Xian is completely introverted. She doesn't speak, or eat unless told to do so, and we don't know why. Any questions about her former marriage are sidestepped. While Xian has been quiet and reserved since she was a young girl, she has never been this badly withdrawn. My wife, Talia, is heartsick about her sister. Since Tally is pregnant with twins, I want to place Xian in therapy as soon as possible to ease her mind. Jane, you and Candace have worked miracles with my daughter and wife. I know you're all overworked but I'm hoping one of you will have the time to diagnose and treat Xian."

Immediately, Jane said, "Rich, you can count on us to help."

Rich smiled at his neighbor and lifelong friend. "Thanks, Jane. Thanks all of you. I just want to mention two things. You all know that my wife and I have a few bucks so money is no object. Second, since my sister-in-law has been abused since she was a child, I don't want her treated with 'tough love.' No angry words. My wife and I feel that she's been through too much trauma already. That said, you may handle her as you wish. Any time. Day or night. Move in if you want. There's plenty of room at our home, a gourmet kitchen and a full gym. We have more information about Xian for the therapist who will work with her." Rich glanced at his watch. "I have another meeting but I can cancel or clear my day if you need any more from me."

"I think we're all set for now," Jane said, looking around the table for confirmation from her colleagues. "We'll call you before the end of business today."

Rich smiled and left the conference room. When the door closed, Candace scolded, "Did you have to agree to take on the patient without discussing it with the rest of us?"

"The Sedgwick family means a lot to Kane & Teasdale," Jane replied. "I'll treat her."

Anabelle piped up, "Jane, I took your patients while you were on maternity leave and I was hoping you'd take them back. I've been juggling all of our clients while you and Candace were out having your babies."

3

"She's right," Candace added. "Anabelle is overloaded. Jane, I had my baby three months before you, and I'm still having a difficult time getting back in the swing of things. You're going to be overwhelmed between your new son and the job!"

Standing, Dagmar announced, "This is all fascinating but... I've gotta go."

"Maybe we wouldn't be so overworked if you contributed a little more," Candace growled.

"Oh? I don't contribute?" Dagmar questioned as she handed Candace a business card.

"What's this?"

"Our latest patient! That's what I was doing in L.A."

Candace raised her eyebrows and said quietly, "I love his movies."

"Look," Dagmar continued, "I caught the red eye into Kennedy and spend the entire flight catching up on my expenses. I drove like a bat-out-of-hell to make this meeting and now, after a lunch date, I'm going to bed."

"Going to bed... with your lunch date?" Jane asked slyly.

"Not likely. First date."

"Who is he?" Anabelle asked.

"Jason Summercrest."

Candace, as usual, made no attempt to hide her opinion. "What is he... twenty-one? Ten years your junior? By the way, I went to school with his brother. The whole family is a waste!"

"Thanks, but I like to make up my own mind. Later," Dagmar said as she left the room.

Jane turned to Candace. "There's always been a rivalry between you two but it's been getting out of hand lately."

"What?" Candace exclaimed! "When is the last time Dagmar took a patient? She's not pulling her weight!"

Suzy, who had been silently observing from the corner of the room, joined the others at the conference table. "Two thirds of our clients were brought in by Dagmar. She's a 'rain maker' and, like it or not, has become the face of Kane & Teasdale."

"Our 'rain maker' is getting us water logged, and I don't even know that she can handle patients anymore."

"I know that the four of you were in the same study group in school. I also know she had better grades than any of you," Suzy said, needling her bosses.

"Yes," Candace relinquished, "Dagmar has the academia down, but she's taken precious few patients. I think she lacks experience and Dagmar's been gone when we needed her the most."

Suzy snickered, "Half of the team has been out on maternity leave. Anyone planning on getting knocked up again?"

Jane smiled. "I guess that's what happens when you have an all-chick shop."

"Dagmar is the only one of you who hasn't had a baby," Suzy observed.

"That sure surprises me," Anabelle said. "You should see the way guys go after her!"

"I don't get that," Candace stated which made everyone look at her in disbelief. "Well I'm sorry, but I don't think Dagmar is all THAT beautiful."

"Candace pul-lease!" Jane moaned. "Men would throw rocks at Halle Berry after seeing Dagmar! That face has brought Kane & Teasdale MOST of our patients."

"Not to mention her boobs and buns," Suzy added.

"Enough!" Candace exclaimed as she checked her watch. "My first patient of the day will be here in five minutes. We have to make a decision about this Xian woman."

Haltingly, Anabelle said, "I… guess I can take on one more."

"I know the family," Jane interrupted. "I'll take her."

Suzy spoke up, "As office manager, I think you should give her to Dagmar. She can knock off the recruitment for a while. Besides, Candace is treating

5

her sister, and Jane is treating her niece. Since Anabelle needs time to help transition Jane's patients back, Dagmar is the logical choice."

Looking steely-eyed at her blonde, petite, and scrappy office manager, Candace admitted, "You're right. I hate it when you're right, even when you agree with me… but you're right."

As Dagmar pulled her car into the restaurant parking lot her cell phone rang. She sighed as she saw Jane's name on the caller ID. "Hi, Jane."

"Hi, Dag. We all agreed that you should back off trawling for patients and take Xian's case."

Hiding her displeasure, Dagmar said, "Fine. No problem."

"Great. I'll give you a hand if you need it. I've arranged for you to stop by Rich's place tomorrow at eight."

"Eight?" Dagmar repeated. "In the morning?"

"They're early risers. You can make any arrangements you want after your initial meeting. Dag, this is an important case both to the practice… and to me."

"It's covered, Jane. I'll stop by the office after my assessment."

## Chapter Two

# One of the Good Ones

All eyes focused on Dagmar as she walked into the restaurant. She immediately caught the attention of her lunch date sitting at the bar off the main dining room. As Dagmar approached him, she noticed Jason was dressed much more casually than the other men. His green Polo t-shirt and khaki shorts stood out among the businessmen wearing suits and ties. He seemed to be posed on the bar stool with a silly smile on his face and a scotch, obviously not his first of the day, in his hand. However, as much as Jason stood out, Dagmar stood out more.

Jason's parents are wealthy so his non-conformity was accepted. Dagmar was the only African-American in the restaurant. Her differences were not as easy to overlook.

"You're late," Jason said smiling.

"But fashionably so," Dagmar charmed.

With an enamored look on his face, Jason continued, "Making me wait. Tease. What are you drinking?"

"Club soda," Dagmar said as she sat on the stool next to his.

"Don't you want anything in it?"

"Hmmm… yes. Two cherries."

Chuckling, Jason flagged down the bartender and relayed her order. He looked at her perfect figure as he rubbed the two days worth of stubble on his chin. "You look fantastic."

"Thank you. So, how many scotches have you had?"

"Three, but I'm okay. How come you don't want a drink?"

"I don't like alcohol early in the day."

"Oh," he said as he sipped his scotch. "You're a light weight."

With a little laugh in her voice, Dagmar said, "Hardly, but whatever you want to think."

Jason looked around the restaurant and asked, "Instead of lunch here, why don't I make you something at home? I went to culinary school for a while. I bet I can make you a better meal than this place. C'mon, lets get out of here."

She wanted to refuse but the twinkle in Jason's eye and the thought of having a guy cook for her changed Dagmar's mind. They walked through the parking lot and Jason opened the passenger door of his Italian sports car.

"I'll follow you," Dagmar said refusing the ride and getting in her Porsche.

Jason smiled and shut the door. "Try to keep up with me."

He sped his way through the winding side streets as Dagmar followed him easily. They rolled up to his gated mansion and flew down the long driveway. As they exited their vehicles in front of the palatial estate, Jason said, "There's something I want to show you."

Dagmar followed him inside through several beautifully decorated rooms until they reached the back of the mansion. Jason pushed open the patio doors and the pair walked outside to a luxurious pool area. The water seemed to hang out over the end of the patio.

"An edgeless pool," Dagmar acknowledged. "Very nice… and expensive."

"Let's go for a swim before lunch."

8

"I don't have my bathing suit with me."

"So?" Jason charmed with that boyish twinkle in his eye.

Returning a smile, Dagmar replied, "We only met once at a party and agreed to do lunch today. If you think that means I'm going to go skinny dipping with you, or more, well, you really don't know me."

"Jason!" came an irritated voice behind them. Both looked around and saw Jason's mother. She was a woman in her late fifties with hair that was dyed black and lacquered into non-movement. Her disapproving expression seemed etched on her face. "I thought I heard you drive up."

"Mother! I didn't think you were going to be home."

"Obviously. Who is this… person?"

Offering her hand, she said, "Dagmar Lamont."

Mrs. Summercrest looked revolted as she extended her hand allowing Dagmar to shake it. "What are you doing here?"

"I was invited for lunch."

She looked Dagmar up and down and then turned to her son. "Jason. A word." Mother and son walked back into the house but their conversation was heard outside through the open windows.

"What were you thinking bringing one of THEM here?"

"C'mon, Mother."

"Is this another rebellious phase you're going through?"

"Mother, it's just lunch," Jason sighed.

"You're going to allow HER to eat from my plate? Use my silverware? Drink from my glass? I can't control you outside this house but I won't allow your bizarre fetishes and mistakes into my home."

The words spoken by Mrs. Summercrest were hurtful and confusing to Dagmar.

"But Mother," Jason said, "She's one of the good ones."

Those words made Dagmar smile; not because they were complimentary, but because her hurt and confusion was gone and she knew what to do.

"She's a doctor... a psychiatrist," Jason continued.

"Really? And how hard do you think it is for one of *THEM* to become a doctor? They get all the breaks while we have to work for everything. Under those designer clothes, she's no different than one of our domestics."

"I know... but it's not like I'm going to marry her or anything."

Huffing, Mrs. Summercrest said, "Have your fun if you must. Just don't bring it here. And, for God's sake, wear a condom!"

Dagmar walked back into the house and approached Jason and his mother. "Excuse me but I had a long flight this morning. I'm very tired and I've completely lost my appetite. Jason, would you mind walking me to my car?" As they began to leave Dagmar turned to Mrs. Summercrest, who was braced for a nasty comment. Instead, Dagmar said, "You have a lovely home."

Jason led Dagmar through the house and to the front where the cars were parked. When he was sure his mother could not hear him, Jason said, "Let's go to your place or..."

"My place? No. That is NOT going to happen."

"Did you hear Mother?"

"Every word."

"I'm sorry about her. She's old and doesn't understand," Jason explained.

"I wouldn't want to put your relationship with your parents in jeopardy, even if I am 'one of the good ones'."

"I *HAVE* to talk to her like that. That's what she and Father understand."

"And that's why I will never see you again. A *MAN* would stand up to his parents... if it were something he really believed in. Sorry. You're going to have to satisfy your jungle fever with someone else."

As Dagmar opened her car door Jason said with some anger in his voice, "Hey, you sound like you think you're better than me!"

Smiling a confident smile, Dagmar said, "Baby, I *AM* better than you," and drove off the property.

# *Chapter Three*

# Haven

Dagmar guided her car to an apartment building and took the overnight bag from the L.A. trip to her second floor walkup. The studio apartment was the epitome of efficiency. There was a bedroom, bathroom, kitchen area and little else, which fit her lifestyle well. Home was just a staging area to prepare Dagmar for her appointments and travels. After the long, sleepless flight home, the meeting, and the drama with Jason, Dagmar was tired but not sleepy. She unpacked and repacked her carryon with tomorrow's clothes. Next, she took off her business suit, showered, and changed into comfortable sweats and cross-trainers. Dagmar put her carryon in her car and drove a few blocks to the apartment building that housed her grandparents and parents. She knocked on the first floor apartment and an elderly black woman answered. Her face lit up at the sight of Dagmar. "Hi, Mama Rue. I'm back from my trip."

"Give me some sugar," Dagmar's grandmother said as she gave her a hug and kiss on the cheek. "I thought you weren't coming home until tonight."

"I caught an early flight. There was a meeting at the office I had to attend."

Mama Rue sighed. "My grandbaby. Always on the go!"

An older male voice came from the kitchen, "Rue? Who's at the door?"

"Come say hello to Dagmar."

Dagmar's grandfather came into the room and gave Dagmar a kiss on the cheek. "It's been a long time since we've seen you. Sit down."

"I have to go upstairs. I just stopped by to say hello."

Dagmar's grandmother took her hand. "Can't you stay for a little while?"

"Mama Rue, I've been awake for thirty-six hours and I've got to get some sleep. I'll come by when I have more time, okay?"

Dagmar exchanged hugs with her grandparents and then took her carryon to the second floor. At the top of the stairs, Dagmar's mother was waiting for her. Mrs. Lamont looked like an older version of Dagmar. She was a lean and beautiful woman with short white hair. "I thought I heard you," she said as Dagmar hugged her. "Why are you here?"

"Do I need a reason?"

Mrs. Lamont took Dagmar's shoulders and gently pushed her out to arms length. Looking her daughter in the eye she repeated, "Why are you here?"

"I had a bad day."

"C'mon," Mrs. Lamont said, and led Dagmar into the apartment. "What do you want to eat?"

"Grilled cheese sandwiches. You know how I like them."

"I sure do."

"Thanks, Mommy," Dagmar said, and noticed her father in the living room. "Daddy? What are you doing home?"

Mister Lamont turned down the volume of the television and answered, "Oh… I'm not feelin' too well today."

Dagmar knelt beside him and took his hand to disguise that she was taking his pulse. "What's wrong?"

"I just got a little dizzy this morning. I'm feelin' better now, Baby."

"Are you taking your blood pressure medicine?" A confirming nod was her answer. "We may have to adjust it."

Dagmar stood and walked into her parent's bedroom. She came out with a blood pressure cuff and began strapping it on his arm. "Baby, I don't need that!"

Looking at the results of the test, she said, "Daddy, your blood pressure is too high! You got to lose some of that gut," Dagmar said poking her father's stomach. "Hey, do I smell smoke on you?" Her father just averted his eyes from her. "Daddy! You have to quit! I'll get you the nicotine patch but it won't work if you don't try."

"A man's got to have SOME vices," he grumbled.

"Not when they threaten your life! Daddy you have to take this more seriously!"

Mrs. Lamont entered the room with a plate of grilled cheese sandwiches and asked, "What's all the commotion about?"

"Daddy!" Dagmar said with her hands on her hips.

"Oh," Mrs. Lamont said to her husband. "You told her how you fell off the ladder at work?"

"What?!" Dagmar exclaimed as her father looked away. "You're going to the doctor... tomorrow!"

"I just need to rest," he explained but after looking at his daughter's stern face relinquished. "All right. I'll go."

"Come here, Baby," Mrs. Lamont said as she sat on the couch and put the plate on the coffee table. Dagmar sat next to her mother and picked up one of the sandwiches. It had three types of cheese, a fresh tomato slice, two strips of bacon and the bread was toasted to a golden brown with the crust trimmed off. She ate three-quarters of the sandwich and lay on the couch with her head in her mother's lap. "Baby, tell me, what's wrong?"

"Nothing really, Mommy. I had another argument with Candace."

"You mean the skinny white bitch with no ass?"

Dagmar smiled. "That's her. Of course, they're all white bitches except for me... who's a black bitch."

"Now, Baby, don't be calling my little angel a bitch. How are you getting along with the other white girls?"

"Honestly, Mommy, I've known them so long that I don't even think of them as white. We're all really open and honest with each other. Candace cuts me no slack and I don't want her to. But I AM different from all of them… and it's not because of color. They don't have the family I have. Candace's parents don't care about her at all, Jane's parents are a couple of lowlifes, and Anabelle's parents disowned her when she married and divorced a black man. I'm the only one with a real family."

"That's not the only way you're different. There are some neighborhoods around here where you can't buy a house because of your skin."

Dagmar nodded as her mother played with her hair. "Sometimes when we're out at a restaurant, I'll catch someone giving me a dirty look. If one of the girls sees it, she'll say something or we'll leave. I just ignore ignorant people."

"I wonder how many of those people that look down their noses at you are smart enough to be a doctor. I thought you were going to be a plastic surgeon."

"I didn't have the heart to operate on the victims of abuse I saw everyday in my plastics rotation." Dagmar sighed. "And… I had a lunch date. I went to a guy's house and his mother bad mouthed me to him."

"Did he stand up for you?"

"He said, as far as black people went, I was 'one of the good ones'."

Dagmar's mother shook her head. "Baby, why don't you start going out with black men?"

"Mommy!"

"I know it's not supposed to matter… but you've dated a lot of white boys who turned out to be fools."

"I've dated a lot of black guys too! Believe me, fool knows no color."

Mrs. Lamont implored, "Baby, don't you want the comfort of a man… and love?"

Dagmar laughed. "When you say, 'comfort of a man' do you mean sex? I have no problem finding a man for sex. Sex is easy. Love is hard."

Dagmar's father spoke up. "Dagmar Rochelle Lamont! I don't want to hear that kind of talk in front of me!"

Both Dagmar and her mother chuckled and Dagmar apologized, "Sorry Daddy." She wrapped her arms around her mother's hips while still resting her head in her lap and said, "Can I sleep over? I have an early day tomorrow."

"I'll make up the guest room."

"I just want to sleep on the couch."

Stroking her hair again, Mrs. Lamont said, "Sure, Baby. What are you doing tomorrow?"

"It's professional. I'm not supposed to say… but… Jane's friend, Rich, has a sister-in law that just came out of an abusive marriage and she needs help. I don't know much about it but I'm going to assess her early tomorrow," Dagmar answered as her tired voice trailed off.

"Close your eyes, Baby. Close your eyes."

Dagmar slept soundly for hours.



Ten-thirty that night, Dagmar woke up alone in the living room covered by a quilt. She stood and walked into the kitchen where her parents had finished washing the dishes and began putting them in the cabinets. "Baby, are you all right?" her father asked.

"I'm still hungry."

"I'm not surprised. You didn't eat much," Mrs. Lamont said. Turning to her husband as she washed her hands, "Cut her a piece of Icebox cake."

Smiling as Dagmar sat at the table, "You made Icebox cake?"

Her father placed a plate of Icebox cake and a glass of milk in front of her. "Don't eat too fast. You won't sleep well."

"Okay, Daddy. Mommy, when are you going to make my favorite, a Red Velvet cake?"

"You know I only make it on special occasions."

"No one makes Red Velvet cake like you!"

Dagmar ate her Icebox cake and finished her milk. She trudged her way back into the living room and lay back on the couch. When her mother entered the living room Dagmar was fast asleep. She placed the quilt back on her daughter, tucked her in and turned out the lights.

# Chapter Four

# The Arrangement

She woke at six a.m. relaxed and full of energy. Dagmar checked her cell phone and saw a text message from Candace reminding her to write a full report on Xian's condition. Bringing her carryon in the bathroom, Dagmar took a vigorous shower, applied her makeup and dressed in a conservative woman's business suit. When she left the bathroom the smell of bacon and coffee lured her into the kitchen. As Dagmar sat at the table, her mother placed a plate of rye toast, bacon and scrambled eggs in front of her as her father added a cup of coffee. "I hope I didn't wake you up early," Dagmar apologized as she added a dollop of milk and three sugars.

"Just eat your breakfast before you start your day," Mrs. Lamont said. Dagmar flipped through the newspaper as she ate. When finished, she went to the bathroom, brushed her teeth and packed her toiletries in her carryon. Dagmar went back to the kitchen and began to help clear the table. "Why don't you go on to work?" Mrs. Lamont asked. "We'll finish up here. Your father decided to take a few days off."

Mister Lamont snorted, "Your mother decided FOR me."

"I approve, Daddy. Don't forget to call the doctor!"

"Are you coming by after work?" Mrs. Lamont questioned while rinsing the dishes.

"You don't need my butt hanging around you all the time… unless you're going to make a Red Velvet cake."

"I told you, Baby… only special occasions!"

"Thanks for the use of your couch," Dagmar said as she gave her mother a kiss on the cheek. She kissed her father's cheek and commanded, "Doctor. Today!"

"All these women tellin' me what to do," Mister Lamont grumbled.

"That's 'cause all these women love you. I'll call later," Dagmar said and left the apartment.

She drove to the newly built home of Rich and Talia Sedgwick. Dagmar had been there a few times and marveled at how this house could be so large yet so homey and comfortable. The front door swung open as she stepped on the porch. Rich was waiting for her with a big smile. "Am I late?" Dagmar asked.

"You're right on time. So, the girls chose you to help my sister-in-law."

"Disappointed?"

"Just surprised that Jane didn't volunteer."

"Jane is going to need some time to catch up with her old patients, so we figured I'd be the best choice to start with someone new. Again… disappointed? Jane has offered to step in if you have a preference."

Rich brought Dagmar into the house and led her to the spacious living room. "Of course I'm not disappointed. Jane trusts you and that's all I need to know. Take a seat. Can I get you some breakfast? Coffee?"

"Thanks, Rich, I'm good."

"My wife wants to talk to you before you meet Xian. She'll be here in a minute," Rich said as he left the living room.

20

Dagmar sat for a moment and checked her cell phone for messages. "Hello, Dagmar," came a voice from the entry. Talia Sedgwick was dressed in a beautiful blue maternity dress. Even though she was five months pregnant it did not show in her walk. Her pageboy cut hair was the color of spun onyx and her complexion was radiant. Pregnancy agreed with Talia. What brought a smile to Dagmar's face was Talia's eighteen-month-old son, George. Talia placed him on the floor, and with staggering steps, he walked to Dagmar. She scooped the child up in her arms and hugged him tightly. When Dagmar pulled him back to look at him, George's face had a big smile and he leaned forward to give her an awkward kiss.

"He loves you!" Talia observed.

"And I love him! He's grown so much since I saw him last!" Dagmar rocked back and forth with George and whispered, "You'll never break a girl's heart, will you?" He pulled back, looked at Dagmar, and gave her another kiss. She laughed and said, "I could hold you all day but I have to start work, okay?" As Dagmar nodded her head up and down George mimicked the movement. She handed the baby back to his mother who placed him in his playpen. Talia offered Dagmar a seat on the couch as she sat in a nearby chair. "So, where is Xian?"

"She is in her room," Talia answered. Dagmar could hear the sadness in Talia's voice when she mentioned Xian. "I want to talk to you before you meet my sister. Have you spoken to Jane or Candace about MY therapy?"

"Your files are the only ones at the practice marked as private and confidential. Information about your case is on a need-to-know basis."

Talia took out her cell phone and tapped out a quick text message. "I just gave my approval for you to read my file. It may shed some light on Xian's condition." Talia sighed, and with a glance, checked George to make sure he was playing quietly. When she was satisfied her son did not need her, Talia turned her attention to Dagmar. "I am the middle of five gifted sisters. My youngest, my little bunny Rini, is a surgeon at Yale New Haven Hospital. Next is Aiko, who with my older sister Valentina, runs my father's international business. Finally, there is our oldest, Xian. As a child, she was nervous… anxious. She could never sit still. She had nightmares and would wake up screaming at all hours. My parents hired several psychiatrists to secure control of my sister. One psychiatrist used a combination of drugs on her that calmed her… permanently. The concoction made her docile… and mute. She was able to regain her speech when I spent time reading to her. Eventually we read aloud together. I always felt close to Xian. We had a more difficult childhood than our siblings. Her young years were like mine except I was more resistant to the drugs my doctors used to calm me."

"What age was Xian when she was administered the combination of drugs that temporarily muted her and changed her life?"

"Eleven."

Dagmar thought back to her life as an eleven-year-old girl. She thought about her friends, her growing interest in boys, her happy participation in school and her loving family. Xian had none of that. "She was so young to have her life blunted. How did she find her husband?"

"My father was always inviting businessmen to the compound to make deals. One such man was from Japan. He was extremely wealthy and Father was eager to create a partnership with his organization. A sumptuous meal was prepared for him attended by my parents and sisters. During dessert, the girls were all persuaded by the businessman to speak their mind on anything they wished… a rarity in our household. After dinner, the businessman and my father retired to one of the living rooms overlooked by a balcony. I hid on that balcony, as I have many times, and spied on their conversation. I remember every word… every intonation."

Talia began her story:

Mister Tamislav and his guest entered the beautifully decorated and airy living room. He picked up a small handmade box and offered the Japanese businessman a cigar. The lean, wiry man was in his mid fifties with gray and black hair. While he was not tall and broad like Mister Tamislav, his confidence made him seem imposing. He clipped the ends and accepted a light from his host's monogrammed cigar lighter. "Cuban?" the guest asked.

"I have a few boxes a year smuggled across the border," Mister Tamislav said as he prepared and lit his own cigar.

"Border?"

"From Canada. Canada has no embargo with Cuba. It's still illegal… technically."

"Ahh, but that illegality makes them so much more enjoyable, does it not?"

Mister Tamislav smiled as he and his guest settled into their overstuffed chairs. "We think very much alike, Mister Kami. Your name; it means 'spirit' does it not?"

"My name translates to God… or spirit if you prefer."

"Personally, I prefer neither. I don't believe in God."

22

"I do," Mister Kami answered. "WE are God! Through our wealth, we employ people. We put food on their table. We provide medical care. We protect our family. The wealthy are God on earth."

Mister Tamislav nodded. "An interesting point of view." Yuri Tamislav smiled at his guest. "You have a remarkable grasp of the English language."

"Thank you. English is very important. It's the language of commerce. Your daughters seem to speak several languages including my native Japanese."

"We have an innate ability to learn languages although I've fallen out of practice."

"You do not travel much, do you?"

"I let the world come to me."

"This is where we disagree. I enjoy going to different lands and observing people in their natural habitat. I especially like the United States of America. In fact, I have satellite dishes at my home to watch American television. Your country wears its flaws like a lavish suit of clothes. Swaddled in their own depravity, your countrymen appear on television and flaunt their moral deviances."

Mister Tamislav grumbled, "Not here. I keep my environment very… controlled."

"Yes. I can see that. Every piece of furniture looks like it was hand built for its spot. There is not a speck of dust anywhere. The food was nothing short of a masterpiece. You have five charming daughters and a beautiful wife. My home is much like yours except I have one son and no spouse."

"You've been married twice, yes?"

Mister Kami nodded as he placed his cigar in the ashtray. "My first wife loved the view from the observation tower. She… fainted and fell through an open window to her death. My second wife was very… troubled. She suffered gravely with depression. My doctor tried everything to help. Despite his best efforts, she hanged herself in our bedroom."

Yuri Tamislav commiserated, "My condolences on your tragedies." Mister Kami simply lowered his eyes.

Hidden on the balcony, Talia clenched her fists so hard she trembled. Through her empathic nature, she knew every word Mister Kami said about his wives was a lie.

"I have never been one to dwell on the past," Mister Kami said. "Let us discuss the future."

"Very well. I assume you've read my business proposal."

"Yes I have," Mister Kami said as he took his cigar from the ashtray and puffed it back to life. "I must be honest. I have received many business proposals from all over the world submitted by men who wish to exploit my businesses and connections. Each proposition has sound reasons for me to work with them. To be blunt, most of the proposals are better than yours. I like you Yuri, but you need an edge."

"Edge?"

Mister Kami smiled and asked, "Do you drink cognac?"

In a booming voice Yuri Tamislav called, "Perez!" One of the butlers waiting outside the room entered. "Cognac. Our best."

Interrupting him, Mister Kami said, "Ah, might your eldest daughter bring our brandy?"

Returning his attention to the butler, Mister Tamislav ordered, "Tell Mrs. Tamislav to send Xian in with the bottle and two glasses... NOW!" The butler scrambled from the room as if his life depended on it. Looking at his guest, Mister Tamislav said, "You were about to mention an... edge."

"You purposely... what is the expression... 'low balled' me in your proposal, did you not?"

"I was trying to get my best price. If you are asking me to sweeten the pot..."

Chuckling, Mister Kami said, "Not at all. I do business with the man... not the money. Find the right man, with the right thinking, and the money will come. The truth is that the others bid too much. You are smart, perhaps as smart as myself. I do not need another smart man. I need a reason to do business with a smart man over men who will pay me too much money." Mister Kami extinguished his cigar and sat quietly formulating his next words. "Your daughters are most exceptional... one in particular."

"Oh?"

"During dessert, I listened to each speak. While Rini and Aiko are very intelligent, they are still children. I have no interest in children. Valentina is well-read and very business savvy. Someone who could argue with my decisions also has no interest to me."

"Talia?" Mister Tamislav asked as his spying daughter again tensed in her balcony hiding place.

Mister Kami hesitated. "Pardon my candor, but that girl is trouble."

"Agreed," Mister Tamislav sighed.

"Now, Xian is a rare woman. She is quiet and unassuming. She speaks only when spoken to. She averts her eyes in conversation. Modern Japanese women have become too... Americanized. Xian is a woman of a different time. A time when women knew their place." The door opened and Xian walked into the parlor with the cognac and two glasses on a sterling silver tray. As she sat the tray on the small table between the two men, Mister Kami said, "Thank you. Would you pour for us, my dear?" Xian froze, not knowing what to do. She directed her gaze toward her father. Mister Tamislav nodded and Xian poured two glasses of cognac. Smiling broadly, Mister Kami spoke as if Xian were not in front of him. "She looks to the man of the house for permission. Wonderful! Her face is breathtaking. It is impossible to find a woman so beautiful yet so humble."

"Leave," Mister Tamislav said to his daughter. Without a word or hesitation, Xian left the room.

"Her name is Chinese, is it not?"

"Yes. She is named after my great, great grandmother."

"Mister Tamislav, I am a man who is blessed with knowing his mind... knowing what he wants. I want Xian. I could travel the earth and not find a woman more suitable to be my wife. I would like to take her back to Japan to show her my homeland... and my heart." Kami could see his host shift in his chair as he considered his words. "Am I being inaccurate in saying that she does not have the mental fortitude of her sisters? Am I being inaccurate in saying she has... disappointed you?"

"You are not... inaccurate."

"Then her best destiny lies with me. She would have anything her heart desired. She would be surrounded by the luxury and beauty of my home and I would expose her to all the arts from the written word to plays to paintings. I am a world traveler. Your daughter would see every corner of the earth in lavish comfort.

She would want for nothing.  Besides, if Xian were my wife it would make us family.  Your… edge."

Talia soundlessly bolted from her hiding place and ran through the house.  When she saw Mrs. Tamislav talking to one of the maids Talia approached her.  "Mother!  MOTHER!  I *MUST* talk to you… NOW!"

Mrs. Tamislav looked at her daughter with annoyance on her face.  "Go," she said to the maid without looking at her.  "What IS it Talia?"

"Father is making arrangements for Xian to marry Mister Kami in exchange for a… a… business deal!"

"And how would you know this?"

"Does it matter?!!!  Essentially, Father wants to SELL Xian!"

With anger, Athena Tamislav said, "I'm sure you have this all wrong, but I shall speak to your father and Mister Kami when they finish their cognac.  Happy?"

"No, Mother!  I will not be happy until that man is gone from this house!"  Talia raged and stomped away.

The next morning, Mr. and Mrs. Tamislav were reading the newspaper and eating breakfast as Talia stormed into the kitchen.  "Where is Xian?!!!  She is not in her room!  She is always in her room!  Where is Xian?!!!"

Mister Tamislav gave her a stern look.  "I understand you were spying on my business meeting," he said and sipped his coffee.

Talia ripped the cup from her father's hand.  She flung it against the wall, shattering the cup.  "You will answer my question or I will call the police and file a missing person's report."

Mister Tamislav stood and slapped Talia with the back of his hand so hard that she flew against the wall behind her.  "I have nothing to hide," he growled.  "Do your worst!"

"You have just said the wrong thing to the wrong person!!!"  Talia hissed.

26

Slamming her hand on the table, Mrs. Tamislav said, "Stop it, both of you! Yuri! Explain it to her!"

Mister Tamislav took a moment to calm himself. "Last night Xian agreed to go to Japan with Mister Kami."

"She agreed?!!!" Talia exclaimed. "She agrees to EVERYTHING!!! Why did you send her with that old man?!"

"Mister Kami is going to show her his homeland, and after a proper courtship, they will be married."

"Are you insane?!!!" Talia screamed.

"TALIA!" Mrs. Tamislav interrupted. "Don't speak to your father that way!"

"And YOU," Talia said now directing her ire to her mother. "I came to you. I WARNED YOU!"

Mrs. Tamislav stood and walked to her daughter. "I spoke to your father about the arrangement. Mister Kami is a well-respected international businessman who is enthralled with my eldest daughter. I questioned him about his intentions… and they are honorable. Xian will have a separate room and her virginity will remain intact until her wedding night. They will come here to Los Angeles to be wed. Before the wedding we will verify with Xian that Mister Kami kept his promises." Mrs. Tamislav sighed and asked, "Talia, what better future do you see for Xian? She expresses an interest in nothing. She barely graduated from high school. She sits in her room all day and does nothing. There ARE no other suitors. Mister Kami will give her a comfortable life."

Talia was seething. "Forgetting the fact that Xian's mental condition is directly due to the drugs your psychiatrist forced into her as a child, I have one question." Turning to her father, Talia asked, "What do you get?"

"What do you mean?" Mister Tamislav asked.

"What is the quid pro quo? Father, you never give anything unless you get something."

"This isn't a business arrangement."

"LIAR!!!" Talia shrieked.

The reward for her outburst was another backhanded slap from her large and imposing father. This slap was much harder than the first and sent Talia sprawling to the floor.

"You need to learn respect!"

Talia jumped to her feet and took a set of car keys from her pocket. "Where are you going?" her mother asked.

"I now come and go as I please," Talia announced. "Since you care so little for Xian's whereabouts I can not imagine you will be concerned with mine. Mother, you said that old man was a well-respected businessman. Is he respected because he is good to his family or because he makes money for his business partners? Your firstborn daughter's future is at stake and your biggest concern is with her virginity? Father, I know you used Xian as leverage to sign a lucrative business deal. She was your 'edge,' was she not? I have completely lost any respect I had for both of you!"

Talia ended her story.

"Damn!" Dagmar whispered.

"When I saw Xian was at my wedding, I insisted my parents look for signs of abuse. During the reception, my mother took Xian aside and discovered bruising under her kimono. Mother took photographs with her cell phone and showed them to Father who decided to keep her in the United States. Unfortunately, Xian's assistants whisked her away. It took Father five years and involvement with both governments to secure Xian's divorce and return her to the States. Yesterday, Xian arrived directly from Japan. Since my parents did not know what to do with her, I kept her here under our care. She is more withdrawn than ever and I am frightened for her. I will take you to Xian as soon as I get Richard to watch the baby."

"Let's bring George with us," Dagmar suggested and Talia lifted her son from his crib.

28

# Chapter Five

# The Fog

*Where am I? This is not Japan. This is not California. This room. These people. And where are the monsters? I have not seen them for some time. Has it been a long time? Are the monsters coming back? This cloud... this fog... it makes the world hard to focus. The fog IS my world. Two people enter the room. No. Three people. One is small. One is familiar. One has dark skin. Who are they? Do they want to hurt me? The fog will protect me. The fog will shield me. It will dull the pain. It will obscure the memories. The familiar one... I believe she is my sister Talia. She wants to speak to me.*

Xian was sitting on her bed staring into space as Talia, holding her baby in her arms, approached her. "Sister, there is someone I would like you to meet. This is Doctor Lamont."

"Hi, Xian," Dagmar said as she purposely extended her hand. Dagmar liked to begin her analyses of her patients by their handshake. Xian did not meet her eyes and did not take her hand.

"Hello, Doctor Lamont." Xian's greeting had a rehearsed sound that made her welcome generic and unrevealing.

"Doctor Lamont is a family friend.  She is here at my request to help you."

Pointing her head in her sister's general direction, Xian said, "That is very gracious… but I am fine."

Dagmar looked at George who returned the look and waved his arms excitedly.  "May I?" Dagmar said to Talia and reached out to take the baby.  "I love your nephew," she said to Xian.  "Would you like to hold him?"  A confused look crossed Xian's face and before she could answer, Dagmar placed the baby in her arms.  Xian held her nephew with no more emotion than if she were holding a bag of sugar.  George stared at his aunt with questioning eyes.  This person looked like his mother, but he felt no more emotion from her than he would from a coat rack.  "Talia, would you mind taking George in the other room so that I may speak with Xian?"

Talia took George and left.

# Chapter Six

# Ring

       Sitting in a chair near the bed, Dagmar observed her patient.  Xian was a reflection of her four heritages; Greek, Japanese, Russian and Chinese.  Her long black hair was like spun onyx and her eyes were either blue or violet depending on how the light hit them.  Despite her innate beauty, she was very thin and her face had a vacant look.  Xian's hands started to shake as she tucked them in opposing sleeves of her white kimono.  She also had the faintest twitch in her face.

       "Do you know what kind of doctor I am?" Dagmar asked.

       "No, Doctor Lamont."

       "I'm a psychiatrist.  Does it bother you that your sister thinks you need a psychiatrist?"

       "No, Doctor Lamont."

       "Oh.  Then you think Talia was correct in seeking me out?"

       "No, Doctor Lamont.  My sister means well… but I am fine."

"Do you remember your youth?  Do you remember your life before your parents had you sedated?  Do you remember how you were so heavily medicated that you couldn't even speak?"

"No, Doctor Lamont.  My early years are… foggy."

"Okay, then tell me about your marriage."

"I was married to a businessman and lived in Japan."

Dagmar waited for Xian to elaborate but she volunteered no additional information.  "But you're divorced now."

"Yes, Doctor Lamont."

"Why?"

Xian trembled but regained her stoic facade.  "Father wished me to be divorced and returned to the United States.  My husband agreed."

"Why?"

"I do not know.  That was between the two men.  It had nothing to do with me."

Xian's words stunned Dagmar.  As the patient removed her hands from her sleeves, Dagmar noticed a gold band around one of her fingers.  "Is that your wedding ring?  May I see it?"  Xian's eyes darted back and forth as if the question were a major decision.  Then, she held her arm straight out in front of her.  Dagmar gently pulled Xian's hand toward her to get a good look.  The ring, composed of yellow and rose colored gold, was hand made; a one of a kind piece of jewelry.  Deeply cut patterns encircled the large wedding band whose ornate design was both beautiful and disturbing at the same time.  "It's an impressive ring," Dagmar said as she released Xian's hand.  "But you're no longer married.  Why haven't you removed the wedding band?"

"I… can not."

"Of course you can.  Xian, your ex-husband has no control over you.  You don't need to wear the ring.  You can take it off if you want."

"I… can not."

Trying to control her exasperation, Dagmar said, "CAN not or WILL not?"

"I… can not."

"Can not?" Dagmar repeated. She moved to sit beside Xian on the bed. Dagmar took her hand to examine the ring again. It looked like a normal, if ornate, piece of jewelry. Then, Dagmar turned Xian's hand over to look at the backside of the ring and what she saw horrified her. The skin of Xian's finger looked like it had been burned into the ring. Flesh and scar tissue seeped through the deep etchings and holes in the ring locking it on Xian's finger. Dagmar was so shocked she jumped from the bed and screamed. Rather than being startled, Xian turned her cheek in Dagmar's direction. "Oh Jesus!" Dagmar exclaimed. "Is this what you went through in your marriage?!!!"

Still staring off into the distance, Xian said, "I am… fine."

"Talia!!!" Dagmar hollered.

A moment later, Talia came flying through the door. "What is it? What is wrong?" Dagmar took Xian's hand and showed the mangled lump of flesh that was bonded with the ring. "What…? What…?"

With a trembling voice, Dagmar said, "Your sister has been abused by a sadist. I want to take her to the hospital… NOW. It'll be expensive if she has no medical coverage."

"Help her! I will BUY the hospital if I must! Help her!"

"I'll call for an ambulance. Get someone to watch your kids. You need to come along to sign some papers."



Dagmar and Talia rode in the ambulance while Rich followed in his car. When they arrived at the hospital, Dagmar sent Rich and Talia to the receptionist to do paperwork and keep them busy. Following the gurney into the emergency room and plucking a pair of gloves from the dispenser, she walked up to a friend of hers. "Bryce!"

The square jawed confidant doctor put down his chart and smiled. "Hey Dagmar! I knew you would come back to me eventually. I just started my shift but…"

"This isn't social. I have a hot one."

"Hotter than you?"

"A hot case."

"And here I was getting my hopes up that you wanted to date again."

"This is important. I have a thirty-six year old female victim of abuse."

Bryce's charming smile disappeared. "Where is she?"

Dagmar led Bryce to Xian's hospital bed. Before he could say anything Dagmar showed him the ring. "I want a full work up on her. Blood. Tox screen. EKG. Full body MRI."

"I'm sure she's been through a lot but bringing her to the ER…"

"I'm not going to wait three weeks for an appointment with a GP only to bounce her around from specialist to specialist. Bryce, I knew you were working today. You were a lousy boyfriend but a great doctor. Help her body so that I can help her mind."

Bryce thought for a second, and then asked, "Will you assist?"

Dagmar held up her hands. "Gloved and ready. Let's go."

"By the way, 'lousy boyfriend' is a little harsh, don't you think?"

"How about, 'inattentive with a wandering eye'?"

"Much better. Let's get to work."

While Bryce ordered the tests, Dagmar drew the privacy curtain around the bed and began helping Xian out of her kimono. As more skin was exposed Dagmar saw more and more abuse. She called for Bryce who entered the curtained area. What he saw stopped his breath. With Dagmar's help, Xian was turned away from him standing naked. Her entire back was discolored from bruises and covered with long red marks, scars, burns and shoe prints. The inside of her thick kimono was covered with dried blood and puss. Bryce had seen abused women in his emergency room but nothing prepared him for this.

At four-thirty, Dagmar, exhausted, entered the waiting room where Talia and Rich bolted to her. "The doctor has a few more tests to run. We're admitting her into the hospital overnight."

34

"Why can we not take her home after her tests?" Talia asked with concern.

"Xian is malnourished and she has some infections that we are treating. I know a good plastics man who will be here tomorrow to remove the ring and repair her finger. I'm getting a osteo guy to check some broken bones to see if they healed properly."

"Infections? Broken bones? What has happened to my sister?!!!"

Dagmar hesitated and then replied, "I don't know yet."

Talia began trembling and tears streamed from her eyes. Rich put his arm around her and said, "It's going to be all right. Xian is with us now. She's safer now than she has ever been." Stroking his fingers through her hair, Rich smiled at Talia. "We'll fix this."

"Did the police come by to talk to you?" Dagmar asked.

Rich nodded. "A couple hours ago."

"By law, the hospital has to report cases of abuse."

"We made an official report telling them what little we know. The officers said there wasn't much they could do."

"They came into the ER to talk to me and I explained Xian couldn't answer questions yet." Dagmar sighed and said, "Why don't you two go home? Xian can't receive visitors today. I'll be here a little longer and I have a friend who is in charge of the ER looking after her.

"Is there not something we can do?" Talia asked.

"If you wouldn't mind, you can bring my car to the hospital parking lot," Dagmar said as she held out her car keys.

Taking the keys, Talia said, "Your car will be waiting for you washed, waxed, and filled with gasoline."

"That's not necessary, but thank you. Come by the office tomorrow morning around eleven. I should have a full report completed by then."

Next morning, Candace Kane arrived uncharacteristically early at her office. Pushing her sunglasses to the top of her head she greeted her receptionist and office manager by saying, "Coffee. Hot and strong."

"Er, g'morning boss," Suzy said.

Candace stopped and looked at the expressions on her employee's faces. "What's wrong? I saw Dagmar's car in the lot. Where is she?"

"Doctor Lamont is in her office. Have you checked your email yet?" Harmony asked.

"No. Why?"

"You should read it before you talk to her," Suzy advised.

Noting Harmony and Suzy's grave faces, Candace proceeded to her office repeating the word "coffee" over her shoulder. She flipped open her laptop computer and checked her email. "Xian Tamislav assessment," she read. "About time! She was supposed to do this yesterday." Candace's eyes widened as she read the report.

# Chapter Seven

# The Assessment

*Report follows:*

*This is the initial medical assessment of Xian Tamislav.*

*The patient is riddled with physical maladies diagnosed by Doctor Bryce Harrington and Doctor Dagmar Lamont. Observations and treatment are as follows:*

*Malady: Patient is dehydrated and malnourished.*
*Treatment: Administered IV saline and IV "banana bag" (magnesium sulfate, thiamine and folic acid.)*

*Malady: Patient's wedding band was burned into her finger using an unknown instrument.*
*Treatment: Plastic surgeon scheduled to remove the ring and reconstruct left ring finger.*

*Malady: Various scars, burns, and sores on the patient's back, sides, legs, arms and buttocks. Long red scars consistent with whip marks. Small bits of gravel, glass and splinters imbedded in scuffed skin on the patient's back, arms, stomach, and upper thighs. Some sites were infected and becoming gangrenous.*

*Treatment: Dead skin debrided.  All particulate matter removed.  Skin thoroughly irrigated. Topical antibiotic cream and IV antibiotics administered.  Dressings changed hourly. Oral antibiotics after hospitalization.*

*Malady: Three cracked ribs, number eight and nine on left, number nine on right.*
*Treatment: None.  Restrict movement.  Dressing to cushion area.*

*Malady: Patient has recently contracted Gonorrhea.*
*Treatment: IV antibiotics.  Oral antibiotics after hospitalization.*

*Malady: Vaginal tear.*
*Treatment: Three stitches.  Topical antibiotic cream.  IV antibiotics.  Oral antibiotics after hospitalization.*

*Malady: Rectal tear.*
*Treatment: Five stitches.  Topical antibiotic cream.  IV antibiotics.  Oral antibiotics after hospitalization.*

*Other:*
*Sexual assault test kit administered to gather forensic evidence.*

*Vaginal and rectal scarring from previous assaults.*

*Patient has had tubal ligation.*

*Both forearms have been broken (radius) and set, twice on her left and once on her right.*

*Left cheekbone and orbital socket cracked.  Healed.*

*Evidence of at least two concussions.  Healed.*

*Faint ligature marks on throat, wrists and ankles.*

*Toxicity screen shows trace amounts of various prescription and non-prescription drugs including barbiturates, amphetamines, psychotropic drugs and opiates. Punctures on backs of legs indicate patient did not self-inject.*

*Brain scans show no activity in certain parts of the patient's brain involving memory, judgment, coordination and pain.*

*Conclusion:*
*Patient is the victim of physical, sexual, chemical and psychological abuse.*

*Recommendations:*
*Plastics consult to minimize scars.  Osteopathic consult to examine healed bones.*
*Nutrition consult to fortify body.  Weekly neuroimaging to track brain deterioration.*
*Daily psychotherapy exceeding fifty-minute hour.*

## *Chapter Eight*

# Bearer of Bad News

Candace walked directly from her office to Dagmar's and opened the door without knocking. In all the years she had known her, Candace had never seen Dagmar less than "camera ready" wearing perfect clothes, perfect makeup, and perfectly coiffed hair. Today, Dagmar was sitting on the floor of her office leaning against her couch. Her eyes were bloodshot, her hair was a mess, and her clothes looked like she had slept in them... which she had. "Sorry the assessment was late," Dagmar said with hoarseness in her voice. "I didn't leave the hospital until two this morning."

"My GOD, Dagmar! Is all this about Xian Tamislav true? I had no idea! What did she tell you?"

"Nothing. She told me nothing," Dagmar said, half asleep. "Xian's been docile since she was eleven years old. In some ways, she's never progressed beyond that age. She speaks intelligently, but underneath she's an abused child. What kind of animal takes advantage of such an innocent soul? Rich and Talia are coming here at eleven this morning and I have to tell them about Xian's condition. Then I have to be with Xian when the plastics guy removes the ring."

Candace looked at her friend/rival/employee exhausted on the floor and said, "You look like a hot mess." She went to the door and waved Suzy into the office. Taking a credit card from her pocket, Candace handed it to Suzy and said, "Get Doctor Lamont a new woman's business suit. Do you know her sizes?" A baffled look was Suzy's only response. With a disgruntled huff, Candace took a piece of paper from the desk and jotted down all of Dagmar's clothing sizes. She handed the paper to Suzy and said, "Be back before ten forty-five. Remember, office attire similar to her style. If you come back with any of that kooky shit you wear outside of work I'll fire you! Hurry up!"

Suzy got to the door but turned back to ask, "How do you know Doctor Lamont's sizes?"

"Darling, there's more to me than just a raging bitch. Aside from being one of the best psychiatrists you'll ever see, I'm also a fashionista ninja."

Suzy opened the door, stopped and turned back again. "What size bra do I wear?"

"You need a 32 B but you wear an 32 C and stuff it."

"Damn...!" Suzy whispered in amazement.

Clapping her hands, Candace said in elevated voice, "Tick Tock! GO!"

As Suzy left the room Candace commanded, "Take a shower and rest until Suzy gets back."

"I'll pay you for the clothes when I get my next check," Dagmar mumbled as she lifted herself to her feet.

"No need. It's on Kane & Teasdale." Candace went to the door. As she was leaving she said, "Good job, Doctor Lamont."


The bathroom in the former Kane & Teasdale office barely had a working sink and toilet. With the success of the practice, Candace and Jane could afford to buy a building with large offices, a conference room, a plush reception area, and a beautiful bathroom. Dagmar peeled off her clothes and slipped on a shower cap. The hot water pelted her like hundreds of thousands of tiny explosions. Using the liquid soap she thoroughly washed every square inch of her body. As she rinsed,

Dagmar allowed the hot water to blast the muscles in her back. She stepped from the shower and patted herself dry with a plush towel. Then, removing the shower cap and wrapping herself in a robe, Dagmar exited the bathroom. The way to her office was past the reception area and as she walked behind Harmony's desk, the only person in the reception area was older gentleman patient who did a double take as he watched Dagmar cross the room. Dagmar saw his stare and his pleased look out of the corner of her eye. She did not return the look, but the unexpected attention brought a smile to her face. As Dagmar stepped into her office she saw a printed copy of the report she had written on her desk. She approached it to go over the assessment but stopped and placed a book on the papers to hide the words. Suddenly, the couch seemed very inviting.

Dagmar woke from the sound of a knock on her office door. She stood and let Suzy into the room. It appeared that Suzy was a bit of a fashionista ninja herself. The clothes were exactly the style she would wear to work… maybe a little better. Dagmar thanked Suzy and asked her to pull Talia's file and hold it for her. When Suzy left, Dagmar put on her makeup, brushed out her hair, and dressed.

Ten minutes later the intercom buzzed. "Mr. and Mrs. Sedgwick are here for you."

"Thanks, Harmony. Send them in."

Rich helped his wife into the office. Talia was shaking so badly she had trouble walking. "She barely slept all night," Rich said with concern.

Dagmar touched the intercom. "Harmony, is Candace with a patient?"

"Yes, Doctor Lamont."

"Is Jane in yet?"

"Doctor Teasdale just arrived."

"I need her now!"

Jane urgently came into Dagmar's office. She took one look at Talia and ran to embrace her. "It's going to be all right. Let's go to my office."

"Talia stammered, "But… But… the report…"

"The report isn't going anywhere. Let's just take a minute," Jane said and led Talia out of Dagmar's office.

After Talia was gone, Dagmar said, "I have GOT to read her file." She looked at Rich and said, "Maybe I should let you look over the assessment first," and handed the report to him.  Rich was a pleasant and even-tempered man, but as he read the assessment his face became grimmer… harder with each word.  When finished, Rich did not say anything.  "Rich?  Are you okay?  What are you feeling?"

Rich took all the thoughts in his head and expressed them in one word.  "Revenge."

"Rich…"

"I know you're going to tell me that's wrong, but…"

"No, your feelings are your feelings.  There IS no wrong.  As I examined Xian, I felt the same thing.  I wanted to beat the living hell out of that bastard, but there are bigger issues here."

Rich's face was still grim as he looked at Dagmar.  "What could possibly be more important than punishing that man?"

"Your sister-in-law's health is more important.  Then, there's Talia.  Your wife isn't handling this well.  You have to think of her emotional state and how it will affect the unborn twins she's carrying.  In most cases of abuse, there is more than one victim.  The loved ones go through mental trauma too."

Rich looked disappointed in himself.  "How could I be so thoughtless?"

"The assessment IS overpowering.  I'm most concerned about Xian's brain scan.  There are areas of her brain that have no electrical activity.  We're going to keep a close eye on them to see if they spread.  Through therapy, I'm going to try to find out exactly what happened to her, but you have to keep your wife stable for the sake of your born and unborn children."

Rich sighed.  "Agreed.  Let ME explain Xian's condition to Tally."

Jane helped Talia back into Dagmar's office.  Still shaking but more focused, Talia could tell from her husband's expression that he had been updated on Xian's condition.  Talia went straight to Rich and took his hands.  "Tell me," she whispered.  Dagmar motioned for Jane to join her in the corner of the room to allow Rich and Talia to speak privately.

"I had her meditate," Jane whispered to Dagmar.  "It helped a little."

The two psychiatrists watched as Rich explained to his wife, as delicately possible, Dagmar's assessment.  With each word, the anguish on Talia's face grew until she fell to her knees in a sobbing heap.  As Rich sat on the floor and held Talia, Jane began to step toward them.  Dagmar took Jane's arm and said quietly, "Let her absorb what she just heard.  Have you read your email yet?"  Jane shook her head no and Dagmar took the printed copy from her desk and handed it to Jane to read.

Jane's eyes widened as she read the assessment.  "Good God!"

"I know.  I'm surprised Xian is alive."

After several moments of sobbing, Talia looked at Rich through tear-filled eyes and said, "I am going to kill him!"

"Oh shit!" Jane exclaimed.

"C'mon," Dagmar said to Jane.  "That was my first reaction, too."

"No... she means it!"

Through clenched teeth, Talia said, "If Mister Kami likes the idea of torture I will show him the meaning of the word.  After a few hours with me he will BEG me to kill him!"

Rich held her face in his hands.  "We have other priorities.  Your first obligations are your sister's health, your children... and your husband."

"But Richard, he can not go unpunished!"

"He won't."  Rich turned to Dagmar.  "I want all forensic evidence of my sister-in-law's abuse.  Every test... every photograph... everything!"

Dagmar took a folder from a locked desk drawer and handed it to Rich.  "I have a file started.  This is a copy of everything I have so far."

"Good," Rich said as he thumbed through the folder.  "Keep me updated.  I'll talk with our lawyers today."

Talia insisted, "I will defer to your judgment, but Richard, this man MUST suffer for his deeds!"

"Whatever is done, Xian's health comes first," Dagmar said.  "If you'll all excuse me, I'm going to the hospital to help with Xian's surgery to remove the ring burned into her finger."

"I am coming with you," Talia said.  "At least I will feel like I am doing SOMETHING to help her."

Jane clicked on Dagmar's intercom. "Harmony, reschedule my day." Turning to Talia she said, "I'm coming too."

While Jane kept Talia occupied, Dagmar helped the plastic surgeon remove the ornate gold ring and sew Xian's finger. After a couple of hours, Dagmar went to the waiting room and sat with Jane and Talia. "It went well and she is resting quietly in her room. You can bring Xian home tomorrow. I have instructions for follow-up care and several prescriptions you can pick up today." Dagmar handed Talia a folder with the paperwork. Then she took out a small, yellow envelope. Inside was a wad of gauze that Dagmar opened enough to reveal the sinister gold wedding band completely cleaned and sterilized. She placed it back in the envelope and handed it to Talia. "As her guardian, I'm giving this to you for safe keeping. Would you like to see Xian?"

Choked with emotion, Talia only nodded.

The three women went to Xian's room to find her being removed from intravenous drips. When the nurses stepped back they saw Xian stock still as if she were a life-size doll lying in bed. "How are you feeling?" Talia asked.

"I am… fine," Xian said without looking at her sister.

"As long as she can walk, eat and take pills she will be released tomorrow. You can pick her up at 10 a.m. and I will come to your home at two for a session. Make sure Xian eats and she needs exercise. Walk around the house with her before I arrive."

# Chapter Nine

# Letter from Home

The next day, Dagmar went to check up on Xian and to have her first formal session. Rich answered his front door and ushered Dagmar inside. In the living room was his five-year-old daughter Jaynette. She most closely resembled her mother especially with her silky, pageboy cut, jet-black hair. Also like her mother and her Aunt Xian, Jaynette's extreme intelligence caused her to have difficulties with socialization. Her mind would race and she would wake up at night screaming from nightmares. However, Jaynette's psychiatrist, Jane Teasdale, was her Godmother and she used talk therapy and meditation to relax the hyperactive mind of the brilliant child. Jaynette walked directly up to her guest. "Hi Aunt Dagmar."

"Hi yourself, Baby."

"Why are you here?" the young girl asked.

Dagmar sighed, "Gotta love kids and their directness. I'm here to see your Aunt Xian."

"Oh," Jaynette said and immediately looked withdrawn.

"Jaynette? What's wrong?"

"Aunt Xian… scares me."

Dagmar and Rich looked at each other.  She dropped to one knee to be on eye level with Jaynette and asked, "Why does she scare you?"

"She's there… but not there.  She's like a doll."

"Jaynette, Aunt Xian has a problem with her brain.  She can't help the way she is."

"Will she get better?"

Dagmar took Jaynette's hand.  "I don't know Sweetie, but I'm going to do everything I can to help her."

Jaynette looked at Dagmar's hand and asked, "Why is your skin that color?"

Dagmar smiled and said, "You know how your rag dolls are all different colors?  Well, this is the color God wanted for me."

Considering what Dagmar just said, Jaynette smiled with understanding.  "You're smart.  And you're pretty!"

"You're pretty pretty yourself!  Just remember, pretty is nice but being smart is great!  And being a good and kind person is… awesome!  I'll bet you're going to be all three!"

"Just like you!  You're all three.  I can tell!"

"Jaynette, tell Mommy Aunt Dagmar's here," Rich said, and Jaynette ran out of the room.

A moment later, Talia entered.  "Hi Talia.  I assume Xian is home and settled in?"

"Yes," Talia said.  "Come.  I have to make the baby's bottle."
Dagmar and Rich followed Talia as she headed toward the kitchen.  "I made Xian scrambled eggs and we walked around a bit, just as you instructed.  I even gave Xian her mail."

"Mail?  What mail?" Dagmar questioned.

"She received an envelope from Father."

"What was in the envelope?"

48

"I do not know. I handed it to Xian and told her to read it. Then I took George to his room. I assume it was a get well card of some sort."

Sternly, Dagmar said, "She isn't ready for contact with the outside world… even your parents. If she gets any more mail, I want to see it before it's given to Xian."

As they entered the kitchen, Talia noticed the envelope on the counter. "Here it is. There is another envelope inside… that was sealed with wax. It is in Japanese."

"Where's Xian?!!" Dagmar asked with nervousness in her voice.

"I… I do not know. I left her at the kitchen table."

Knowing his wife was fluent in several languages Rich asked, "What does the letter say?"

"It looks like Father's staff forwarded the unopened letter." Paraphrasing, Talia read, "It is from her ex-husband. He said she was an embarrassment to him. He said that he is an honorable man and Xian brought dishonor to his family. He goes on to say that there is only one thing she can do to bring honor back to his name." Talia's eyes widened as she read the word, "Seppuku!"

"What's that?" Rich asked.

Dagmar yelled, "It's the Japanese form of ritual suicide! WHERE IS SHE?!!!"

"I'll check her room!" Talia said and bolted from the kitchen. Dagmar began to follow but Rich was delayed for a moment as he noticed a knife was missing from the butcher block.

Rich reached the room and a frantic Talia said, "The door is locked! Do you have the key?!!!"

He kicked the door in and they found Xian on the floor. The kitchen knife was in her gut and she was lying in a widening pool of blood.

"Get that out of her!!!" Talia screamed.

"NO!!! Talia, get me clean towels and if you have a medical kit, bring it! Rich, call 911! We need an ambulance, NOW! Tell them she's lost a lot of blood!!" Dagmar put her bare hands around the knife to reduce the bleeding. She also had to be careful to avoid moving the knife and causing more damage. Talia ran back with an armload of towels and a large first-aid kit. "Open ALL the sterile gauze and hand them to me." In a flash Talia began ripping open the packets and handing them to Dagmar, who arranged them around the wound. Next, Dagmar placed the towels around the knife and she used the tape from the medical kit to hold everything together. When Dagmar was done, the knife was immobilized.

Rich ran back into the room with the phone in his hand. "The operator says an ambulance is on the way. She wants to know what's going on."

"Hold the phone toward me," Dagmar said, still applying tape to the small mountain of towels. With raised voice, she said, "Tell the ER to expect a 36 year old female with a knife wound to her abdomen! She's lost a lot of blood! Have type 'O', universal donor, waiting and hurry the ambulance!!!"

Then, they all heard something that made their hearts freeze.

"Daddy? W-What's going on?"

Dagmar, Talia, and Rich turned to see Jaynette standing in the doorway with tears in her eyes.

Rich scooped her up in his free arm and ran out of Xian's room. He brought Jaynette to the nanny and quickly explained there was an emergency as the 911 operator could be heard saying "hello" over and over.

"Daddy what's going on?! Daddy?!!!"

Rich heard the ambulance siren and ran to the front door. He flashed the porch lights and the ambulance drove directly to the main house.

The paramedics went inside with a stretcher. They rolled Xian just enough to fit a backboard under her. She was then placed on the gurney and rushed into the ambulance with Talia and Dagmar. Rich followed the ambulance to the emergency room and held his wife as her sister was removed from the vehicle.

Dagmar jumped out of the ambulance and looked at her bloody hands. "Talia, I'm going to scrub in and work with the doctor. When I have any news, I'll come to the waiting room."

50

# Chapter Ten

# Assurance

The Sedgwick's nanny, Delmare, answered the front doorbell to see Jane Teasdale standing on the porch. "Hi Delmare. Rich called me from the hospital. He's concerned about Jaynette. May I see her?"

Delmare brought Jane to Jaynette's room. The five-year-old girl was crying on her bed. When she saw Jane, she ran to her and sobbed in her arms.

"Your father is worried about you," Jane said in a comforting way. "I'm here to answer any of your questions."

Choking through her sobs, Jaynette said, "You won't lie to me, will you Aunt Jane? You can tell me the truth. I'm old enough. I start school in the fall."

Smiling, Jane said, "Of course I won't lie to you. So, what did you see?"

"I saw Aunt Xian on her back with a knife sticking out of her. There was blood on her robe and the rug. Aunt Jane, is it safe here? Did someone do that to Aunt Xian?"

"If you're asking if someone broke into the house and attacked Aunt Xian, the answer is no."

"Then, who did it?"

Jane sighed. "She did it herself."

"Why?"

"Someone talked her into doing it. Jaynette, Aunt Xian's brain is… broken."

"Is that why I don't feel her in my head like I feel everyone else?"

"Yes, I think so."

Jaynette thought for a second. "Will she do this again?"

"We're going to make sure that no one will talk her into harming herself again. Aunt Dagmar is working very, VERY hard to help your Aunt Xian."

"I wish YOU were helping her. I like Aunt Dagmar but I know you better. You're my Godmother!"

Jane ran her fingers through Jaynette's silky black hair. "I'm helping other sick people who need me, but Aunt Dagmar is keeping me up to date. From what your father told me, she saved Aunt Xian's life. Aunt Dagmar is much better with the medical part of being a doctor than I am. With Aunt Dagmar helping her you should feel a whole lot better! Okay?"

"I guess so."

Jane noticed Jaynette's mind start to wander. Figuring that Jaynette was thinking about Xian, Jane distracted her. "Want to run through your meditations with me?" Jaynette sat on the floor in the lotus position and closed her eyes. "That's right. Say your secret chant," Jane instructed. While watching her Goddaughter silently mouth her chant, Jane wondered how this impressionable and emotional girl would react if it turns out she watched her Aunt die on the bedroom floor.

Dagmar rubbed her eyes as she walked to the hospital waiting room. Rich had his arm around Talia in a vain attempt to calm his wife. Hearing Dagmar's footsteps through the noisy din of the waiting room, Talia ran to her. Holding up her hands to slow Talia's approach, Dagmar said, "She's okay! She is VERY lucky!

Xian is so weak, malnourished, along with having a bandaged left hand, she didn't plunge the knife in the right place. And she must've passed out before she could twist it. There was a lot of blood since she nicked a few organs, but no serious damage."

"Oh, thank HEAVENS!" Talia wept. "And thank YOU! You knew just what to do for her!"

"Let's sit down. We have to talk," Dagmar said indicating the chairs. "For now, we have to manage Xian. No letters, no television, no Internet and no phone calls. Her only contact should be with you two, myself, and any of the doctors from my practice. It's important for your daughter to know Xian is alive and well. Let her see Xian and say hello. After that, no contact with the kids, her parents or her other sisters."

"For… for how long?" Talia asked.

"Until I've made some progress with her, Xian is only to interact with essential caregivers. Clear her room of anything she could use to harm herself. Her robes and kimonos should have no belt. Remove all the toiletries and razors from her bathroom. Make sure she has nothing sharp. I don't know if the blood will come out of the rug in her room but it's best that she isn't reminded of the incident unless I bring it up in therapy."

"I will have a new carpet installed by late tomorrow morning," Talia assured Dagmar.

"Good. I'll come by everyday to make sure she bathes and I'll change her dressings."

"Isn't that something a home health aide should do?" Rich asked.

"Normally yes, but I want to get Xian to trust me. It's human nature to trust the people who take care of you. She is so withdrawn I have to work with her on a visceral level."

"Will she ever become a normal functioning woman?" Talia asked.

Rich added, "We're looking for a glimmer of hope."

Dagmar smiled. "I don't make promises I can't keep. All I can say is that I'm going to give it my best shot." She hesitated for a second and continued. "I know that's not what you want to hear. If it helps, I can say I'm… optimistic. I have nothing to base that on. I just feel I can help. I'm making Xian my only priority. I'll either be working with her or studying up on cases similar to hers… if I can find any. I'm going to run a couple more tests. You both might as well go home. You can pick her up tomorrow morning at ten.  I'll be at your house at two p.m. to change her dressings and get some answers."

# *Chapter Eleven*

# Answers/ No Answers

At noon the next day, Jane Teasdale had finished recording her notes from her previous patient. She was leaving her office to go to lunch when the receptionist stopped her. "Excuse me, Doctor Teasdale. Doctor Lamont wants you to meet her at the coffee shop."

"Oh? I didn't see it on my calendar."

"It isn't, but she said it's important."

"Then… I guess I'm having lunch at the coffee shop."

As Jane started to leave, Harmony added, "Oh, Doctor Teasdale? Doctor Lamont said YOU are buying lunch."

Jane rolled her eyes and preceded to one of her favorite places… the coffee shop. She placed an order for her usual sandwich, the "Turkey Bomb". When she received her food it included a garden salad with grilled chicken. "I'm sorry. The salad isn't mine."

The counterperson told Jane, "The woman at the far corner table said you would pay for it."

Jane looked in the corner of the coffee shop and saw Dagmar with files and her laptop computer monopolizing most of the table. After paying with her credit card, Jane brought the sandwich and salad to Dagmar's table. "Hey, 'Supermodel,' pretty sneaky the way you got me to buy you lunch."

"It's a working lunch, 'Lusty and Busty.' Expense it to the practice. Sit. I need answers," Dagmar demanded as she took her salad. "I've spent last night and most of this morning trying to find a case like Xian's. After coming up with nothing I went to get Talia's file and… it's huge!" Dagmar said indicating the large amount of paper in several folders on the table. "Catch me up on her."

Jane picked at her sandwich as she spoke. "The short version is that Talia and her sisters hit the genetic lottery. They are all strong and intelligent, especially Talia."

"Define intelligent," Dagmar said as she ate her salad.

"Talia's I.Q. is one hundred and ninety four."

"Are you sure? People that intelligent have extreme social problems."

"I'm sure. Talia has a raging anger she keeps under control by fixating on Rich and the kids. When she said she wanted to kill Xian's husband… well… that wasn't an idle threat."

"Where does her anger come from?"

"Her family… her parents mostly. Talia was treated with brain drugs like Xian but her mind was more resistant."

"I don't suppose she remembers what drugs were given to Xian."

Jane sifted through Talia's file and pulled several pages from the report. "No, but this is what Talia was given."

Dagmar looked horrified as she read through six pages of prescription drugs prescribed to Talia. "How is she still alive? This is unbelievable!"

"You may want to read the entire file."

"I will. Tonight. I've got something to show you." Dagmar took a brain scan from a large manila envelope by her chair and handed it to Jane.

"Xian?" Jane asked. "Are these the dead spots in her brain you mentioned in your assessment?"

56

"Yes. Now look at this," Dagmar said as she handed Jane a second scan.

"I'm not very good at reading these…" Jane's voice trailed off. "When was this done?"

"Late yesterday. Same layer. About thirty-six hours after the last one."

"It's different. Some of the 'dead' areas now show electrical activity but other parts that seemed healthy look 'dead'. What the hell is going on?"

"That's what I've been trying to figure out. I think Xian is unconsciously shutting down parts of her brain to block out memories and pain."

"Is… is that possible?"

"It looks like it's possible for Xian. I doubt even Talia can do that. Do you know what this means? She might be able to get it all back. Memories, emotions… everything!"

"But… how?"

"I was hoping you might have some ideas," Dagmar sighed.

"Dag, you haven't even had a session with her yet. You rushed her to the hospital during her assessment, and the next time you met she tried to kill herself."

"Why do I get all the easy assignments?" Dagmar mumbled.

"Look, if you want me to take her…"

"No," Dagmar sighed. "I've got it. I guess I wanted to hit the ground running with this one. She's lost so much of her life already."

"You know how this works," Jane said. "This isn't like putting a bandage on a scrape. You need to invest the time. When do you see Xian again?"

"An hour and a half from now."

"Email your raw notes to me when you're done."

Dagmar arrived at the Sedgwick home with her doctor's bag and Talia showed her to Xian's room. "The door has been repaired already?" Dagmar asked referring to the day before when Rich kicked it open.

"Yes, and the carpet has been replaced. The workers left an hour ago," Talia said.

"Just make sure the lock is disabled. Please bring in her prescriptions and a plastic cup," Dagmar said as she knocked and entered the room. Xian was sitting on the bed with her hands folded. "Good afternoon, Xian."

"Hello, Doctor Lamont," Xian said without looking at her.

Dagmar took a thermometer from her bag and said, "I'm going to take your temperature." She brought the thermometer to Xian but she sat still. "Open your mouth. I'm going to place this under your tongue." Xian complied and Dagmar took her wrist to check her pulse. Then, Dagmar took out her blood pressure cuff and sat beside Xian. While checking her blood pressure, Talia walked into the room with several pill bottles. "Would you get your sister some water?" Dagmar asked and Talia went into Xian's bathroom to fill the plastic cup. After checking her temperature and listening to Xian's heart, Dagmar took out two small paper cups and began filling them with the various pills.

"Should I leave?" Talia asked.

"No. I want you here while I change her dressings. Xian," Dagmar said as she held up one of the paper cups, "These are your medications. This cup has various antibiotics. Please take them now."

Talia handed Xian the water and Dagmar held the cup of pills. One by one, she took each pill from the cup and swallowed it with a sip of water. Xian never looked at her sister or her doctor. She simply took the pills obediently.

"Very good," Dagmar complimented. She took the other paper cup and explained each pill before handing it to Xian. "This is a multiple vitamin. This is a 'B' complex. Timed-released vitamin 'C'. Vitamin 'D'. Vitamin 'E'. Calcium." When Xian finished the last tablet, Dagmar said, "None of these pills will affect your brain. They are to heal and fortify your body. Do you understand?"

"Yes, Doctor Lamont."

"I want to examine you and change your dressings. I'm going to give you a shower today. Tomorrow, I want you to shower by yourself after I remove your bandages. I'll apply fresh dressings when you're done." Dagmar turned to Talia. "Let's help her into the bathroom." Once in the bathroom Dagmar said,

"We're going to remove your kimono." After donning latex gloves, Dagmar and Talia removed Xian's kimono and let it drop to the floor. One by one Dagmar removed the bandages and inspected each sore, cut, abrasion and bruise. Then, they helped Xian into the shower. Dagmar adjusted the temperature of the water and washed Xian's long, silky black hair. She then took the shower massage and began rinsing her patient's back. Dagmar took the back brush and placed it in Xian's hand. Slowly, she showed Xian how to raise lather with the soap and the brush. She guided her patient's hand, teaching Xian to wash her back without disturbing her sutures. Dagmar quickly washed Xian's face, arms, and legs. Then, handing her the washcloth Dagmar said, "I'm going to give you some privacy to wash your chest and between your legs." Closing the shower curtain, she turned to Talia. "Would you please get a protein drink for your sister?" When Talia returned, they helped Xian out of the shower and towel dried her. Carefully, Dagmar reapplied her dressings and placed her hands on Xian's lower ribs. "Does this hurt?"

"I am fine."

"That's not what I asked you. Are your ribs sore? Are they getting better?"

"Yes. Better."

"Okay. I won't pad your ribs but let me know if they become uncomfortable."

"Yes, Doctor Lamont."

Placing a fresh, clean robe around her, Dagmar led Xian back to her bed. As Xian sat, Dagmar poured the protein drink into the plastic cup. "This is a low calorie protein concentrate. Before we start our sessions I want you to drink one of these. You're very thin and rundown. I want to build you back up." Dagmar turned to Talia, "Before I came here, I emailed a list of food I want you to buy for Xian. I want you to make sure your sister gets good nutrition. I know you have a fitness room in your home. I'm going to email you an exercise routine for Xian to follow before I arrive each day. Email me everyday on her number of reps and the amount of weight used on each machine."

"I will."

"Exercise may not seem important to your sister's recovery but it is. I'm using this in place of what my colleagues and I call 'brain drugs' which were improperly prescribed to Xian, and you, in the past. In most cases, breaking a sweat is better than taking a pill." Turning back to Xian, Dagmar handed her the cup with the protein drink. "Here you go." Xian drank the liquid in small sips and returned the cup to Dagmar without looking at her. "It comes in different flavors. I had your sister pick up vanilla. Do you like the taste?"

Stoically, Xian answered, "It is fine."

Dagmar turned to Talia and said, "Would you excuse us? I'd like to start our session." Talia collected the pills, cup and yesterday's kimono and then left the room. Dagmar sat in a chair opposite the bed her patient sat on. She took a note pad and pen from her bag. "So, how are you feeling today?"

"I am fine."

"I usually begin by asking why my patient came to me. I'd like to hear what my patient thinks is wrong with them. So... what's wrong?"

"Nothing is wrong. I am fine."

"You may think so, but your sister and parents are worried about you."

"I realize that, Doctor Lamont, but their fears are unfounded."

Uncertain to how to proceed, Dagmar thought for a second. "Okay... let's start from the beginning. Tell me about your childhood."

"I was born in Los Angeles, California and lived in a mansion in the hills on the outskirts of the city."

"Parents? Grandparents?"

"My grandparents died before my birth. My parents are Yuri and Athena Tamislav. Doctor, since you know Talia, I believe you know all of this."

"Just humor me. Siblings?"

"I have four sisters... Valentina, Talia, Aiko and Rini."

Dagmar made some quick notes and asked, "How was your childhood?"

"It was fine."

Cocking her head and looking skeptical, Dagmar returned, "It was? Your sister told her therapist something different. She said you would wake up in the middle of the night screaming from nightmares and a racing mind. You would throw things. You resisted going to school. Never obeyed your parents."

60

Without flinching, Xian replied, "That must have been long ago when I was a child. I do not remember the details of my childhood."

"You don't remember your father beating you?"

"No, Doctor Lamont."

"You don't remember the psychiatrists and the drugs they administered? You don't remember how the drugs removed the spark from your life?"

"No, Doctor Lamont."

Dagmar made more notes and leaned back in her chair. "Do you remember your sister's wedding?"

Xian thought for a second and said, "I remember that she is married. I believe I was in attendance."

"During the reception, do you remember your mother taking you aside and inspecting your arms for abuse?"

"No, Doctor Lamont."

Dagmar made another note and paused. "Do you remember yesterday's suicide attempt?"

"Yes, Doctor Lamont."

Dagmar's thought process was jolted for a second. She expected her patient to deny it happened. "Why did you do it?"

"To restore my husband's honor," Xian said casually.

"EX-husband," Dagmar corrected. "How did you cause him to lose his honor?"

"That is something only my husband… my ex-husband can answer."

"Speculate for me."

"I assume he lost honor because of our divorce."

"Did you initiate the divorce?"

"No, Doctor Lamont."

"Then how can you be the cause of his 'dishonor'?"

"Again, I do not know his reasons. It was a decision made between my ex-husband and my father."

"Will you try to kill yourself again?"

"There is no point. I failed at suicide as I failed in my marriage."

"Since you were married to a wealthy man you didn't have to work. What did you do all day?"

"Each day was different."

"Give me an example."

"I would read. I studied the art collection. I sat in the garden. I saw all the forms of kabuki."

"Did you see kabuki with your husband?"

"No, Doctor Lamont."

"Why not?"

Xian hesitated. Her eyes darted back and forth for a moment, then she answered, "My husband is a very busy man."

"He's got to have some time off. Doesn't he like the kabuki?"

"It is his favorite form of entertainment."

"Then, why didn't he see it with you?"

"He would go with… others."

"What others?"

"I don't know. It was not my business."

It took a moment for Dagmar to process Xian's response. "You were his wife! How your husband spends his leisure time IS your business!"

For the first time, Xian turned her head in Dagmar's direction and almost looked at her. Each word dripped with venom. "How little you understand traditional Japanese culture… Doctor Lamont."

Dagmar sat in stunned silence. Looking at her notepad Dagmar read the words "No Answer" over and over in response to her questions. She put her pen and pad back in her doctor's bag. "I think that's it for toda…"

"Good bye, Doctor Lamont," Xian said, before Dagmar could finish her sentence; as if rushing her to leave.

Dagmar walked to the door. She stopped and turned back to Xian. "Do you remember being raped?"

As cool as always, Xian said, "No, Doctor Lamont."

"Do you remember being sodomized?"

"No, Doctor Lamont."

"How did you get Gonorrhea?"

"Sorry, Doctor Lamont. I don't know what you're talking about."

Dagmar suppressed a sigh and left the room. As soon as she closed the door to Xian's room, Talia came running to Dagmar. "How did it go?" Talia asked.

Dagmar looked at a face radiating hope. Completely at a loss for words, Dagmar said, "See you tomorrow."

# *Chapter Twelve*

# Direction

For eight days they settled into a routine.  Dagmar would change Xian's dressings after a shower.  Xian would drink her protein concentrate and take her pills after which Dagmar would question her and get no results.  One morning as Dagmar was in her office, poring over one of her medical books for a fresh idea to help her patient, the intercom buzzed.

"Doctor Lamont, you're wanted in the conference room."

Dagmar left her office and went to the receptionist.  "Who?"

"Everyone," Harmony answered.

As she opened the door, Dagmar saw Anabelle, Jane and Candace on one side of the conference table with a single chair on the other side facing them. "What's going on?" she asked as she sat down.

"Dag, how are things going with Xian Tamislav?" Jane asked.

"Slow.  Frustrating.  I've been updating all of you with my emails. You all know how difficult this case has been."

"We know," Anabelle said. "Everyone in this room thinks you've done a fantastic job."

Skeptically, Dagmar said, "Thanks. Why do I feel there's a 'but' coming?"

"We're concerned about your lack of progress," Jane said.

"What?! Jane, YOU had to remind ME to be patient, remember?"

"There's new factor," Candace said as she took out her micro recorder and placed it on the table. "This is from my last session with Talia." Candace played back part of their session.

Candace: *Talia, you're agitated again. You seem to be worsening each session.*

Talia: *I... I cannot help myself. I am growing angrier every day!*

Candace: *Why?*

Talia: *I cannot stop thinking about my sister, Xian, and the agony her life has been. Even though we have rescued her from her husband she is still a prisoner of her own mind. I want to find him! I want to find that cur she called a husband and rend him limb from limb!*

Candace: *Jane told me Rich would take care of him.*

Talia: *Richard had our lawyers contact the Japanese government. They say there is nothing they can do.*

Candace: *I doubt he is going to give up that easily.*

Talia: *No, Richard is not giving up, but each day that I see my sister, a mere shell of a woman, I am more convinced that my way to solve this is the right way!*

Candace: *Your way?*

Talia: *I want to take the next flight to Japan, go to his home, and torture him in ways he cannot imagine! Would you like to know what I would do?*

Candace switched off the small device. "She went on to explain in lavish detail what she planned to do to him. Talia… scared me," Candace admitted with a shudder.

Choosing her words carefully, Anabelle said, "It might be time to… shuffle the deck. A different therapist could be just what Xian needs."

Nodding, Jane added, "You can go out and canvas for new patients again."

"No!" Dagmar shot back. "You are not taking me off this case!"

"There is more at stake here than your patient," Jane said. "You've read Talia's file. I can tell you that she is capable of carrying out her threat, pregnant or not!"

"Listen, I've been busting my shapely butt for this woman and I'm not giving up on her! Candace, how did the rest of that session with Talia go?"

"We spent the remainder of the time meditating and working on relaxation techniques."

"Good! You do your job and I'll do mine!" With those words, Dagmar left the conference room and slammed the door. As she walked past the reception desk she barked at Harmony, "Coffee! Dark and sweet!" Dagmar slammed the door to her office, grabbed her book and threw herself into one of the chairs. A couple of minutes later there was a soft knock on the door. "Come in, Harmony." Instead of Harmony, Anabelle Loomis brought in her coffee. "Anabelle, I'm not in the mood!"

Never losing her smile, Anabelle placed the coffee on the table beside Dagmar and sat down. "The bosses are very impressed with you."

"Then, why do they want to take me off the case?"

"None of us WANT to take that case over! You heard the recording. We're just worried that her sister might do something crazy. Candace doesn't want to admit it, but Talia's relaxation stuff isn't working as well as it has."

"I know I can help Xian. I can feel it in my soul. I just need more time!"

Anabelle smiled. "For two people who are such good friends you and I approach work so differently. You're so analytical! You think you're going to find your answers in a book. I'm just the opposite. I go by my woman's intuition. It hasn't always been right, especially with men, but it works most of the time."

"What are you saying?"

Anabelle stood and walked to the door. "I'm saying it might be time to take a new approach. Think about it."

Dagmar continued her routine of speaking to Xian and not accomplishing anything with her therapy. The lack of progress was beginning to weigh on her. To clear her head Dagmar went to visit her parents' apartment.

"Hi, Mommy," she said as she kissed her mother's cheek. Dagmar walked into the living room and saw her father sitting in his favorite chair, perspiring. "Daddy? Why are you sweating?"

"I just got home from work and, I swear, someone is adding more stairs to this building! It's nothing, Baby. I'll be all right."

"I'm making coffee for your father. Want some?" Dagmar's mother offered.

"Yes, please. It's been an exhausting day."

The two women went into the kitchen. As Dagmar's mother began spooning coffee in an old style percolator she asked, "What's wrong, Baby? Problems with work?"

"It's my patient," Dagmar admitted as she sat at the kitchen table. "She's locked up tight. She's been through some horrible abuse but sits across from me as cool as a cucumber and says that she doesn't remember anything. I reword the same questions everyday hoping I'll get something different from her."

Sitting at the table while the coffee began to perk, Dagmar's mother said, "I don't know anything about all this psychology stuff, but I know that the best way to help someone is to give them what they need."

Smiling, Dagmar said, "I think she wants me to leave her alone."

"No. Don't give her what she WANTS. Give her what she NEEDS."

"She's living in her wealthy sister's home. She doesn't need anything."

Dagmar's mother checked the coffee and turned back to her daughter. "How old was this woman when she first had her problems?"

"Eleven. Xian is thirty-six now."

"Seems to me your patient must've missed out on a lot in all those years… maybe in her lifetime. She's lost a lot so she needs a lot. You just have to figure it out. You make sure you help this woman!"

"I will," Dagmar relented. "Another problem is that… well… I don't like her."

"Baby?"

"When she does speak, she's… snotty and condescending. She doesn't look at me when I talk to her. She's standoffish."

Mrs. Lamont placed cups and saucers on the table. "Let me tell you something about yourself Dagmar Rochelle Lamont… you got a way about you. People LIKE you… even if it's just a little bit. What's the word for all that?"

Dagmar smiled. "You mean charisma?"

"That's it! Charisma! You've got that. Just one look and men fall in love with you. Just one look and women want to be your friend. If this woman doesn't like you… she's workin' at it!"

Mister Lamont walked in the room. "I smell coffee. What are you women talking about?"

"Dagmar thinks her patient doesn't like her."

"Ain't no one doesn't like my Baby," he said as he sat at the table.

Dagmar laughed, "I think my boss, Candace, would disagree with you."

"She's jealous, but she likes you," Dagmar's mother said as she poured three cups of coffee. "Stay for dinner, Baby?"

"I thought you'd never ask."

Dagmar and her parents had an early dinner and they did not mention her job again. She was smiling as she drove home still basking in the warm glow of her parents company. Then, on the radio, she heard a song by the singer Sade called

"Soldier of Love." Even though Dagmar had heard the song many times, the first lyrics stuck in her head:

*"I've lost the use of my heart. But I'm still alive."*

She thought about Xian and how those words applied to her. Dagmar now understood her patient, and she knew how to treat her.

# Chapter Thirteen

# Open & Honest

The next day, Talia was surprised as she answered her door. Dagmar arrived as usual but instead of her business suit she wore jeans and a plaid blouse. "Come in Dagmar. You look different today."

"I'm changing it up a little. Before I see Xian, could I talk to you for a second?"

Talia was tense as they walked into the living room. "Is something wrong with my sister?"

"Nothing like that," Dagmar said as they sat. "I just wanted to see how you're doing."

"Me? I suppose I am all right."

"Let me be direct. Candace told me about your growing obsession with punishing Xian's ex-husband."

"It weighs… heavily on me," Talia said with intensity.

"We still don't know if her husband is responsible for what happened to Xian in Japan."

"It does not matter. If her abuse was done by another, her husband should have protected her."

"I agree, but your fixation is affecting you."

Sounding dark and ominous, Talia said, "That will change once I have my revenge."

"It's not your revenge to have! If ANYONE should have ANYTHING to say about revenge, it's the woman in the other room! We MUST wait for Xian to come to us about her abuse. Sometimes therapy works fast, but usually it's slow. I know the process of helping your sister is agonizingly slow to you but that's how it works. Talia, give it time. Everything will unfold AS it should, WHEN it should."

"Well…"

"You have so much in your life. A handsome husband, two perfect children with two more on the way, and you're wealthy! Don't let thoughts of revenge, which isn't even yours, poison all that you have."

Talia was silent for a moment and then said haltingly, "You… have given me… much to think about."

"I read every word of your file. You've had a lot of anger and rage buried inside of you. But since you've met Rich and had your children, those negative emotions have been far overshadowed by generosity, joy, kindness and love. You've made a conscious choice to bring that into your life. Despite the horror your sister has gone through, I'm sure you'll continue to make the right choice."

Talia could not suppress a small smile. "Whatever Kane & Teasdale is paying you… it is not enough."

"True that!" Dagmar said with a little laugh in her voice. "C'mon. Let's see someone who REALLY needs my help."

They went to Xian's room and began their ritual. As Dagmar inspected Xian's injuries she said, "You're healing better than I expected. You don't need dressings anymore and we'll start to phase out the antibiotics. The protein drinks, exercise and proper nourishment are making you look much more healthy. From your ability to snap back it looks like you have Talia's constitution."

"All the sisters heal quickly," Talia informed. "Jane says it is in our genetics."

"No doubt. Talia, I'm ready to start the session. Will you excuse us?"

"Of course," Talia said and exited the room.

Dagmar sat in the chair across from Xian and asked, "How are you feeling today?"

"I am fine."

Looking at Xian with a smile on her face, Dagmar said, "Xian, I have a confession. I didn't like you very much. You've made my job very difficult. I've spent a lot of time and effort trying to help you but you haven't made any attempt to help yourself. Then, I heard a song on the radio and the first words were, 'I've lost the use of my heart, but I'm still alive.' Your heart was lost… your soul has been crushed over and over since you were an eleven-year-old girl and after all you've been through… you're still here. You're still alive. The way you've stayed alive is by retreating into your own mind. When you must speak you're cool and aloof to push people away as a defense mechanism. I suspect you aren't convinced that you won't go back to that hell… or some different hell. For twenty-five years you've become more and more withdrawn just to survive. And here I am. Your therapist. The one person on earth who is supposed to understand. Instead, I get angry with you. I thought of you as someone trying to fight me. I forgot that you're a victim. For that, I'm sorry. I'm the doctor and I should have known better."

If Xian agreed, disagreed, or felt anything, it was not visible on her face. Dagmar continued. "Also, I walked in this room, told you I was your therapist and started questioning you. I didn't intend it, but that was rude of me. How can I expect you to answer these personal questions if you don't know me? My name is Dagmar Rochelle Lamont. I graduated magna cum laude and went on to med school. In college, I stumbled on three crazy but brilliant girls; Candace, Jane and Anabelle. We formed a study group and became very close. After med school, Candace and Jane decided to open their own office. When their practice took off, they offered a job to Anabelle and me. For the last few months I've been bringing in new patients. Some fly in from all over the country just to talk to us. We're kinda chic in Hollywood circles. What else can I tell you? Anabelle is divorced, Candace and Jane are married to amazing guys who treat them like gold, and I'm single. There've been a couple close calls but I never married. Most of my money goes toward student loans and to help my parents and grandparents. Do you remember much about your family?"

Xian gave no answer.

"Your parents are wealthy and your family business is run by your sisters Valentina and Aiko under the scrutiny of your father. Your sister Rini is a surgeon right here in Connecticut and Talia married a great guy. I don't know how much you remember about Talia but I can tell you she is an amazing woman. Your sisters all have very high I.Q.'s but Talia is at the high-end genius level and she's extremely intuitive. Talia is also much stronger than she looks and all of her senses are heightened. She has amazing eyesight and keen hearing. Between her sense of smell and taste she can eat at a restaurant and replicate the meal at home. Some, or all of these gifts may be locked inside you. Do you remember being anything like Talia?"

A shudder passed through Xian's body. It made her appear as if she shook her head no.

"I've been thinking about what you need to get better. You've needed a family, a real family, since you were a kid. Since you don't recall your childhood, I'll share memories about my childhood and family with you."

## Chapter Fourteen

# Baby, Girl, Lady, Woman

Dagmar sat back in her chair and spoke causally to Xian. "I want to tell you a story about how Mommy helped me. And, yes, even though I'm an adult, I still call my parents Mommy and Daddy. I was fourteen and came home from school hurt and upset."

Dagmar began her story:

The young girl entered her apartment through the kitchen door with eyes that examined the floor. Mother was folding laundry on the table as her daughter trudged by. "How was school, Baby?"

"Okay," young Dagmar mumbled, and without a look, shuffled out of the kitchen and to her room.

When Mrs. Lamont took an armful of clean clothes to her daughter's room, she saw Dagmar's face buried in her pillow as she tried to stifle her sobs. Mrs. Lamont let the laundry fall out of her arms and went to the bed. "Baby, what's wrong?" she said, stroking her daughter's hair.

"I can't tell you."

"Baby, I'm your Mama.  You can tell me anything.  What's making you cry?"

"It's… a boy, Mommy," Dagmar sniffed as she sat up in bed.

Mrs. Lamont stiffened and said, "What did some boy do to make my Baby cry?"

"It's not what he did, it's what he said."

"Oh," Mrs. Lamont said and relaxed.  After thinking a half a second she tightened up again.  "What'd he say?"

"Remember D'shaun… in my class?  I… kinda... like him.  All the girls like him.  I was trying to get him to talk to me, but he said he didn't like me. He said he only liked white girls.  Sometimes… I wish I were white."

An unusual streak of anger shot across the mother's face.  She cupped her hand under her daughter's chin and raised her head so their eyes met.  "Don't you ever, EVER say that again!  Don't even THINK it!  This is the color God wanted you to be, and God don't make mistakes!  Understand?"  Looking at her daughter's hot tears running down her face, Mrs. Lamont brushed them away and took a seat on the bed.  "You're too good for that 'D'shaun' and I'm going to prove it to you.  It looks like we have to have a talk about being a woman."

"Mommy, we already had that talk."

"I'm not talking about sex.  I'm talking about growing up.  A female matures from baby to girl to lady to woman.  You start from the bottom and work your way up.  When you're a baby, you cry when you're hungry because you don't know anything else.  You don't care if mother is out of formula or busy making dinner.  A baby thinks the world is all about her needs and doesn't care about anyone else.  If YOU were only interested in white boys and this 'D'shaun' asked you out, would you say you only want to date white boys?"

"No."

"Why not?"

"Because it would hurt his feelings."

Mrs. Lamont projected her radiant smile.  "That's what makes you better than D'shaun.  He's a baby.  He only cares about his own selfish needs.  You

76

aren't a baby. You're a girl. Do you want to be a young lady?" Dagmar nodded. "You don't carry it around. You get over it. You don't let him bother you."

"But Mommy, how do I do that?"

"You take a day. You take a day to be angry, to grieve, to be sad, to scream. Do what you got to do to let it all out. The next day you start out fresh 'cause you've let out all that pain. You may still feel sad or angry, but the worst is behind you."

"I'll never get a boy to like me. I'm too skinny and plain."

Mrs. Lamont stood and said, "Come with me."

Dagmar followed her mother into her parents' bedroom. Mrs. Lamont opened her dresser drawer and took out a snapshot. "Baby, did I ever show you this picture?"

Dagmar examined the photograph closely. "When did you take that picture? I don't have those clothes."

"That's not you, Baby. That's me when I was your age. Look at me now. Do you think I look skinny and plain?"

"Mommy, you're beautiful!"

"You're going to grow up to look like me. Probably better! In the meantime…" Mrs. Lamont said as she examined her daughter's face. "You can use a little foundation… just a little. I think you're old enough."

"Really?!!!"

"Sure, Baby. Maybe we'll shorten and straighten your hair."

"You said I went from baby to girl. When I put D'shaun behind me I'll be a young lady. When do I become a woman?"

"A woman puts her family and her loved ones before everything else. A woman is responsible. A woman is compassionate and, most of all, a woman is strong of heart. You become a woman when you face adversity… REAL adversity… and survive it."

"Is that what D'shaun will have to do to become a man?"

"Sometimes, people get stuck where they are and they never get out. D'shaun may be a baby all his life or he may grow out of it. Understand?"

Young Dagmar nodded. "I think so." She thought for a second and asked, "What about Daddy? Was he a baby when you met him?"

Mrs. Lamont smiled. "Your Daddy was, and is, and always will be, all man! I think he was born that way. He's been a strong man as long as I've known him. When we met, there was electricity in the air. That man would do anything for me. He hated to dance, but he danced with me 'cause I loved it." Mrs. Lamont turned on her radio and 'Ain't Too Proud to Beg' by The Temptations was playing. As Dagmar watched, her mother began dancing... showing off. She reached out to her daughter and they both began dancing.

Supper was late, but young Dagmar was smiling when she went to sleep that night.


Dagmar concluded her story:

"The next day," she said to Xian, "I came home from school and found Mommy made me my favorite... a Red Velvet cake. She said a little Red Velvet chases the blues away. Nobody makes it like she does." Dagmar sighed and continued, "That's my story about how my mommy taught me to get over boys that didn't like me. My parents are very wise. The older I get, the more I appreciate them."

Xian sat quietly but she seemed different. The vacant look where she would retreat into her own world was somewhat missing. Though the difference was subtle, Dagmar could tell that Xian had followed her story... with interest.

## Chapter Fifteen

# Goodbye

Dagmar returned to the Sedgwick home day after day and cheerfully relayed stories about her family. Xian heard about Mrs. Lamont's wisdom and understanding. She learned about Dagmar's strong father who could make his daughter feel like a million dollars with a smile but could express more disapproval with a look than most men could with a lecture. Through all the stories, Xian never looked at her therapist once. However, several times it seemed as if she was going to say something… maybe ask a question… but backed off. The process was slow but Dagmar knew she was on the right track by sharing her family with her patient. Xian was becoming… involved.

The morning was like any other. Dagmar was sitting across from Xian about to tell another story when her cell phone buzzed. Annoyed but curious, Dagmar excused herself and checked her phone. She was surprised when she saw that her grandmother was calling.

"Mama Rue? Is everything all right?"

"I… I don't know. This morning, I woke up from a dream where I heard sirens and people running up and down the steps. Your granddaddy had the same dream too! I called your mother and father but there's no answer. I… I'm going to try to climb the steps to see where they are."

"No, Mama Rue! You and Granddaddy stay right where you are! I'll be there as fast as I can!" Dagmar quickly grabbed her doctor's bag and said to Xian, "I have to go! I'm sorry!" Seeing Talia as she left the house she yelled, "Family emergency! I'll call later!" Dagmar jumped in her car and sped off the property.

Stopping in front of her parents' two family house, Dagmar ran inside to her grandparents' apartment. "Mama Rue… Granddaddy… are you both all right?!!"

"We're fine, Baby," Dagmar's grandfather said with a shaky voice. "Why aren't they answering the phone?"

"That's what I'm going to find out. Stay here!" Dagmar bolted up the stairs and saw the door to her parents' apartment open. No one was home and at first glance it seemed like nothing was wrong. One of the throw rugs was askew but nothing else was out of place. Dagmar went into her parent's bedroom and saw the bed was unmade. As she looked around the room her heart froze. Dagmar noticed her mother's purse was missing and one of her father's pill bottles was open and spilled on the dresser.

"Oh my God… Daddy?" she whispered.

Dagmar ran down the stairs and out of the building. She hammered her Porsche's gas pedal and flew down the street toward the hospital. Doctor Lamont slammed her brakes and skidded to a stop in front of the emergency room entrance. Charging past the front desk Dagmar ran into the emergency room yelling "DADDY!" over and over.

Her former boyfriend Bryce stepped away from his patient and went to Dagmar. "Dagmar! Stop! There are patients in here!"

"I want Daddy! Where's my Daddy!"

"He 's right there," Bryce said and pointed to one of the beds.

Dagmar's father was sitting on a hospital bed wearing an oxygen mask. She ran to her father and embraced him. "Thank you God! Thank you Jesus! Daddy, you gave me such a scare!" She leaned back and saw tear tracks on his face and on the mask. "Daddy? What's wrong?" Dagmar was about to look at her father's chart when she noticed her mother's purse next to him. As long as she had known him, he had never touched his wife's purse. An icy fear gripped Dagmar's heart. "Where's Mommy?" All Mister Lamont could do was shake his head and cry.

"MOMMY!!!" Dagmar shrieked. Bryce came over to her.

"Dagmar, keep it down! Your father said he was taking his pills when he heard your mother fall. He called 911, took your mother's purse because it had their insurance card, and rode the ambulance here. It looks like she had a cerebral hemorrhage. She probably died before she hit the floor. I'm sorry."

"No! NO!!! There's nothing wrong with Mommy! She's strong… healthy! MOMMY! Where ARE you?!!! MOMMY!!!" Bryce tried to hold her in his arms but Dagmar pushed him away. "NO! Don't TOUCH me! What's wrong with you?!!!"

Bryce motioned to a couple of orderlies and said, "Put her in bed seven and restrain her."

As the orderlies dragged her to the bed she screamed, "No! NO!!! Daddy needs me! NO!!!"

While being restrained, Bryce turned to a nurse and said, "five of Haldol." The nurse prepared the syringe and handed it to the doctor. "This is for your own good," Bryce said as he injected her.

Immediately, Dagmar began thrashing, trying to fight off the effects of the drug. After a half a minute she collapsed into a fitful twilight sleep.

"That's right. Relax. I'll take care of you," Bryce said as he stroked her hair.

Fifty minutes later, Jane came running into the emergency room. "Where's Dagmar Lamont?!" she asked the first nurse she saw.

Before the nurse could answer, Bryce walked up to Jane and said, "Just a minute! Who are you?"

"Doctor Janasha Teasdale. I'm her boss and her friend! Dagmar ran out of a therapy session due to a family emergency. I called her cell, her home, her parents, the police, and finally your ER said she was here. Now… where is she?"

"I have everything under control. Why don't you take a seat in the waiting room? I'll talk to you later."

The tomboy in Jane was beginning to bubble up to the surface of her emotions. As she opened her mouth to tell Bryce off she heard her name being called in a garbled voice. Jane threw back the curtain on a nearby bed and saw Dagmar with leather straps on her wrists and ankles.

"Help…" Dagmar mumbled.

Looking at Bryce, "What the hell happened?!!!" Jane demanded.

"I told you to go to the waiting room!"

Jane grabbed the chart and read that Dagmar was agitated because of the death of her mother. She looked at Dagmar and said, "Oh my God! Your mom? Dag… I'm so sorry." Jane looked farther on the chart then fixed an angry stare at Bryce. "You gave her an antipsychotic?!!!"

"She was in shock," Bryce said coolly.

"Of course she was in shock! She just lost her mother!!! Where's her father?"

"He's right over…" Bryce looked around and saw Mister Lamont's bed was empty. "Nurse," Bryce snapped, "where's the patient that was in this bed?"

The nurse said, "He walked out a few minutes ago. I couldn't stop him."

"So," Jane said with anger radiating from her face, "You've got everything under control, huh? What were your plans on treating Dagmar?"

"We used to date. I'm going to bring her back to my place to sleep off the drug."

"The hell you are!" Jane said and began to unbuckle the restraints.

Through her haze, Dagmar slurred to Jane, "Mommy. I have to see Mommy."

Jane looked at Bryce with steely eyes and said, "Where's her mother?"

"The morgue."

Jane turned to a nurse and said, "Get her release papers."

Since Bryce was going to sign Dagmar out at the end of his shift, the papers were in the chart ready to sign. "Hey!" Bryce exclaimed, "You can't sign her out!"

Scribbling her signature, Jane said, "I have permissions at this hospital."

"I'll see that you lose your permissions!"

Jane handed the papers back to the nurse then turned to Bryce. "And I'll see that you lose your license… fucker!" She helped Dagmar to her feet and they walked to the elevator.

Steadying Dagmar as they slowly walked into the morgue, Jane said to the doctor, "Can we see Jennifer Lamont?"

The doctor brought them to a wall of large drawers. He tugged one open and a covered form rolled out. The morgue doctor waited until both women got close. Jane nodded and he pulled back the sheet.

"That's… that's not her."

"Dag…"

"No, Jane. Mommy is full of life and energy. This looks like a mannequin… a doll."

"Let's go," Jane said quietly.

They turned away, took a couple of steps, and Dagmar stopped. She walked back to the body and looked at her mother's face. From a certain angle, it looked like she was sleeping. Dagmar gently placed her hand on her mother's cold cheek and then allowed her fingertips to nestle in her hair. There it was. Dagmar found the small scar no one knew about, just above Mrs. Lamont's hairline. There was no longer any doubt to Dagmar that this was her mother. "Goodbye, Mommy," she whispered, and walked back to Jane's steadying embrace.

## Chapter Sixteen

# A Little Help from My Friends

Jane took Dagmar back to her building and helped her upstairs. Taking Dagmar's keys from her bag, Jane opened the apartment door and guided her inside.

"No, no, no," Dagmar said as Jane took her to her bed. "I have to tell Granddaddy and Mama Rue about Mommy. I have to go."

"You're in no condition to drive, Dag. Sleep for a couple hours. I'll make sure they know what happened."

"But, where's Daddy? What happened to him?"

"I'll figure it all out. Close your eyes."

When Dagmar drifted off to sleep, Jane took out her phone and called the office. "Harmony, are Candace and Anabelle between patients?"

"Yes, Doctor Teasdale. They both have appointments in ten minutes."

"I want you to call everyone into the conference room, yourself and Suzy included, and put me on speaker phone."

When everyone was in the conference room, Candace asked, "What's wrong, Jane?"

Over the speaker, Jane said, "Long story, but to bottom line it, Dagmar's mom died this morning from a cerebral hemorrhage."

Anabelle was visibly shaken by the news. "Oh my God! Dagmar was so close to her mother. She must be out of her mind!"

"Bryce, that ER doc she dated for a couple months, shot her up with Haldol."

"Asshole!" Candace exclaimed. "Where is she now?"

"I brought Dagmar to her apartment and she's sleeping. Someone has to pick up her car from in front of the emergency room before it's towed. Her grandparents need to be told the bad news and Dagmar's father left the hospital. No one knows where he is."

Anabelle spoke up. "I know her grandparents. I'll tell them about Mrs. Lamont."

"Good," Candace said. "Jane, you can't leave Dagmar alone so stay put. Call Talia and tell her to continue the exercise and nutrition routines Dagmar put in place for Xian. One of us will step in if she needs help. Harmony, we're closing the office for the next three days starting now. I need you to reschedule the patients. Suzy, get your ass to Dagmar's apartment, pick up her keys and bring her car home. Can you drive a stick?"

Suzy smirked, "Since I was twelve."

Candace nodded, "I'll look for Dagmar's father." Pausing a second, Candace continued, "At Kane & Teasdale we go the extra mile to help our patients. One of our own needs help during the worst time of her life and we're going to do a goddamn good job for her. Everyone go! Get crackin'!"

One thing Doctor Candace Kane knows like the back of her hand are the area bars. Starting from the hospital and working her way outward, she planned to check every watering hole within walking distance. Fortunately, she found him in the first place she tried. Dagmar's father was bent over the bar wearing old work pants and pajama top while holding a shot glass in his hand and clutching his wife's purse in the crook of his arm.

"Mister Lamont?" Candace asked.

"Go away," he said without looking at her.

Candace sat on a bar stool next to his and watched as he drank down a double shot of whiskey. "We have to talk."

With effort, he turned his head toward Candace, showing a tear stained, pained face. "Nothin' means anything to me anymore."

"Dagmar was in an automobile accident on her way home from the hospital."

Mister Lamont jolted and shook at the news. "What?!!! Where is she?!!! Is she all right?!!!"

"Oh," Candace said casually. "I guess there IS something that means something to you. There was no accident. Dagmar is fine."

Half angry and half relived, he said, "Why would you say that to me?! Who ARE you, you…?!!!"

"'Bitch?' It works for me. But did you notice, with that one sentence, I reminded you that there IS something that's meaningful to you? Your daughter. The daughter who needs you."

"She's grown up with a fine education. She don't need me no more."

"You're SO wrong. You're daughter needs you more than ever." Candace took a breath and continued, "Look, as someone who essentially doesn't have parents, I can tell you that Dagmar is going to need your strength. I don't care how old she is, or how successful, or how many friends she has, Dagmar needs her father to help her through this."

"Who did you say you were?"

"I'm Candace. I'm one of her bosses."

"You're the one that doesn't like her."

Candace sighed and continued. "Let me tell you something about your daughter. Dagmar is gifted. She breezed through college and med school dragging me and my friends along with her. If it weren't for Dagmar my practice would not exist.  She knows how to handle people, even stupid people.  Your daughter rises above racism with ease and grace.  And her beauty?  I spend a lot of money on creams and spa treatments to look as good as she looks naturally.  Everyone loves Dagmar and very few people 'get' me.  Because her career, her looks, and her social skills came so easily to her, she can be complacent.  I have to push her to excel and needling people is my forte."

"I noticed."

"Mister Lamont, I like your daughter very, VERY much.  My only problem, and it IS my problem, is that I'm… jealous.  My enormous ego is bruised by Dagmar and it hurts like hell to admit that out loud."  Candace paused as if to flush out her thoughts.  "Getting back to what's important, your daughter is going to need to talk and you're going to need to listen.  Do YOU have someone to talk to about your feelings?"

"Men don't talk about their feelings."

Candace sighed.  "You sound like my husband."  She took out her business card and handed it to Mister Lamont.  "I'm sure you don't believe in therapy but I want you to call me.  We'll meet someplace and discuss those feelings you don't want to talk about.  No office.  No therapy.  Just two people having a conversation."

Mister Lamont stared at the card and said, "I don't know about this."

"I'm sorry, did I give you the impression that you had a choice in the matter?"

The bartender walked over to them and said, "Another round?"

Candace took out her credit card and said, "His next round is black coffee and keep it coming.  I have his tab."

As the bartender walked away, Mister Lamont said, "You don't have to do that."

Ignoring him she said, "You're going to drink at least three cups of coffee.  Then, we are going back to your house so you can change clothes.  First, I'm going to take you to the men's room so you can splash cold water on your face."

"You… you can't go into the men's room!"

For the first time since he saw Candace, she smiled.  "Darling, before marriage, I visited many men's rooms."

88

Dagmar woke to the sound of voices. For a moment, she forgot where she was and what had happened, but the moment was fleeting. Crushing reality sat on her shoulders like two anvils. As she sat up in bed, Jane, Suzy, and Harmony went to her side.

Jane bent down and looked at Dagmar's eyes. "How are you feeling, Dag?"

"Horrible. What time is it?"

"Seven p.m. Can you stand?"

Dagmar slowly stood and looked around. On the kitchen table of her studio apartment she saw a platter with meats, poultry, cheeses, bread and condiments. "Where did this come from?"

Suzy said, "Harmony and me didn't think you were in any mood to cook."

Offering a weak smile, Dagmar motioned them closer and gave each a hug. "You shouldn't have spent the money."

"It's the least we could do, Doctor Lamont," Harmony said.

"When we're outside the office, my name is Dagmar."

"Okay, Dagmar, I'm going to make a sandwich for you."

"Thanks, but I'm… not hungry, Harmony."

"Make the sandwich," Jane said. "Dag, you haven't eaten since breakfast. Food but no booze. Not tonight."

"I just remembered, I left my car at the hospital!"

"Gotcha covered, Dagmar," Suzy said handing her the keys. "Your car is right outside."

There was a knock on the door. Jane answered it and Anabelle walked in. She ran directly to Dagmar and hugged her tightly. "I'm so sorry about your mom," she whispered. "I brought someone who wanted to see you." Behind Anabelle stood her thirteen-year-old daughter. She was a thin girl in the middle of a growth spurt. Her hair was long and frizzy like her mother while her complexion was a cross between her white mother and her black father.

"Maya," Dagmar said as the young girl ran to embrace her.

"I'm sorry your mother died, Aunt Dagmar. You must be sad."

"I'm all right, pretty girl. How's school?"

Maya tightened her grip on Dagmar. "I don't care about school right now. I care about you. You've been crying."

Dagmar brushed the hair from Maya's face. "I'm a big girl. I'll be all right. Hey, why don't you make a little sandwich for you and your mom?"

"But..."

"Maya, I can't talk about it right now. We'll sit down in a few days and have a conversation. Please, have something to eat."

"Okay, Aunt Dagmar," Maya said reluctantly and walked to the kitchen table.

Waiting until Maya was busy, Anabelle said to Dagmar, "I told Granddaddy and Mama Rue about your mother. They're handling it as well as can be expected."

"I should call them."

"Why don't you call your grandparents tomorrow? I told them you were sedated. How are you feeling? You look awake."

"I slept half the day."

"And how are you feeling... otherwise?"

Dagmar looked Anabelle directly in the eye and said, "I pray that you never feel what I'm feeling right now."

There was another knock on the door and when Jane answered it, she saw Talia and her children. After giving Jane a quick hug Jaynette ran into the room and stopped just short of bumping into Dagmar.

"Is it true?" Jaynette asked. "Did your mommy die?" With a lump in her throat, Dagmar nodded. "Why? How did it happen?"

90

Dagmar swallowed hard. "My mommy was sick and I didn't know it."

"What are you going to do without your mommy?"

Trying to keep her lips from trembling, Dagmar said, "I don't know, Sweetie. I don't know."

The sound of Jaynette's eighteen-month-old brother crying interrupted their conversation. Talia looked surprised as her son began kicking and wailing.

"What is wrong, little one?" Talia asked. "You never behave like this. Do you want to walk?"

George kicked and twisted even harder, and Talia gently placed him on the floor. Immediately he took staggering steps to Dagmar. He cried as he stood in front of her with raised arms, beckoning to be picked up. Dagmar lifted George and held him in her arms. The baby who was throwing a tantrum a second ago was now gently cooing as he wrapped his arms tightly around Dagmar's neck.

Tears began to well up in Dagmar's eyes as she whispered, "You know, don't you? You know I'm hurting. How do you know?"

No one spoke. They all watched Dagmar quietly cry as little George gave her his reassuring hug.

Finally, Talia approached the pair. "I am sorry to hear about your mother, Dagmar."

"Thank you, Talia."

"Richard wanted to come but he is watching Xian."

"Oh... with all that has been happening I didn't get a chance to call about her."

"I will keep Xian on her routine. She seems to be doing well." Talia looked at her son in Dagmar's arms. "He has developed a bond with you."

"Oh... I'm sorry," Dagmar said and began to hand George back to his mother.

"No, no, no..." Talia said. "Please hold him as long as you like. I've trusted you with my sister's life. My son could not be in better hands."

Jane walked to Dagmar and said, "I'm not sure this is the right time, but I have made some calls about… arrangements for your mom. I'm trying to take some of the burden off you, but if you want to do it yourself…"

"Thanks, Jane," Dagmar said. "What have you done so far?"

"While you were sleeping off the drug, I took the liberty of looking at the address book in your cell phone. I called your minister and he gave me the name of a good local funeral home. He said he could have the wake as early as tomorrow and the burial the next day. I don't know if this is too soon for you."

Dagmar took her free arm and wrapped it around Jane. "Thank you. I don't know how I could have arranged all that."

"Are you sure it's not too soon?"

Dagmar smiled. "Mommy always said, 'When I die, plant me in the ground as soon as possible and get back to dancing!' She wouldn't want the arrangements to linger. We have a small family plot where she can be buried."

"It's too late now but I'll be here first thing in the morning and we'll give the details to the funeral director. Would you like me to stay the night? I can call my husband and…"

"I've kept you from your family too long as it is. I'll be all right tonight."

There was a knock on the door and Anabelle answered it. Standing in the doorway was Candace with Dagmar's father. He was cleaned up and wearing new clothes but the most striking thing about him was that he was standing tall and exuding his usual quiet confidence.

"Daddy?" Dagmar said quietly.

"Baby," he said walking into her apartment. "I was shocked. I was grieving. My world was crushed. It hurt so bad that I forgot. I forgot that I wasn't just the husband of the most wonderful woman who ever lived. I'm also the daddy to the best daughter a man could have." He looked at Candace but continued talking to Dagmar, "I lost my way and I needed a little help." Then turning back to Dagmar he said, "Are all these people here for you in your time of need?"

"We're here for both of you, Mister Lamont," Anabelle said.

"Thank you. My baby chose her friends well. I would like to spend some time alone with my daughter."

One by one everyone in the crowded studio apartment walked by Dagmar and her father to say good-bye. As Talia approached, Dagmar leaned back to look George in the eye. "You have to go home now. I'll be all right." As if he understood every word, George released his grasp and leaned into his mother's waiting arms. Dagmar walked straight to Candace and threw her arms around her. "I don't know how you did it but thanks for finding my daddy."

Candace smiled and said, "Don't worry about a thing. We've shut down the office until this is all over and any one of us will be available to help you at the drop of a hat."

"You're going through a lot of trouble."

"If the situation were reversed, would you have done the same for me?"

"Candace, you know I would."

"Then don't be surprised at what I'm doing for you. Anything you need... ask."

When the last guest left and her apartment door was closed, Dagmar began to cry. Mister Lamont beckoned his daughter to him and held her tightly. "Daddy..." Dagmar choked, "it hurts so much!"

"I know Baby, I know. Let it all out. During the wake and the funeral we're going to hold our heads high and be the family your mother would want us to be. We had her for a short time, but forever wouldn't have been long enough. We'll make your mama proud of us. That's what she'd want."

# Chapter Seventeen

# Awake

At five o'clock the next day, Xian was sitting quietly, listening to the voices outside her room. She heard her brother-in-law leave the house and drive away. A few moments later her sister, Talia, knocked on her door and opened it. "Dinner will be ready in an hour," she said. "Is there anything you need?" The question was rhetorical. The answer was always "no."

Xian hesitated and then said, "Where is Doctor Lamont?"

Talia's eyes opened wide with surprise. This was the first question Xian asked since she arrived. Talia rushed into the room and sat in front of her sister. "Why do you ask?"

"Doctor Lamont left early yesterday and it is far past her arrival time today."

"Oh… I am not sure what to tell you…"

"Tell me… the truth."

Talia sighed and said, "Doctor Lamont's mother… died yesterday. Richard is going to the wake today. Tomorrow, he will stay with you while I go to the funeral."

Xian's brow furrowed which was the most emotion Talia had seen her demonstrate. "Mommy… is dead?"

Confused, Talia asked, "Who?"

"Mommy. Doctor Lamont's mother. Mommy."

"Oh… yes… Doctor Lamont's… 'mommy' died."

Xian continued, "And this 'wake' you mentioned… what is it?"

"It is a gathering of family and friends. It is a time to offer condolences to the surviving family."

Xian paused for a long moment, and then suddenly stood. "We must go to Mommy's wake. Is my black kimono suitable?"

"Well, yes, but, I am not sure you should attend."

"I MUST go. I MUST offer my condolences to Doctor Lamont. It is… appropriate."

Talia was not sure if she was doing the right thing, but she said, "Very well. We shall change our clothes and I shall get the nanny to watch the children."

An hour later, Xian and Talia arrived at the funeral home. Talia was amazed at the long line waiting to pay their respects. It seemed that everyone from the church and some out-of-town family was there to offer support. Dagmar's father was standing tall and strong, offering a solemn face. Although it was not intentional, Dagmar looked beautiful and even sexy wearing a black form fitting satin dress ending just below the knee with small slits on either side. Her black opera gloves reached midway between her elbows and her bare shoulders. She wore a black pillbox hat and a black veil covered her face.

As they waited in line, Xian began rubbing her temples. "Is something wrong," Talia asked.

"Pain!"

Xian felt waves of sadness and anguish assaulting her brain. She peered toward Dagmar, the direction of the onslaught and, slowly, the fog in her brain start to dissipate. "Aaaagh," Xian shrieked as her knees began to buckle. Talia grabbed her before she fell, and the commotion caught the attention of Dagmar. She looked down the reception line and recognized her patient wincing. Dagmar ran to Xian and helped her to stand. As Xian looked at Dagmar she felt another stronger wave of burning pain searing her from the front to the back of her head. And in it's wake… clarity… cool, calm… clarity. The fog had lifted and the world was now completely clear to her for the first time.

Xian placed her hand on Dagmar's cheek and said, "You… You are real! You're real to me!!!" She paused and said, "Doctor Lamont… the pain… the agony you are going through… I can feel it! How… How do you stand it?!!!" Xian looked around the room and her eyes fell on Talia. Immediately, Xian threw her arms around her sister and hugged her tightly. "I feel you! I feel you in my heart!"

"I'll bring you to the front of the line and we will talk," Dagmar said.

"No," Talia returned. "We will wait our turn in line like everyone else. We will be all right. Everything will be all right now!"

Dagmar walked back to join her father and Xian looked around the room almost birdlike. "The colors are so bright," Xian told her sister. "The flowers are so… pungent! Is it… always like this?"

"Yes. Maybe there are more flowers in one place than usual, but this is normal."

"Amazing," Xian said as she continued to look around the room. "Talia, I can still feel sorrow from everyone but I feel excitement from you."

"This is a miracle! The coldness, the aloofness is gone. I can not wait to tell Father, Mother, and our siblings!"

The line ahead got shorter until it was Xian and Talia's turn to view the body. They stepped forward and peered into the casket. Mrs. Lamont was wearing a white dress and her folded hands held two perfect red roses; one from her husband and one from her daughter. Laced between her fingers was a beaded bracelet Dagmar made for her as a child. The lettering on the beads spelled "Mommy."

"It's hard to believe the corpse lying here is the vibrant woman Doctor Lamont spoke of," Xian whispered.

"That is because the body is a shell for the spirit. When the spirit is gone it leaves behind an earthly vesicle devoid of personality and character."

"Then, why do we place such importance on the body of the deceased?"

"Because it is the physical face of the spirit and its last earthly home. We are holding up the line while discussing philosophy. A short prayer is in order."

"Talia, I do not know how to pray. What do I say?"

"Whatever comes to your heart."

"Then, I will pray for Mommy's friends and family... especially Doctor Lamont," Xian said and closed her eyes.

When their prayers were finished and the two sisters began to walk away, Talia noticed a stand covered with cards. She was embarrassed because she had no card to give due to her lack of "wake" knowledge. She then smiled as she noticed a card saying, "The Sedgwick family" in her husband's handwriting. "My man thinks of everything," she whispered to herself. Talia walked up to Dagmar and hugged her. "I am so sorry for the loss of your mother." Before she could say anything, Xian stepped up with open arms. Doctor and patient embraced tightly.

"How is this possible?" Dagmar whispered.

"I don't know. I felt the pain of your loss and now... I feel everything!"

"Please don't leave. I'll come to talk to you as soon as possible." Dagmar took the sibling's hands and led them to her father. "This is Xian and Talia... my patient and her sister."

Mister Lamont extended his large hand and shook each woman's slender hand. "Thank you for coming."

With a look of recognition, Xian said, "You... You are Daddy! Doctor Lamont has told me much about you. I'm glad we are meeting face to face."

"Xian," Dagmar said and indicated an elderly couple sitting down but staring into space. "This is..."

"Mama Rue and Granddaddy," Xian finished. "I recognize them from your stories." She walked closer to the seated couple and said, "I am sorry for the loss of your daughter."

"It ain't right," Mama Rue said quietly while staring straight ahead. "It just ain't right. A child shouldn't die before her mama." Dagmar's grandfather

98

took off his glasses and rubbed his eyes with his handkerchief.  They both appeared as if they were still in shock.

Xian and Talia walked toward the back of the room to find a quiet place to sit and saw a familiar face.  Rich was there with a surprised look on his face.  It was immediately apparent that his sister-in-law was different.  "Xian?  Is that you?"  Xian just smiled at him.  "My God!  What…?  How…?"

"It just happened a few minutes ago," Talia said.  "She is… awake."

Also sitting in the back of the room was Jane.  "Oh my God!" Jane whispered loudly.

"I don't know who you arc," Xian said.

"I am Doctor Lamont's employer and friend, Jane Teasdale-Belesco.  We met at your parents California home and at Talia's wedding.  Don't you remember me?"

"I'm sorry."

"Don't be," Jane said as she waved over some other seated attendees.  "One step at a time.  Xian, I'd like to introduce you to my husband, Nick Belesco."

"Hi, Xian," Nick said.  "You look a lot like Talia."

"High praise.  Thank you Mister Belesco."

"And this guy," Nick said pulling his brother next to him, "is my bro, Frank."

Frank took Xian's hand and softly kissed her knuckles.  "My pleasure," he said as Candace stepped up and removed Frank's hand from Xian's.

"Hands off, darling.  He's all mine," Candace vamped.

"My wife, Candace Belesco," Frank said which earned him a poke in the ribs.  "I mean Candace Kane-Belesco.  If she isn't chasing women away from me, she's threatening to divorce me."

"I am also Doctor Lamont's employer and friend," Candace said.  "You don't seem at all like Doctor Lamont's description."

"Isn't it wonderful?!!!" Talia said as she hugged her sister.  Xian smiled as she leaned into the warm embrace.  Finally, two more women walked up to Talia and her sister.  "Oh, Xian, I'd like to introduce you to two more friends.  This is Vanessa Lanski and Silva Sorrel-Linville. This is my sister Xian. The three of you have something in common. You have all been treated by Doctor Lamont."

"You are very fortunate," Silva stated. "She takes very few patients but she's an excellent therapist! I had problems with acceptance and self worth. Through our sessions, Doctor Lamont guided me to make important life decisions, and now I'm now happier than I have ever been."

Vanessa smiled and said, "What she means is that our doctor gave her the green light for a boob job. Silva is a lawyer so she uses lots words. I can simply tell you that Doctor Lamont saved my life when I was ready to throw it away. She's one of the best women I know and you're very lucky to have her as your therapist."

Hesitantly, Xian said, "I think… somehow… I've known that all along."

Xian was also introduced to others from Dagmar's workplace, Suzy, Harmony, and Doctor Anabelle Loomis. They all took their seats and sat quietly watching the long line of people pay their respects.

When there was no one else in line, Dagmar walked to the back of the room directly to Xian. The doctor looked at her patient and saw clear, bright blue eyes looking back at her. "Amazing!" Dagmar whispered and then turned to her friends. "I'd like to speak to Xian alone for a minute." She took her patient to another corner of the room then Dagmar asked, "How did this change happen?"

"I… I am not sure. When you were missing…"

"Missing?"

"Yes. When you were missing from our appointment I became curious… then concerned."

Dagmar smiled. "You were worried about me?"

"Yes, I was. I came to expect… and look forward to… your stories about your family… and your visit. When Talia told me Mommy died I felt… I felt… I'm not sure what I felt."

"Was it sadness? Was it pity for me?"

"Yes. Those. And I believe I felt… cheated."

"Cheated? Why?"

"I felt cheated that I would never meet… Mommy. Doctor Lamont…"

"It's Dagmar. Please call me Dagmar."

Xian smiled. "What a curious name. Dagmar… this may be a big imposition in light of your loss, but… is it possible to see where Mommy lived?"

"Oh. Of course. Why?"

"I'm not sure. I think I want to get a sense of her life. Through your stories, I feel close to her. I feel like she was my mommy too."

Dagmar brushed a tear from her eye and said, "When would you like to see the apartment?"

"As soon as possible. Tonight? Just for a few minutes. Before her things are disturbed."

While Dagmar thought this was an odd request she was happy Xian was coming out of her shell and exploring something that mattered to her. "I'll ask Daddy if it's all right. I'm sure he'll say yes."

## Chapter Eighteen

# Last Fan

Xian, Talia, Dagmar and her grandparents, stood with Mister Lamont in front of his apartment building. He sighed at the prospect of climbing the stairs. When Dagmar's grandparents were settled in their apartment, Mister Lamont loosened his tie and began trudging upstairs.

Xian turned to her sister and said, "Would you mind waiting in the car? I will not be long and I wish to do this… alone, with Doctor La… Dagmar."

Talia smiled and said, "Take as long as you like," then walked back to her car.

"Daddy, can I help you?" Dagmar asked. Her father waved off the offer and continued the climb. Mister Lamont opened the door to his residence and sat in his living room chair mopping his brow with his handkerchief. "Are you all right, Daddy?"

"I just have to sit for a minute."

Xian said to Dagmar, "If Daddy is all right, may I see where Mommy slept?"

"This way," Dagmar said, and led Xian to her parent's bedroom.

"Are you sure you don't mind me looking at Mommy's things?"

"No. You're… special. As you saw by the number of people at the wake, my mother had a lot of fans. You are the last fan Mommy will make."

Xian slowly walked around the room looking at every picture and item on the dresser. "Everything is so neat, but the bed is unmade. Daddy has left things as they were." Walking to a spot in the room where the rug was askew, Xian continued, "This is where the medics tried to help Mommy. Nothing else is disturbed. They knew Mommy could not be revived because they took their time leaving. There are no nicks on the door. No chips off the furniture." Dagmar would be impressed with Xian's observations if she were not so saddened by the story of her mother's last moments in the bedroom. Looking at some pictures on the wall, Xian said, "Mommy and Daddy have several graduation pictures prominently displayed. They are proud of you." Xian smiled as she was drawn to one picture on the dresser. "Dagmar, what's this? I've never seen the like."

The picture made Dagmar smile. "That's an old picture of Mommy, me, and my Coco Puffs."

"What are Coco Puffs?"

"See those two fuzzy balls on either side of my head? That's my hair… my Coco Puffs. It's a black thing."

"Oh. Your hair, it doesn't look like that today."

"Lots of processing. A black woman's hair is a long story."

"I understand. Shall we see how Daddy's feeling?"

As the pair walked back into the living room they smiled upon seeing that Mister Lamont had recovered from his climb upstairs. "How are you Daddy?"

"I'm tired, Baby. It's been a long day today and it's going to be a longer day tomorrow. I'm gonna turn in."

The women watched as Mister Lamont closed the door to his bedroom. Dagmar said, "This is about everything there is to see. The apartment is only four rooms."

"Mommy spent much of her time in the kitchen, correct?"

Dagmar led Xian into the kitchen. "This is where she cooked and baked. God, what I wouldn't give for her to make one more meal for me." Her eyes fell on the old domed ceramic cake dish. "When Mommy made a cake, she would put it in here."

Dagmar lifted the top and jumped when she saw a freshly made Red Velvet cake.

Xian saw a note by the cake. She picked it up and read, "Everyday is a special occasion when my Baby comes to visit me."

Mrs. Lamont wanted to surprise Dagmar. It was the last thing she did for her daughter. Overcome with emotions, Dagmar collapsed to the floor in a sobbing heap. Immediately, Xian ran to her and cradled the crying woman in her arms.

Mister Lamont, wearing his pajamas, came running into the kitchen to see what was wrong. As soon as he saw the cake, all questions were answered. The man who showed such strength at his wife's wake was now crying. He kneeled down and his daughter wrapped her arms around him. Xian sat back, awash in the searing hot emotions radiating from father and daughter.

Xian stumbled to her feet and said, "I will see myself out."

Dagmar got off the floor and caught her patient before she could leave. "No, Xian. Wait… are you… crying?"

Xian's face was wet with tears. "I… feel her too. I feel what you feel."

As Mister Lamont braced himself on a chair to stand, he said, "There's only one thing to do. We're gonna have a piece of that cake."

"But… But…" Dagmar stuttered.

"What you gonna do, let it go to waste? Your mama made this cake for us to enjoy and that's what we'll do. Xian, I would like you to join us."

Xian hesitated. "I… don't want to intrude."

"Daddy's right," Dagmar said. "The cake was made to be enjoyed and we want you to enjoy it with us."

Wordlessly, Dagmar and her father placed plates and silverware on the table. Three glasses of milk were poured and the cake dish was brought to the table. Mister Lamont cut three slices of cake and placed them on three dessert plates.

Dagmar and her father closed their eyes and mouthed a silent prayer as Xian watched. Then, they all took their first forkful of cake.

"This is delicious," Xian said.

Dagmar gave her a weak smile. "Thanks. It's a shame that this will be the last Red Velvet cake. Mommy never showed me how she made it."

They ate in silence. Xian's dish still had half of her cake slice left when Dagmar and her father were finished. As they took their plates to the sink, Xian quickly took her paper towel napkin and surreptitiously wrapped her remaining cake. As she stood, she slipped it into a pocket in her kimono and brought the empty plate and glass to the sink.

"I should leave and return to Talia."

"I forgot your sister is in the car waiting," Dagmar said. "I should have thought to invite her in for cake."

"I am sure she is all right. I will see you both at the funeral."

"Let me walk you out," Dagmar said as she went with Xian to the apartment door.

"No thank you. I know the way. Stay with Daddy."

Xian walked down the stairs, to her sister's car and entered the passenger seat. Before Talia could say anything, Xian asked, "Is it true that you are an excellent cook and baker? In one of our sessions, Dagmar said you could eat at a restaurant and recreate the meal at home."

"Yes, I can."

Xian took the wrapped cake from her pocket. "You must make this cake."

When Xian and Talia returned home they were greeted by Rich who smiled as he looked carefully at his sister in-law. "I still can't believe it," he said. "You look so different!"

At that moment, Jaynette came running into the room. She stopped and gaped at Xian. "You're real! I can feel you in my head! Aunt Xian, you're real!"

106

Xian looked at Jaynette quizzically. "Rini?"

"No," Talia laughed. "She looks like our sister Rini used to look but this is my daughter, Jaynette. Do you not remember?"

"I'm sorry. I have no recollection of your daughter… but I'm delighted to meet her. Come little one," she said as she fell to one knee.

Jaynette ran to her aunt's embrace. Placing her hand on Xian's face she said, "Mommy, she's like us! I can tell! She's like us!"

"Talia? What is she talking about?" Xian questioned.

"Nothing, my sister. Jaynette, isn't it getting close to your bedtime?"

"But I want to stay up and play with my new aunt."

Rich scooped his daughter up and said, "C'mon. You need to go to sleep. You'll have lots of time to talk to Aunt Xian tomorrow."

As Rich and Jaynette left the room, Talia said, "Come. We have a cake to bake."

# Chapter Nineteen

# Second Sight

       The day after Mrs. Lamont's funeral, Xian, Talia and Jaynette were in the waiting room of the psychiatric office of Kane & Teasdale. They were meeting Rich and waiting for Jane Teasdale to finish a session with one of her patients so that they could all go to lunch.

       Talia and Jaynette looked at each other knowingly as Harmony and Suzy talked at the reception desk. Turning to Xian, Talia quietly asked, "Do you see anything unusual about those two?"

       "No," Xian replied. "Should I?"

       "Show her, Mommy. Show her the magic," Jaynette said.

       "Look at Harmony," Talia said to her sister.

       Xian peered at the receptionist and said, "I see nothing unusual."

       Talia placed her hand on the back of Xian's head, threading her fingers through her hair until they were in contact with her scalp. "Keep looking. Open your mind. Open your soul. And open your heart."

As Xian concentrated, she felt a tingling in her head. When it stopped, her eyes widened. Surrounding Harmony were ghost-like shapes. They were geometric forms that hovered around her, interlocking without touching. "What… is that?"

"What do you see?" Talia asked.

"Orderly shapes hovering around her."

Talia smiled. "Harmony is very disciplined… organized… logical. She handles the phone calls, appointments, and scheduling in a very efficient manner."

"There is a glowing reddish white pinpoint of light in the center of her chest."

"Harmony is a very religious young woman. You are seeing her deep seated faith."

"Amazing," Xian whispered. "It's like I know her with just a look. The other woman…"

"That is Suzy, the office manager."

"Wild, psychedelic colors… like a Peter Max painting."

"Suzy is a fun loving free spirit."

Xian smiled. "Yes. I see that."

Talia removed her hand from the back of her head. "Do you still see the images?"

"Yes, if I concentrate."

Jaynette piped up, "See! She's just like us!"

"Xian, what do you see when you look at Jaynette and myself?"

"Sparkles. I see sparkles around you both."

"And we now see sparkles around you."

"What is this? How does this work?"

110

"I call it… second sight," Talia explained. "I am not sure how it works. It is possible that we are sensitive to psychic emanations. We may also visualize images from clues we pick up in body language."

"It's magic!" Jaynette added.

"Or… it could be magic. Also, if you pay very close attention you can empathically 'read' someone's thoughts." Talia smiled. "For some reason, that part of my gift does not work on my husband, Richard, which is one of the many reasons I love him. He surprises and delights me constantly. As for our siblings, I do not know if the other sisters have this second sight or not."

Just then, Rich entered the waiting room to join them for lunch. Xian gasped. She saw him surrounded by flowing blue silver plating. Beams of pure white light shot out from between the plates. He literally looked like a knight in shining armor.

"Oh, Talia!" Xian whispered. "The strength! The character! The nobility! I… had no idea! No wonder you fell in love with him!"

Rich approached and asked, "Xian? Are you all right?"

As she relaxed her concentration, Rich appeared normal again. "Yes, I am all right."

Talia stood and kissed her husband. "I am so glad you could meet us for lunch. Please sit."

Before Rich could take a seat, Jane walked into the waiting room. Xian concentrated on her and was shocked at the vibrant image she projected. Like Rich, she had glowing plating surrounding her except it was red and white. She was another knight in shining armor. Jane's patient had walked into the waiting room with her, and as he put on his jacket to leave, Xian focused on him. A storm cloud surrounded his head as swirling puzzle pieces circled his body. As two pieces were about to fit, a bolt of lightening would scatter them.

When the patient left, Xian said, "A very disturbed man."

Jane smiled and said, "He's trying very hard."

"Yes, I can see that. Oh, I'm sorry. Hello Doctor Teasdale-Belesco."

"I've kept my maiden name as my professional name. To my patients, I'm Doctor Teasdale. To you, I'm Jane."

"Thank you, Jane. Have you heard from Dagmar?"

"She's taking one more day off but she asked me to make an appointment for you to get another brain scan… today. She'll come see you tomorrow. Now, let's eat. I'm starved!"

# Chapter Twenty

# Invitation

Dagmar heaved a heavy sigh as she sat in her car, parked in front of the Sedgwick home. She was still constantly thinking about her mother. The psychiatrist wanted to take more time off from work, but she had a patient who had just gone through a major change in her life. As Dagmar walked to the front door she dreaded going back to work. This case was fascinating, exciting, and it would distract her from her mourning. It was exactly what she needed... but not what she wanted.

Talia answered the door and ushered Dagmar inside. They walked through the house to the deck where Xian was enjoying the sight of the majestic trees stretching skyward like hands to the heavens. With a look, Talia excused herself leaving doctor and patient alone.

"Good afternoon, Xian. This is the first time I've been here when I haven't found you in your room," Dagmar said, placing a computer bag and her doctor's bag on the deck.

"Good afternoon, Dagmar. Aren't the trees magnificent?"

"Yes, they are. The whole backyard is beautiful. Let's sit and talk for a while."

As they took their seats Xian said, "I don't wish to seem unappreciative of all this beauty but I am a little… bored."

"That's not surprising. Since your suicide attempt, I've kept you away from outside stimuli."

"'Suicide'?"

Dagmar leaned closer to Xian. "You don't remember your suicide attempt?" Xian shook her head 'no'. "Try. Try to remember."

Xian's eyes darted back and forth as if scanning the pages of a book. "I remember following an order. An order I felt I had to obey. You… you were there."

"Yes."

"You… saved my life."

"Well… I stabilized you until the ambulance came."

Persistent, Xian repeated, "You saved my life." She starred at Dagmar and smiled at what her second sight revealed about her. "You are intelligent and wise. You are a strong and noble woman. There is so much love inside you and so few outlets for that love, especially now that Mommy is gone. Your professional demeanor cannot hide from me the sadness you feel. If there is anything I can do to lessen your pain… please tell me."

"The little girl in me thinks the pain of Mommy's death will never go away, but the psychiatrist knows it will be more bearable with understanding and time. There's no way to speed that along. I'll go on. It won't be easy, but I'll go on." After a second or two, Dagmar snapped back to her professional self. "I'm not here to talk about my problems. I want to know what happened to you at the wake."

"I can't explain it. At Mommy's wake I could feel your sorrow like an undeniable tidal wave washing over me. The rawness of your emotions seemed to unlock my own."

"Xian, from previous brain scans I saw that there were parts of your brain that had no electrical activity. From the scan done yesterday, I can see many more areas have become active, but there are still sections of your brain that are dormant. To help, I bought a present for you." Dagmar placed the computer bag on the patio table. "This isn't from Kane & Teasdale. This is from me personally. I stopped by the Apple store and bought you a notebook computer."

"You… you bought a computer for me?"

"Yes, and this thing is called an 'iPod.' I want you to use it to listen to music. There is a theory that listening to music helps build pathways between the left and right sides of the brain. I'm hoping it will help to stimulate your mind to heal." Looking in the kitchen window Dagmar saw Talia. She waved until Talia saw her and joined them outside. "I'm partly lifting the suicide watch," Dagmar said to Talia. "Xian can be exposed to media but I still don't think she should have contact with the rest of your family, phone calls or mail."

"Very well. Is that a computer?" Talia questioned.

"I got it for your sister. I want to set up an account so that she can download and listen to music."

"That is a wonderful idea!" Talia exclaimed. "But I could have purchased anything you think she will need."

Looking at Xian, Dagmar said, "I wanted to do this for her."

"Richard and I have our own iPods, so I am familiar with the set up. Here," Talia said as she handed Dagmar a credit card. "Buy as much music as you like."

After connecting with the home Wi-Fi network, Dagmar set up the computer and began downloading songs. "I'm getting a lot of classical music for you, but I want to get something more personal. You lived in Japan but I'm not familiar with Japanese music."

Xian said, "What type of music do YOU like?"

"I like soul… rhythm and blues."

Xian smiled. "From your stories, I remember that is what Mommy liked. That is what I want to hear!"

"Really?"

"Yes, really."

"ALL RIGHT! This is going to be fun."

Dagmar was like a kid in a candy store. She downloaded music for over a half an hour as Xian and Talia watched. The enjoyment Dagmar felt was infectious. Finally, she said, "The downloads aren't finished, but you're going to have a great little collection! I've got you some Sam and Dave, Al Green, James

Brown, Sam Cooke, The Four Tops, The Temptations, Otis Redding, Cannonball Adderley, Harold Melvin and the Blue Notes, Ben E. King, Chubby Checker, Bill Withers, The Dells, The Supremes, Wilson Pickett, Stevie Wonder, Aaron Neville, and my favorites, Aretha Franklin, Chaka Khan, and Marvin Gaye. For some blue-eyed soul you have some Johnny Rivers, Simon and Garfunkel, and Righteous Brothers. Have you ever heard of these artists?"

"No," Xian confessed.

"Nor have I," Talia echoed.

"I envy that you are going to discover this wonderful music! Oh, I almost forgot," Dagmar said and tapped the keyboard a few more times. "You're going to like the smooth and sultry sounds of Sade."

"I am eager to listen to this music and I can imagine you as a young girl dancing with your mother," Xian said. She noticed the look of sadness begin to encroach on Dagmar's face. "Thank you for the computer and this 'iPod.' My sister and I have a gift for you as well."

Surprised, Dagmar asked, "A gift? For me?"

"Come with us," Xian said. As they walked into the kitchen, Xian asked Dagmar, "Have you had lunch?"

"Just before I came."

"Then you should be ready for dessert," Xian said and pointed to a homemade Red Velvet cake.

Dagmar was speechless as she saw the cake frosted exactly as her mother would. A small wedge had been cut and placed invitingly on a plate. Slowly, Dagmar approached the cake and picked up a fork sitting neatly on a cloth napkin. Carefully cutting a small corner, Dagmar closed her eyes as she brought a forkful of cake to her lips. The taste was so perfect that for a second she thought she could hear her mother's voice. Looking at the sisters, tears began to well in her eyes. Dagmar said in a shaky voice, "This is a amazing! How…?"

Smiling at Talia, Xian said, "My talented sister did it. I sneaked a piece of Mommy's cake back home and she was able to recreate it."

Still amazed, Dagmar said, "Talia, your file said that your taste and sense of smell was so accurate that you could copy any dish. I thought it was an exaggeration."

"It took a few attempts to get it right but I am happy I could do this for you. In fact," Talia said handing Dagmar a folded piece of paper, "I wrote down the recipe."

Xian noticed Dagmar looked a little disappointed as she reached out. Intercepting the recipe, Xian said, "However, I believe part of what makes the cake so good is that it is made FOR you instead of making it for yourself. We will recreate this cake for you whenever you wish… and at random… as a surprise." Handing the piece of paper back to Talia, Xian continued, "However, if you ever wish to have the recipe, you need only ask."

"How do you know me so well? Why don't you keep this cake since I have one at Daddy's apartment?"

"Are you sure?"

"Yes, Xian. And I can't wait to see when you're going to surprise me with another Red Velvet cake!"

"Thank God!" Rich said entering the kitchen. "I've been lusting for a piece of this cake all morning." He hastily sliced a wedge and popped a piece in his mouth. "Mmmmm! This is GOOD! Did I see a laptop on the deck?"

Talia walked to her husband and used a napkin to dab some frosting from his lips. "Doctor Lamont…"

"Dagmar," Dagmar interrupted.

"Dagmar… bought it for Xian and she is downloading music for her."

"Really? Who are you downloading?"

"R&B and soul mostly," Dagmar said, "Wilson Pickett, Marvin Gaye, Cannonball Adderley…"

"Do you mind if I hook the computer up to the sound system so I can hear the music?"

"Mind?!" Dagmar exclaimed. "Let's do it… if it's all right with Xian. It IS her computer."

"Of course it's all right. I'm excited to hear a sample!"

Rich took the laptop and went to the media room as everyone followed. While making the necessary connections, his daughter Jaynette walked into the room. "What are you doing, Daddy?"

"We are going to listen to some music Aunt Dagmar picked for Aunt Xian." Everyone sat in the comfortable chairs patiently until Rich finished the connection. "What should I play?"

"Hm," Dagmar thought. "Something by Marvin Gaye. Your choice."

Rich clicked on "I Heard It Through the Grapevine." Dagmar and Rich had heard the song but it was new to Xian, Talia, and Jaynette. Dagmar smiled as the three listened intently. Xian and Talia closed their eyes while Jaynette had a big grin on her face. When the music ended, Xian said, "I like it!"

"As do I," Talia said.

"Yeah! Let's hear another!" Jaynette exclaimed.

"I can't sit still while this music is playing," Dagmar said as she jumped out of her chair and walked to the computer. She clicked on the song "That's the Way Love Is" and started moving to the music.

"Wow!" Jaynette said. "I wish I could dance!"

Dagmar walked to Jaynette, took her hand and led her to the center of the room. Rich went to the sofa his wife was sitting on and held her hand.

"Put your arms in the air real casual like," Dagmar instructed. Jaynette complied and Dagmar continued, "That's it. Now, move the lower half of your body in time with the music. Don't think about it. Just do it. And if you're having a good time… smile!" Jaynette grinned ear to ear as she mirrored Dagmar's moves exactly. "There you go! All right! You're shakin' your cute little rear like a black girl!"

"Mommy," Jaynette said as she continued dancing, "I'm shakin' my cute little rear like a black girl!"

While Xian and Rich laughed, Talia was less amused. "Richard," she said quietly, "I am not sure I want Jaynette exposed to such suggestive music and dancing at her young age. I am not comfortable with her… shaking her… 'cute little rear'. I am also uncomfortable with her noticing race."

"Sister!" Xian whispered. "Dagmar's mother used to dance with HER like this. I would be proud if Jaynette grew to be like Dagmar."

"Well, of course, but…"

118

"Tally, she has already asked Dagmar why her skin is a different color," Rich interrupted. "She's very well aware of racial differences. As for the music and dancing, we'll make sure it doesn't go too far. Until now, she's only listened to classical music. It's good for her to be exposed to different things, and people. Look at how much she's enjoying this."

"As always, you are right, my love," Talia acquiesced with a smile. "It is just a sign of my baby growing up. I want to keep her a little girl forever… but I can not."

When the music stopped Dagmar and Jaynette clapped. "Did you like that, Jaynette?"

"Yes Mommy… oops, I mean Aunt Dagmar."

It wasn't until Jaynette's slip that Dagmar realized she was instinctively acting like her mother. She wanted to cry but forced herself to smile. "I'm gonna put on some Chubby Checker and teach you how to dance The Twist!"

As the music played and Dagmar and Jaynette danced and laughed, Talia leaned over to her husband and whispered, "Richard, you are familiar with this music, yes?"

"I used to listen to it on the 'oldies' station on the car radio."

"And you know these artists? Marvin Gaye? Wilson Pickett? Chubby Checker?"

"Yes, I do. Why?"

"Richard, can you tell me who or what a 'Cannonball Adderley' is?"

They danced and laughed through several more songs, and then Jaynette ran to the sofa so hard she crashed into her father saying, "I LIKE TO DANCE!"

Talia smiled and asked, "Do you wish to take dance lessons, little one?"

"I want Aunt DAGMAR to teach me to dance!"

Dagmar picked up Jaynette and held her at eye level. "You already know how to dance like me. Just move like you feel. You know, if you really,

REALLY like to dance there are all kinds of styles. I think that's what your mother's talking about. You could take lessons and teach me!"

"Wow! That would be great! More, more, more! Let's dance some more!"

Realizing his daughter was starting to get overly excited, Rich said, "Jaynette, you'll wear Aunt Dagmar out! Why don't you show us how you meditate?"

"Could you do that?" Dagmar asked. "I've never seen you meditate."

Jaynette lowered herself to the floor without using her hands and sat with her legs crossed. She chanted quietly with her eyes closed while her hands rested on her knees. After running through several chants that had a meaning only to her and Jane, her therapist, she silently mouthed a secret chant that was hers and hers alone. With eyes still closed, she sat quietly, and then smiled. She opened her eyes and stood gracefully.

"How do you feel, my sweet?" her mother asked.

"Good."

"Jaynette," Talia continued, "Could you excuse us? We have to talk to Aunt Dagmar and she has to talk to Aunt Xian."

Jaynette walked to Dagmar with her arms open wide. Dropping to one knee Dagmar embraced her and said, "Give me some sugar before you go."

"Thank you for teaching me to dance," Jaynette said as she hugged her tightly.

"Any time, Baby."

She looked over her shoulder at her mother's sister, turned back to Dagmar and whispered, "Thank you for helping Aunt Xian." Without waiting for a reply, Jaynette ran off to her room.

"I am sorry my daughter took up so much of your time," Talia apologized.

"I loved every second of it! You have a wonderful little girl."

"I know you want to get to your session with Xian but before you do, I just wanted to let you know that my heart is completely filled with joy now that I have my older sister back in my life. I am so happy that I am planning a celebration. I want to have a… ladies night!"

"What is a 'ladies night'?" Xian questioned.

Talia smiled. "One week from this Saturday, I am going to rent a limousine and we are going to go to a hot club in Manhattan and celebrate. We will have a VIP table with a nice view of the club and we will eat, drink and dance! Jane told me her receptionist will turn twenty-one the day before so we can also celebrate her birthday! I am inviting everyone from Kane & Teasdale."

Dagmar looked a little uncomfortable and said, "I… really don't feel much like celebrating. I can't see dancing so soon after… well… my Mommy… well…"

"But, you were just dancing!" Rich said.

"That was for your daughter and in remembrance of my Mommy."

Xian added, "Then don't dance. Please come!"

"I'm sorry. I just can't. Xian, if you're ready, I'd like to start your session."

Xian nodded and they walked to her room. Talia, who was so excited, now looked sad. Rich put his arm around her and said, "She'll come."

"Richard, you heard what she said."

He kissed his wife gently on the lips and said, "I'll handle it. Just make sure you include her in the reservation."

Smiling, Talia said, "Yes, my love."

"And don't go dancing with any guys!"

"Richard, I am five and a half months pregnant. Who would want to dance with me?"

Rich walked to the computer and played the song, "Swayin' to the Music" by Johnny Rivers. He returned, took his wife in his arms and said, "I would. I would like to dance with you." They rocked back and forth and Talia smiled as she melted into her husband's strong embrace.

Doctor and patient sat in opposing chairs in the bedroom. Dagmar went through her ritual of taking Xian's temperature, pulse and blood pressure. "For someone who barely graduated from high school you are very well spoken."

"In spite of my silence and lack of interest in school, it seems I absorbed the knowledge. Also, I've been exposed to my sisters and parents who are quite intelligent."

"It sounds like your memory is improving. Do you remember your marriage?"

"I remember that I was married… but little else."

Looking at how straight Xian was sitting; Dagmar walked behind her and felt her neck and shoulder muscles. "Your neck and back are as tight as a drum. I think meditation would help you. I'm going to consult with Jane. She's more familiar with meditation techniques than I am. I also want you to begin daily therapeutic massage. I'll make an appointment for you tomorrow." Dagmar took her seat and said, "So… you remember my stories."

"Yes. I liked the stories about your family. Dagmar, I know you are feeling sad about the death of Mommy, but I wish you would come to the party my sister is planning."

"It's going to be a while before I can feel like celebrating anything again. I've told you stories about my family that no one has heard. You, of all people, should know how devastating this has been for me."

"I just want to help you heal… as you have helped me."

"Thank you, Xian. It's… going to take a lot of time for me. But if you want me to feel better, go and have a fantastic time at the club. Make sure you tell me all about it! I don't want you to drink alcohol yet but, other than that, go crazy. Don't wear a kimono. Have Talia buy you a hot, slinky dress! Hit the dance floor and have fun!"

122

# Chapter Twenty-One

# Day to Day

It had been a little over a week since Dagmar's mother died, but it felt to her like it just happened. Yesterday, Anabelle helped her box up her mother's clothes and donate them to charity. Today, Dagmar had a shopping bag filled with shirts and pants for her father to help fill the emptiness of his closet. She went to knock on the door of her father's apartment and found it was partially open. As Dagmar walked into the room, she saw him sitting in his favorite chair with his hand covering an exhausted face, wet from crying.

"Daddy?"

Mister Lamont shook with surprise at the sound of his daughter's voice. He forced a smile and stood. "I didn't hear you come in, Baby. I was just taking a nap."

"I bought you some new clothes," Dagmar said as she took the shirts and pants and laid them out on the coffee table in front of him.

"Those look nice. Those look real nice."

Picking them up, Dagmar said, "I'm going to put your new clothes in your closet." She neatly hung the clothing and went to the kitchen.

"Baby?  What are you doing?"

"I'm going to make you dinner."

"Don't do that," Mister Lamont said as Dagmar returned to the living room.  "I gotta learn to cook for myself.  I can't do that with you making me dinner.  It's nice that you've been comin' by after work but I really have to be on my own.  What's gonna happen when you go on a business trip?  I got to rely on myself."

"I've been thinking about cutting back on my travel."

Now stern, Mister Lamont said, "No.  You don't do that for me.  Your mama wouldn't want it and I don't want it.  I'm okay.  Gettin' by day to day.  I'm okay.  Just leave me be."

"Daddy, when are you going back to work?" she questioned.

Mister Lamont returned to his chair, looked away from his daughter and said, "Soon.  Real soon."

Dagmar took a kitchen chair and placed it in front of her father.  She sat directly in front of him and asked, "Daddy, what's wrong at work?"

"Nothin'.  I just need a few days."

"My patient Xian had told me for weeks nothing was wrong with her.  I didn't believe HER and I don't believe YOU."

"You're my baby.  I'm supposed to worry about you.  You're not supposed to worry about me."

"We're family.  We worry about each other.  What's wrong at work?!"

"I… I don't want to talk about it.  Not with you."

Dagmar was stunned into momentary silence.  "Daddy, I am your flesh and blood!"

Mister Lamont smiled and said, "I know, Baby.  Look, there are a few things I have to straighten out.  Why don't you go home?  Worry about yourself for a change.  If I need you I'll call."

"I don't know…"

124

"Baby… your daddy said he'd call if he needs you."

"Do you promise?"

"I promise."

Dagmar sighed, got off the chair and kissed her father's cheek. "I'm gonna come back in a few days," Dagmar said as she returned the chair to the kitchen. She went back in the living room and wrapped her arms around her father. "You sure I can't cook for you?"

"Look," Mister Lamont said walking his daughter to the door, "You should go to dinner with one of your friends. Why don't you give that Anabelle girl a call?"

"Maybe I will," Dagmar said as she walked through the door. "Bye, Daddy."

"Bye, Baby. Never forget… I love you."

As he closed the door his smile turned upside down. Mister Lamont trudged into his bedroom. He sat on the edge of his bed and looked at his wife's wedding photograph on the dresser until it blurred through his tears. Mister Lamont ached so much inside, he fell to the ground, doubled over with anguish.

He was on the floor for over an hour before he was all cried out. Haltingly, Mister Lamont stood and looked at himself in the dresser mirror. A beaten and broken man looked back. Returning to sit on his bed, Mister Lamont stared off into space for several minutes. Then, he opened his bottom dresser drawer and dug through it until he found a pouch. Mister Lamont took out the buried pouch and removed the contents. The .38 caliber Smith & Wesson felt heavy in his hand. Placing the gun on the bed, he opened another drawer and took out a second buried pouch that contained a box of bullets. Mister Lamont spun the cylinder of the double action revolver. He thought about all he had lost and the parts of his life that were never going to get better. Looking at a picture of his smiling wife Mister Lamont said, "Jenny. My sweet Jenny Mae. I did everything the way you'd want. We had a quick wake and funeral. Dagmar and me, we stood tall and did our name proud. It took every bit of my strength to do it, but I did it. Now… I got no more. I can't eat. I can't sleep. I can't earn a living. And I can't look into my woman's eyes and tell her I love her."

Picking up the gun and looking at it, Mister Lamont said, "Just like the old days, I'm taking the train to see my girl." He popped open the cylinder with one hand, picked up a bullet with the other and loaded the firearm. "I've got a box full of one-way tickets, but I'm only gonna need this one." Clicking the cylinder closed he said, "I'm comin' to see you, Jenny. I'm comin' to see you." Mister

Lamont was surprised that his hand did not shake as he brought the gun to his temple. For one last time, he began taking a good long look at each picture on the dresser, remembering the joy and love he felt for his beloved wife. By the time he would look at the last picture there would be nothing left to do but get on board the train and use his ticket. Each photo brought more sadness to his face and as he looked at the last picture he tightened his finger on the trigger. However, that last picture was a photo of his wife and his daughter. Mister Lamont could not help himself. He smiled at the sight of his young daughter… and her coco puffs. The anguished man sat the gun on the bed and picked up the photograph. It never occurred to him how much Dagmar looked like her mother. Then, Mister Lamont realized his daughter would be the one to find his dead body. "I can't do that to you, Baby. I just can't." Carefully, he unloaded the gun and returned it, and the bullets, to the drawer. Looking at the picture of his wife and daughter he choked, "I can't live and I can't die. What am I gonna do?" As if to answer his question, he looked at the dresser and noticed the corner of a business card peeking out of his wallet. He looked at the card, sighed and reluctantly picked up the bedroom phone.

Candace had to think before she introduced herself. At her psychiatric practice, she kept her maiden name, Candace Kane. To her friends, she used her hyphenated name, Candace Kane-Belesco. If her husband had his way, she would simply be Candace Belesco. So, she left her office as Candace Kane but walked through the door of her home as Candace Belesco. Her stride into the living room was halted at the sight of clothes, toys and baby bottles everywhere. Turning to the direction of her crying baby, Candace bolted into the kitchen. Frank, Candace's husband, was walking around the room bouncing her son in a vain attempt to get him to stop crying.

"Hey, Can! What's for dinner?"

"You were home all day! Why didn't YOU make dinner?"

"'Cause I'm the man and you're the woman."

Candace simply folded her arms and smiled as she looked her husband up and down. He was wearing her fuzzy slippers and an apron. Noticing the irony in his words, Frank quickly added, "He threw up on my shoes and I don't want to get my pants dirty."

"Why didn't you clean the house?"

"'Cause that's women's work."

126

"I know you're half kidding. That's why I'm only going to cut off ONE of your balls."

Laughing, Frank said, "You wouldn't do that! You love them too much! Say, lets put the kid to bed early and hit the sheets."

Boiling with anger, Candace exploded, "Listen, idiot, I'm busting my hump trying to run a practice! The last thing I want to see when I come home is a husband who can't pick up after himself and a seven month old! Get it together!"

Frank was about to argue back when his wife's cell phone rang. She looked at the caller ID and her face registered concern. Frank instantly recognized that it was a serious call and said, "Take it in the study. I'll start dinner."

Candace ran to the quiet of the study and answered her phone. "Mister Lamont! What a nice surprise. Are you okay?"

A long silence on the other end and finally, Mister Lamont responded, saying, "I'm about as far from okay as a man can get. I miss her, Doctor Kane. I miss her so much! I... almost joined her."

"YOU WHAT?!!!"

"I couldn't do it. If I joined my wife, it would hurt my Baby. I loved my woman to the depths of my soul. I thought she'd be there forever. And now she's gone. I lost my job, you know. The general contractor said I was a risk with my medical problems. Thank God I never had to tell Jenny. A man isn't a man unless he can work. What am I gonna tell my Baby? I... I don't know why I called you. I should let you get on with your evening."

"Have you had dinner yet?"

"I... I can't eat."

Candace glanced at her watch and said, "I'm picking you up and you're going to have dinner at my place. After you eat, you'll play with the most adorable baby in the world and then we'll sit down and talk."

After a pause, Mister Lamont said, "I can't..."

"I'll pick you up in forty-five minutes."

Candace walked into the kitchen still thinking about the sadness in Mister Lamont's voice and his terrible loss. Frank was busy cleaning and cooking at the same time. "Hey, Can, tell you what, you spend some time with Frankie junior and I'll whip up a nice Polo Ripieno. I already have an Antipasti chilled in the fridge."

Candace walked to Frank and gave him a long, passionate kiss. She pulled her lips away and said, "I just want you to know I love and appreciate you. In no way does that mean I'm putting up with your shit… but I love and appreciate you. Now, get you ass in gear. We're having a guest for dinner."

"Who?"

"Dagmar's father."

"Isn't he the black guy who just lost his wife?"

"No, he's the GUY who just lost his wife… and he needs help. I'm going to give him as many off-the-books sessions as he needs. I hope you have no objections to him coming here on short notice."

"'Course not. The man's in pain. If anyone can help him, you can, Can. Say, his daughter is HOT. Is she coming too?"

Walking close to her husband, Candace gave him a couple playful slaps on the cheek, then one hard slap. "You just can't help yourself. You're SUCH an ASSHOLE!"

Frank grabbed his wife and planted a long kiss on her. When they parted he said, "I may flirt and I may bust'em off on you, but the truth is… I never forget that I'm married to the smartest and sexiest woman I know."

She patted him on his butt then took her car keys out of her purse. "Nice recovery… but you aren't getting laid tonight."

Smiling a confident smile, Frank said, "We'll see."

# Chapter Twenty-Two

# Blue

The Thursday evening before the party in Manhattan, Dagmar was in her apartment wearing her old, but comfortable, pajamas. She was trying to distract herself from thinking about her mother by watching television. While flipping through the channels her phone rang.

"Dagmar, this is Rich," she heard through her phone.

"Hey, Rich. Is something wrong?"

"No, nothing at all. I just wanted to stop by for a visit."

"A visit? You've never come here before."

"I'd like to talk to you face to face. It's important."

Dagmar hesitated, and then finally said, "Sure, c'mon over. When will you be here?"

"I'm on the other side of your door," Rich said and knocked twice. "See?"

"Wha…!  I'm not dressed!"

"You're naked?"

"No, I'm in my pajamas!"

Rich laughed, "My wife and daughter wear 'PJ's'.  I think I can handle it."

Dagmar jumped up, turned off the television and threw on an old robe.  From habit, she ran her fingers through her hair as she passed by a mirror.  When she opened the door, she saw Rich standing in the hall, unintentionally looking sexy, wearing a dark blue shirt and jeans.  A curious canvas bag was at his feet.  "Are you sure everything's all right?" Dagmar asked as she clutched her robe, closing it up even tighter.

"If you invite me in, you'll find out."

As Dagmar stepped aside, Rich picked up the bag and walked through the door.  The studio apartment was essentially one large space that was the living room, dining room, most of the kitchen and the bedroom.  In fact, the queen size bed was the first thing Rich saw when he entered the apartment.  To Dagmar, the bed seemed to grow in size and obviousness as the attractive man looked around the room.  "Er… take a seat," she offered.

"Thanks.  You've got a nice place," Rich said as he sat in one of the chairs.  His eyes followed Dagmar as she sat on her loveseat, folding her arms and crossing her ankles.  "Dagmar, you look nervous."

"I'm in my apartment with a married man whose wife could kick my ass from here to The City.  Why would I be nervous?  Does Talia know you're here?"

"Yes, she does."

"And she's okay with you and me being alone in my apartment?"

Rich flashed his boyish smile and said, "I can be very… persuasive."

"I don't want to be rude, but why are you here?"

"I've been worried about you so I called Jane and asked for a little background on you.  She told me we have something in common… our birthday."

"You're an Aquarius too?"

130

"Yes, February 7th just like you. She told me how intelligent you are."

"Jane exaggerates."

Rich laughed. "You started college at the age of sixteen and a half. I'd say that qualifies you as intelligent. Since your mom passed, I've noticed the spark missing when you come to the house for Xian's therapy so I asked Jane what you needed during this tough time in your life. She said you needed to get drunk and get laid."

Dagmar stuttered, "Er… Rich, I… er…"

"As you said, I'm a married… HAPPILY married man, so I can't help you with the latter. But I CAN help you with the former," Rich said as he took a bottle from the canvas bag.

Dagmar smiled, "Johnny Walker Blue. You've got good taste in blended scotch."

"Glad you like it," Rich said as he took two crystal glasses from the bag and placed them on the end table next to his chair. As he poured the scotch, he said, "We're going to drink, you're going to get drunk, and we're going to talk."

"I have to warn you, I don't get drunk easily."

"Jane told me that you have a high tolerance of alcohol. That's why I brought along two more," Rich said, and took two more bottles of Johnny Walker Blue from the bag. "They're all yours. The scotch. The glasses. Even the bag." Handing a glass to Dagmar, Rich said, "I want to make a toast to Xian and the miracle that returned her heart and soul." They clinked glasses and Dagmar took a sip. "C'mon, drink it down. There isn't THAT much in the glass." Dagmar threw back the scotch and Rich refilled the crystal. "To Mrs. Jennifer Mae Johnson Lamont who left the world too soon."

This time, Dagmar needed no encouragement to drink the glass dry.

"What was your mother like?"

"She grew up poor and left high school before graduating to get a job. She cleaned houses from when she was seventeen until just before I was born."

"She never went back to work?"

"Briefly. When Mommy went back to work after giving birth to me, one of the homeowners began making passes at her. He became persistent."

131

"Was she… assaulted?"

Dagmar laughed. "Mommy could handle herself. She kicked him in the balls. Of course, she was fired. She quit her other cleaning jobs and became a stay-at-home-mom and made some money sewing and hemming clothes for the neighbors and the local cleaners. I'm the only person she ever told. If Daddy knew someone tried to get physical with her, even today, he'd go to that house and beat the living hell out of that man. Damn the consequences." Dagmar paused, looked at Rich and said, "I've never told anyone that story. Please don't repeat it. If Daddy ever found out…"

"I won't say a word to anyone." Rich continued, "When your mother died, I'll bet people were tripping all over themselves to say they were sorry and ask if you were okay. Now that it's been a couple of weeks no one is asking anymore… except me. How are you feeling? Are you okay?"

Looking at the sparkling crystal, Dagmar said, "My favorite weather is a spring day. I love the warm sun and a cool breeze on my skin. That was what it was like for Mommy's funeral. It wasn't hot or rainy or cold… the weather was perfect. Now, every time there's a perfect day, I associate it with burying Mommy. To answer your questions, I'm feeling horrible. It's like I'm not myself. Damn it, Rich, it's not fair! She was healthy! And you're right. No one is asking how I'm feeling. It's like everyone forgot. Am I okay? No. I don't think I'll ever be okay."

Rich gave her an understanding nod. "It feels like no one knows what you're going through. After all, all of your friends still have their parents. That's why I'm here. Remember, both of my parents are gone so I have some perspective on what you're going through. Believe me, your friends haven't forgotten about your loss. They want to help, but there IS no help. The best they can do is to try to get you back to some form of normalcy."

Dagmar shook her head. "Don't they understand…"

"No," Rich interrupted, "they don't." He refilled her glass and motioned for her to drink. As Dagmar sipped the scotch, Rich continued. "They won't understand until they've been through it. And even when they go through it, it won't hit them as hard. Your friends have started their own families. Losing a parent is easier when you ARE a parent. By the way, just because no one knows what you're going through doesn't mean their attempts to bring back 'the old Dagmar' are wrong."

"How so?" Dagmar asked as she finished the scotch in her glass.

Rich explained as he refilled the crystal. "Doing normal things will help you heal. Like a patient who's had an operation, you'll always carry around a

132

scar… but you'll be okay.  This leads me to the second reason I'm here.  I think you should go with Tally and the girls into The City this Saturday night.  Have some fun."

"It… feels too soon."

"It will always feel too soon… until you take that first step.  You know, Xian is very fond of you.  Everyone surrounding her is family except you.  You're her only friend… probably the only friend she's ever had.  She'd be happy if you came along.  Do you know that she cries every night because you won't come to the party?"

"What?  She never told me that!"  Dagmar said holding out her glass.

As Rich filled it he said, "She doesn't want to make you feel guilty… I do."

"You're SURE Xian's been crying because I won't go out with the girls on Saturday?"

"Just ask Tally.  She'll tell you."

Dagmar knocked back a full glass of scotch.  She stared off into space for several seconds and finally said, "All right.  I'll go."  Looking at Rich from the corner of her eye, she smiled and said, "You were right.  You CAN be convincing."  Just then, her phone rang.  Answering it she said, "Hello?  Jane?"  Covering the mouthpiece she said to Rich, "It's Jane."  Turning back to the phone she repeated, "Who's here?  Rich is here.  Say hi, Rich."

"Hi Jane!" Rich said loudly.

"Rich said 'hi.'  What's he doing here?  You told him I needed to get drunk and get laid, right?  Well, he just got me drunk and… I gotta go!"  Dagmar hung up the phone and started laughing.

"You really ARE drunk!"

"Yes… I… am!"

Rich's cell phone rang.  "Hello?  Jane?  I'm sorry but I can't talk.  I'm gettin' busy… I mean I'm busy."  Dagmar laughed as Rich continued.  "Call me tomorrow… late."

"Hey, Rich," Dagmar said loudly, "What do you want for breakfast?!!!"

Trying to contain his laughter, Rich said, "Jane I really, REALLY have to go. Oh, and Dagmar won't be in the office tomorrow morning. Cover for her, okay? Bye!"

They could still hear Jane squawking as Rich hung up the phone. Dagmar held her stomach as she laughed… the first time she laughed since her mother died.

Smiling, Rich said, "It looks like you're pretty smashed so I should probably go."

"You know, I just figured you out," Dagmar said as she helped herself to another glass of scotch. "Here you are being nice, sitting on my chair lookin' all fine and handsome… and convincing. You're using what you got to make me do somethin'. You're a HIMbo… a male bimbo!"

"I really should go," Rich said as he began to stand.

"Sit back down!" Dagmar commanded. Rich complied and she continued, "Don't worry about it. It ain't nothin' I haven't done. What's important is WHY your doin' what your doin'. You're just tryin' to help me." Looking Rich over and smiling, Dagmar said, "I'm seein' a whole different side of you. I only knew you as Jane's hot, if nerdy, friend."

Rich smiled. "What do you mean, 'nerdy'?"

"You always carried around that 'PDA' thing when everyone else was keeping their information in their phones, and you're the last guy on earth to get rid of his beeper!"

Rich rolled his eyes and said, "I see what you mean… but I'm up to date now."

"Yes you are. Up-to-date-and-hot-as-hell. I always thought you and Jane would eventually get together, then Talia came along and locked you up. Rich, did you ever date any black girls?"

"Yes, one."

"Who broke it off?"

"It was complicated."

"Ain't it always? C'mon. Who broke it off?"

"She did."

134

Dagmar gulped down the scotch in her glass and said, "Dumb fuckin' bitch!"

"Dagmar! I've never heard you swear!"

"You've never seen me drunk, either! Let me tell you somethin'... if that black girl were me, we'd be together an' makin' babies. Don't you think we'd make beautiful babies?"

Rich smiled and said, "Yes, we would."

Dagmar smiled as she looked at her empty glass. "I love your kids. Jaynette is adorable and George is as sweet as sweet can be. Rich... I like Talia, I really do, but if something were to happen to her... I've got dibs on you!"

Rich laughed and said, "Thanks. I'm flattered."

"You should be! Look at all this!" she said and looked down at her ratty robe and worn flannel pajamas. "Well, don't look at all this right now. If I knew your hotness was comin' by, I'd have made myself luscious." Dagmar emptied the last of the bottle into her glass and began to sip. She looked at Rich, sat the glass down, folded her hands and said, "I used to date this guy who drove a Corvette. Every time he'd pass another person driving a Corvette he'd wave. I asked him if he knew these people and he said he didn't. They were just people who drove Corvettes. No formal club. No meetings. Just like minded people recognizing each other. I've always thought that people of great love and passion just... know each other. They sense it. They're drawn to each other. I can see it in Jane and I can see it in Talia. I haven't seen it in many men," Dagmar said, looking Rich up and down. She added with a smile, "At least, I haven't seen it in many SINGLE men. Maybe these people should wave to each other like the Corvette people do... just to acknowledge they're all on the same vibe." Dagmar rubbed her face and said, "Oh God, I'm so drunk!"

Rich put the extra bottles of scotch on the kitchen counter and rinsed out the glasses. "I'm going home now. Will you be all right?"

Dagmar stood and staggered over to Rich. She draped her arms around him and said, "Thanks for coming over. At first, I was afraid you were going to hit on me. Now, I'm sorry you DIDN'T hit on me." She popped her head up and looked Rich in the eye and said, "Not that I would've acted on it."

"Of course not," Rich said with his charming smile. Dagmar buried her head in his chest, wrapped her arms around him and squeezed hard. He spoke in a soft voice, "Any time you want to talk about your mom... or anything else... just call me, okay?"

She looked up at him with a goofy smile and said, "Ten-four, good buddy!  I want to kiss you… but I can't kiss you… you… fuckin' married guy. Rich, give me somethin'!  At least tell me I look good!"

Rich brushed away the hair from her face and said, "I think you're beautiful."

Dagmar threw her hands in the air and said, "Woooo!  Hot guy thinks I'm beautiful!" and fell backwards onto the bed.

"I'll see myself out.  Good night.  I'll tell Tally you'll join everyone on Saturday night."  Rich opened the door, turned back, and said, "Hey, Dagmar!" When Dagmar lifted her head, Rich waved… just like the "Corvette people."

"I know what that means!" she said and waved back.

Rich closed the door which locked behind him.

Several minutes later Dagmar heard a knock on her door.  Giggling and staggering, she got out of bed saying, "Rich, did you forget somethin'?"  When she opened the door she saw Jane's disapproving face.

"What the hell…?" Jane questioned.

Dagmar burst out laughing.

# Chapter Twenty-Three

# Ladies Night

A Harley-Davidson motorcycle made a ninety-degree turn onto the private road "Love Lane". The rider, encased in black leather, wearing a black helmet with a blacked out visor, gunned the engine and shot down the long, tree-lined driveway. When reaching the clearing, the motorcycle slid sideways to a stop in front of a warm and inviting house. Suzy Cohen shut down the engine and pulled off her helmet. She walked on the porch to the front door, pressed the bell, and extricated herself from her black leather backpack.

Rich smiled as he opened the door. "Hi, Suzy."

"Hey, Rich. I'm early. I need time to change clothes. Is that okay?"

"You know you're always welcome," Rich said as he held the door open wide. When she walked inside the beautiful home he asked, "Can I take you to a bedroom?"

Looking at Talia's handsome husband Suzy sighed, "You really know how to break a girls heart, don't you? A bathroom is good enough. I know the way."

One by one the women arrived at the Sedgwick residence. The last to show up was a man driving Harmony in an old station wagon. Looking at Harmony he said, "Yo no sé acerca de esto". ("I don't know about this.")

"Será Poppy bien! Dos de las chicas ni siquiera será potable y vamos a tener una limusina nos trae hacia y desde el club." ("It'll be okay, Poppy! Two of the girls won't even be drinking and we'll have a limo bringing us to and from the club.")

"¿Cómo le va a casa? ¿Quieres que te recoja? " ("How are you getting home? Should I pick you up?")

"Voy a llegar a casa de uno de mis amigas." ("I'll get a ride home from one of my friends.")

Harmony's father looked at all the expensive cars, then pointed to Suzy's motorcycle. "No dejes que se os lleve a casa." ("Don't let THAT one take you home.")

She leaned over and kissed her father on the cheek. "No me esperes despierta." ("Don't wait up.")

Harmony walked up to the front porch and Rich, waiting at the door, led her inside. All of her co-workers were in the living room except Suzy who was just entering and becoming the center of attention. She wore a fitted two-tone gray men's vest without a shirt, tie or jacket. Her pants were pleated men's pants except they had several slits in them exposing glimpses of Suzy's legs as she walked. She abandoned her contact lenses for the evening and wore stylish glasses, multiple earrings, and a diamond stud in her nose. To finish her look, Suzy wore men's wingtip shoes and, cocked to one side, was an expensive gray fedora.

Looking Suzy up and down, Rich said, "That's an… interesting outfit you're sort of wearing."

"Thanks. Why is everyone standing around in their coats?"

"They got here just a minute ago," Rich answered.

"I want to see what everyone's wearing! C'mon! Fashion show! Take off that coat, Candace!"

Candace unbuttoned her coat and let it fall to the ground. Floor length sheer layers of violet, blue and white draped her slim body. Spinning around displayed almost no back to the dress, which was scooped out dangerously low. "I've finally lost the baby weight and I'm going to make sure everyone knows it."

Rich turned to Anabelle and said, "Let's see what you're wearing."

The normally frumpily dressed psychiatrist sighed and asked, "Do I have to?"

"Yes!" Rich insisted.

Slowly, Anabelle began unfastening her coat. She never had what she would consider a flattering figure, however her dress made her look fantastic. She wore a white and maroon empire waisted floral gown.

"Anabelle!" Suzy said in surprise. "Look at the bazooms you've been smuggling under those Moo Moos you wear!"

When Rich saw how uncomfortable Anabelle looked he turned to Harmony. "Okay, time to unwrap the birthday girl."

"I thought you'd never ask," Harmony said and dramatically whipped off her coat. Her skin tight, hot pink dress was just a little too low cut and just a little too short.

"Caliente!" Suzy exclaimed.

"Er... maybe you should put your coat back on," Rich suggested.

"I turned twenty-one yesterday, Mister Sedgwick. I'm now an adult woman."

"Sorry. I still think of you as a young girl. Especially when you call me 'Mister Sedgwick'."

"Okay... Riiiiich," she teased looking at him in a flirtatious way.

"Save it for the club," Rich said and turned to Jane. "I know you're dying to show off your outfit."

She turned away from everyone and took a few steps as she unbuttoned her coat, then spun around. Jane was still in the process of losing the extra weight gained from having her baby. Making the best of her fuller figure, she wore a beige top with black piping, a black belt, and a matching skirt that hugged her legs just past her knees. Adding to the outfit were stockings with a line running up the back. A Veronica Lake style wig and bright red lipstick made Jane look like she stepped out of the 1940's.

"Darling, I have to hand it to you. You never fail to surprise," Candace complimented. "Rich, where are Talia and Xian?"

"They're still getting ready. Okay, Dagmar. Your turn."

Slowly, Dagmar opened her coat to reveal a shimmering white, opalescent, form-fitting gown that was eye catching next to her dark skin. The gown ended just past her ankle with a split on one side that occasionally revealed a long, perfect leg. Matching high heels completed her outfit. The amount of cleavage she was showing was tasteful... but only just.

"GodDAMN!" Suzy whispered. "She looks like a fuckin' angel!"

Jane's eyes widened. "Suzy! Kids in the house!" she scolded.

Still staring at Dagmar in awe, Suzy said, "Sorry... but, Holy Shi... SUGAR! I didn't know you owned anything but business suits!"

Rich walked over to Dagmar and quietly said, "You look absolutely beautiful."

"Thanks, Rich." Dagmar looked down modestly.

"I know this isn't easy for you. Thanks for coming."

Dagmar looked at the charming man. She is never tongue tied with men but she found herself completely wordless and was relieved when she heard someone else enter the room.

"Don't we all look fantastic tonight?!" Talia announced. She was wearing a short, blue, baby doll dress. Cut low, just enough to show off her growing breasts, and bulky enough to help hide her pregnancy. Rich went to his wife and kissed her softly. "God, you look cute!" he said, and then quietly, "Why haven't you worn that to bed?"

Returning quietly, "This isn't sleepwear, silly."

"That's okay," he whispered. "If you wear it to bed, you won't be sleeping." As Talia giggled, Rich continued, "Don't go tonight. Stay here with me."

"I organized this, Richard. You know that I must go. You are going to have to stay here... in anticipation of my return."

The pair stared lustfully into each other's eyes until Talia turned away and said, "Ladies, we have another entrant for our fashion show. Come out, little one."

From the other room came her daughter Jaynette looking adorable wearing her one-piece pink sleeper and fuzzy pink slippers. Everyone clapped as she spun around to show off her pajamas. "Can I come too?!!!"

Talia picked her daughter up and said, "No, Jaynette. But you get to stay home and take care of Daddy for me."

All fell silent as they heard, "I'm ready now… I think."

The voice belonged to Xian. She was wearing a form-fitting red sequined dress that looked stunning. The back of her outfit was full and the sleeves were long covering the immense scarring on her body. No longer the emaciated woman who they first saw, she looked as if she were melted and poured into her curvy dress.

Dagmar rushed to her patient and hugged her tightly. When she leaned back Xian saw tears beginning to form in her doctor's eyes. "Wow!" Dagmar said. "Is this what you look like beneath those bulky kimonos?"

"Thanks to your nutrition and exercise program," Xian complemented.

"Hey, Dagmar," Suzy said, "If you treat me, can I look that good too? I just have to come up with a mental problem."

"Shouldn't be hard," Candace joked flatly.

"Isn't my sister-in-law beautiful?" Rich asked everyone. He turned to Xian and said, "I'm amazed by your growth and progress." He then went to Dagmar and hugged her. "What you have done is nothing short of a miracle."

When he released her, Talia walked to Dagmar. Rather than being mad that her husband just hugged Dagmar, Talia embraced her as well and whispered, "The Sedgwick household will forever be in your debt." Talia leaned back and placed her hand on Dagmar's cheek. "Soon, after our little soirée, we will talk at length." Talia recoiled a bit as she sensed Dagmar's emotions and said, "You feel… undeserving?"

"I appreciate everything you and Rich said about me… but it was the anguish I felt from Mommy's death that unlocked Xian's emotions. I don't think I did so much."

"Stop it!" Jane barked. "Your treatment worked. I know because I've read every word of your notes. The death of your mother sped things along but you were on the right track. In fact, I've never seen a doctor work as hard for their patient as you have for Xian. You can be humble if you like but I won't let you dismiss your hard work, sound judgment, and results! When Rich said you created a miracle, those weren't his words. Those were MY words to him! We are all proud of you, Dag."

Looking stunned, Dagmar said, "I… I don't know what to say…" Then she smiled and said, "Wait. I DO know what to say. Here we are talking about me when we should be celebrating Harmony's birthday!"

"Dagmar is right," Xian added. "How often does a woman turn twenty-one?"

"I think I did a few times," Candace vamped. "So, Harmony, what will be your first legal drink?"

"I don't know. What's good?"

"What do you usually drink?"

"I've never had a drink."

"What? Never?" Candace asked incredulously.

"Candace, I'm a good girl!"

"Not after tonight, darling."

Talia's keen hearing picked up the sound of the limousine pulling up to her home. "Girls, our ride is here."

As the ladies gathered their things to leave, Rich gave his life long friend a look that meant he wanted to talk to her. Jane waited for the girls to leave before she walked to Rich.

"I want you to look after Dagmar tonight."

"Rich, I haven't tasted booze in nine months! I'm going to need someone to look after ME! Why not have your wife keep an eye on her."

"She will. Talia will keep her safe but YOU know Dagmar the party girl. Make sure she has a good time."

"What is it with you and Dagmar, anyway? I ran over to her apartment to make sure the two of you weren't screwing."

"Jane, you know me better than that!"

Skeptically, Jane said, "I don't know. You two sounded awfully chummy over the phone."

Rich paused and said, "I remember how tough it was after my parents death. If I didn't have you in my life… I don't know what I would've done."

Jane nodded with a smile. "Understood. Okay. I'll get her butt on the dance floor at least once tonight. What did you say to get Dagmar to come out with us?"

"Nothing really."

"You flirted with her, didn't you?!"

"Well…"

"RICH!"

"Look, I wouldn't expect you to know this, but after a big loss like Dagmar experienced, you feel kind of… asexual. I figured a couple compliments could help her ego and her libido."

"I can tell you that she didn't feel 'asexual' after you left."

"Good. Let me walk you out before everyone wonders where we are."

Rich and Jane went to the front porch to see the women getting into the limousine. "Hey, look!" Suzy yelled. "Jane talked Rich into coming with us!"

Taking his daughter from his wife's arms he said, "Sorry. I already have a date tonight. Isn't that right, Jaynette?" She wrapped her arms around his neck and squeezed hard. Talia gave her husband a long but soft kiss good-bye.

When their lips parted he simply said, "That dress."

She simply said, "Tonight."

All the girls settled into their seats and waved good-bye to Rich and Jaynette as the limo rolled down the driveway.

When they were underway, Harmony said to Talia, "I give you a lot of credit, Mrs. Sedgwick…"

"Please, call me Talia."

"I give you a lot of credit, Talia. I'd feel insecure if all these beautiful women were throwing themselves at MY husband."

"It is something I have worked through with my therapist," Talia said smiling at Candace.

"Well, Tal, you're a better woman than I!" Jane confessed. "I've known Rich most of my life and I couldn't even meet him for coffee without some chick checking him out or slipping him her phone number. It got to be damned annoying!"

"I have gotten used to it… mostly. Besides, I trust Richard with my life. His heart, body and soul belong to me. And he assures me of that fact when we are… alone."

"God, Talia!" Suzy exclaimed. "You're making him even MORE attractive! I need a fuckin' drink!"

"Suzy! We're supposed to dial back the swearing!" Jane reminded.

"Do you see any kids in the limo?"

"Er… no."

"You mean, fuck no! That's the way you used to talk!"

"I don't want to slip into any old habits."

"Then, I guess you won't be drinking tonight," Suzy said as she took a bottle of champagne and started pouring it into fluted glasses.

"Don't be ridiculous. Give me a glass of champagne."

Suzy handed it to Jane but at the last second withdrew the glass. "Ask for it right."

Jane sighed and said, "Give me the mother fucking champagne!"

Handing her the glass, Suzy said, "I love you, Jane. No one can swear like you!"

Talia turned to her sister and said, "I am sorry, Xian. I should have warned you that the language can get... colorful when the girls get together."

"It IS rather... jarring," Xian admitted. She turned to Dagmar and asked, "Is your language 'colorful' as well?"

Dagmar smiled. "No, Xian, only under extreme circumstances."

When all the women had champagne, except Talia and Xian who had ginger ale, Candace got their attention and said, "I'd like to propose a toast to Talia who is footing the bill for tonight's festivities!" They all sipped their drink and Candace continued, "I'd like to propose another toast. To Harmony! Thank you for allowing us to deflower your liver!" After everyone sipped again, Candace said, "Last toast! To Xian and the first of many outings with the girls. God help her!"

"Thank you everyone," Xian said.

"Are you having a good time?" Dagmar asked.

"Yes, I am!"

"Good. Rich told me about how upset you were."

Xian and Talia looked at each other questioningly.

"You know," Dagmar continued. "He told me how you cried every night because I wasn't going out with everyone this evening."

"Er... my sister certainly was sad that you were not going to join us but... she did not cry every night about it," Talia admitted.

"No, Talia, Rich told me..." Then it came clear to Dagmar. "He lied to me. That fucking asshole lied to me!"

Xian furrowed her brow and said, "I thought you didn't swear."

"Must be an 'extreme circumstance'," Candace smirked.

"It is... my fault. Richard convinced you to come with us to please me," Talia confessed.

"That asshole!" Dagmar repeated, and her face softened to a smile. "That asshole," she whispered with a small laugh in her voice. Sighing, she looked at Talia and said, "I'm sorry for what I said about your husband."

Talia returned the smile and said, "I am fortunate enough to have married the most wonderful man in the world. However. There are a few... a VERY few days where I have been familiar with the emotion you just expressed, even if I do not know exactly what Richard said to you. To put it another way, I do not know the words... but I know the music... if you understand my meaning."

Suzy laughed. "Talia just called her husband an asshole without swearing. I think I love you too, Talia!"

The women laughed and joked throughout the ride until they came to a nightclub with a huge crowd outside. "We'll never get in there," Anabelle said.

The limo driver left the car and ran to the man in charge of security at the door. After a quick conversation, the security guards lined up forming a barrier from the crowd. Talia watched as the driver nodded to her and she passed out dark glasses to everyone. "What's this for?" Harmony asked.

"Talia likes to maintain her anonymity to protect her family. We'll only need them until we get in the club," Candace explained.

As they filed out of the limousine, the curious crowd pushed forward against the line of security men and snapped pictures with their cell phones. The manager met Talia at the front door and personally escorted them through the club to an elevated, private, VIP area with a good view of the dance floor. The sectioned off space had comfortable chairs, plush sofas and glass tables. When the partiers settled into their opulent surroundings, a woman in a black and white party dress walked into the private section and introduced herself.

"Hello. My name is LaLa and I'll be your bottle girl for this evening. May I ask which of you is Mrs. Sedgwick?"

"I am Mrs. Sedgwick," Talia answered.

LaLa directed her attention to Talia. "The owner is out of town, but he asked me to extend his personal welcome. He has, of course, waived entrance and any incidental fees along with credit minimums or maximums. He would also like you to start the evening with two bottles of Dom Pérignon... on the house."

146

Talia opened her purse and handed the bottle girl her American Express Black card. "Please thank the owner for his hospitality. You may run any expenses on this card. I am pregnant and would like ginger ale or 'virgin' drinks."

Dagmar interrupted, "Xian, too."

"Thank you, Dagmar," Talia said and pointed to Xian as she spoke to LaLa. "This is my sister. For personal reasons, what applies to me applies to her as well. Aside from that small detail, these ladies may have whatever they want."

"Very good," LaLa said, and then tried to continue delicately. "Er... Mrs. Sedgwick... I hate to bring this up, but..."

Immediately, Talia turned to the two youngest looking women. "Harmony, Suzy, please show this good woman your driver's licenses."

LaLa glanced at the cards and returned them. She winked at Harmony and said, "Happy Birthday." Turning back to Talia, she said, "Thank you, Mrs. Sedgwick. Again, my name is LaLa. Your party is my only group tonight. I will be close by so if you need anything at all, please let me know." The bottle girl left with Talia's credit card.

"She seems very accommodating," Anabelle remarked. "Do you know the owner?"

Talia smiled and said, "No. He is just a businessman who would like us to buy his club."

"Are you going to buy it?" Anabelle asked.

"I never say never when it comes to investments, but it does not fit in with the other businesses in our portfolio."

"Does the owner know this?"

"Yes, he does, Anabelle. He knows my interest is a... long shot, but he also knows a favorable mention from The Sedgwick's of Darien will increase his business... and his asking price."

"Your file states you are a good business woman," Dagmar said. "I hope you will share some of that expertise with Xian."

Taking Xian's hand, Talia smiled. "It is my intention to have my sister become independently wealthy."

"Thank you, Talia," Xian said. "More importantly, I hope to have a wonderful husband and beautiful children just like you."

Talia and Dagmar looked at each other. Dagmar leaned closer and told her patient, "Xian, you can't have children. You've had a tubal ligation. Your tubes have been tied."

"Oh…" Xian said and stared off into space.

"Don't you remember the operation?"

"No… I don't," she said with sadness.

Candace saw the servers arriving with champagne and said, "I'm declaring a moratorium on gloom and doom for tonight! Let's drink!"

After the champagne was poured, Jane announced, "First toast in the club! Here's to me… because I produced a handsome baby boy a month ago. I haven't touched a drop of booze since I found out I was pregnant, and I'm going to make up for the last nine months… TONIGHT!"

Suzy stood and said, "Second toast in the club! Here's to Anabelle! While Dagmar was hunting patients and while Candace and Jane were cycling in and out of the office with their pregnancy, Anabelle was the rock that held the practice together." They drank and Suzy added, "Oh, P.S., let's also toast the big boobs Anabelle's been hiding."

"Here, here!" Jane exclaimed. "Anabelle, you aren't leaving until you've danced with a man. An, Honest-to-God, potential love interest, hot, Stranger-of-a-Man!"

Looking at her champagne, the modest psychiatrist said, "Then, I'm going to need something a lot stronger than this."

"What's your poison, Anabelle, shots or scotch?"

"Er…"

"Does that mean both?" Jane joked. "Then, both it is! Here comes that LaLa chick."

LaLa came back to return Talia's credit card and Jane said, "I want two lemon drops and two glasses of your best single malt scotch for this big, beautiful woman right here!" Then looking at Dagmar, Jane continued, "And a Johnny Walker Blue for the supermodel over there… or have you had your fill of J.W., Dag?"

"Troublemaker," Dagmar mumbled to Jane. Sighing, Dagmar turned to Talia and said, "You DO know that when Rich came to my apartment, he got me drunk to convince me to come out tonight, right?"

"He told me he bought three bottle of scotch for you but did not give me details. I do not care, as long as you are here." Then Talia turned to her sister and said, "Xian, you have been very quiet. Are you well?"

"I'm just observing… absorbing the loud music. It's different from the songs I've been listening to. I like Jane! She seems like a lot of fun!"

"You ain't seen nothing yet!" Suzy exclaimed. "Hey, Talia, can I see that credit card before you put it away?" Talia handed her American Express Black card to Suzy. "What's it made of?"

"Titanium," Talia said as Suzy returned the card.

"Yeow. That's a whole different level of wealth than I'm used to. Hey, here comes the booze!"

The servers sat the drinks in front of Dagmar and Anabelle. Jane said, "All right, Dag, you first! Show these prissy girls how to knock back a drink!"

Dagmar daintily picked up the glass, and almost faster than the eye could see, threw it down her throat. Smiling and still looking angelic, she placed the glass on the table.

"Rad!" Suzy exclaimed.

"Okay, Anabelle, did you see how Supermodel did that? You're going to do the same thing with the two lemon drops and two scotches."

"Jane," Anabelle began to protest, "I don't think…"

"Drink! Drink! Drink!" Jane chanted and everyone else joined in until Anabelle picked up the first shot. Everyone was now clapping as they chanted.

Anabelle took the lemon drop and drank it in one gulp. Before she could lower the glass, Jane took it from her and handed her the second shot. When that shot was gone, Jane handed her the scotch, and then the second scotch. As Anabelle coughed, all the women clapped and cheered.

"Jane," Talia said, "Why don't you begin scouting a dance partner for Anabelle?"

"Good idea, sis!" Jane said and went to the brass railing to look over the dance floor."

"'Sis'?" Xian questioned. "As in 'sister'?"

"Yes," Talia said. "Jane and I are… sisters. I was going to tell you."

"How can this be?"

"It is… complicated. I will explain tomorrow."

Xian turned to Dagmar. "Were you aware of this?"

"Yes. I found out when reading Talia's file."

Hesitantly, Xian said, "This is… disturbing."

Realizing that Xian was thinking that Jane was a half sister from the an infidelity of one of her parents, Dagmar quickly added, "Jane isn't a blood relative. When you hear the story, you'll be proud of Talia and Jane."

Jane waved to Suzy to join her at the rail. "Look over there. Three guys that Anabelle would like. Bring her over and make the introduction. Stay on the dance floor and bring her back."

"What if she doesn't want to come back? What if she falls in love… er… lust, out there?"

"Look, Talia's paying for this evening and no one's going to ditch her for some guy. It's ladies night, not pick-up-guys night. We go out on the dance floor in two's and return in two's. By now, Anabelle's pretty smashed so watch her."

As Anabelle and Suzy left the private area to go to the dance floor, Dagmar got Xian's attention and said, "Jane scouted out some men that would like Anabelle's 'type' but dislike Suzy's 'type'. Jane, Candace, and their friends used to go out clubbing a lot. They have it down to a science."

"And you?" Xian asked. "Do you have 'clubbing' down to a science as well?"

"I don't like to brag, but Jane and her friends are rank amateurs compared to me. The clubs are one place where I drum up business for Kane & Teasdale."

150

Turning to her sister, Xian continued, "And you, Talia, do you go to clubs like this as well?"

"Sometimes. When invited. I usually like to spend my free time with the children… and, of course, with my Richard."

Placing one arm around Talia, Jane said, "But when she DOES come out with us… she has a BALL!"

Talia smiled and said to Xian, "As you said, Jane is a lot of fun."

"Look!" Candace exclaimed as she jumped to her feet. "Anabelle is dancing!"

Everyone stood and rushed to the railing to watch their modest friend dirty dancing with a tall handsome man. As the women cheered and hooted, Xian felt an overwhelming wave of joy.

Looking at Dagmar, she said, "You are moved… more than the others."

Nodding, Dagmar explained, "Anabelle's life has been a struggle. She was taller than the others in her class all the way up through high school and was teased. Her parents disowned her when she married the man she loved. He then divorced her before Anabelle gave birth to their daughter. She finished med school, worked, and took care of her baby without child support or alimony. It's made her a strong but lonely woman. Her daughter is her only joy. To see her dancing like a horny teenager… it's a little…"

"Overwhelming?"

"Exactly."

"Dagmar, YOU overwhelm me. You are all the things I never saw throughout my life… even in Talia." Smiling, Xian continued, "Maybe we should have Jane 'scout' some men for you!"

"Way ahead of you, but I don't see anyone in here that I like. It isn't about looks. I'm looking for intelligence and a good heart… confidence and humility. I know that may seem conflicting."

"No it doesn't. You deserve a special man. I understand that. You won't find him here, will you?"

"As I said, I use the clubs to get business for the practice… and a little fun now and then."

"She's talking to him!" Candace said excitedly. "Oh my God… she's actually smiling at him! Wait… she's coming back to us."

The women all clapped as Suzy and a sheepish Anabelle reentered the private area.

"Tell us all about him and DON'T leave anything out!" Dagmar demanded.

"His name is Clarke and he's a cardiologist. He seemed… nice," Anabelle admitted.

Folding her hands as if praying, Jane said, "Anabelle please… PLEASE tell me you gave him your number!"

"I… I just met him. I don't know the man well enough to give him my number!"

Jane smacked her hands against her head in disbelief and was about to scream when Suzy said, "Calm down, Jane. I slipped him Anabelle's number."

"You what?!" Anabelle exclaimed.

"Just your office extension."

Relieved but still a bit nervous, Anabelle admitted, "Oh, well, I guess that's all right."

"Good job, Suzy!" Candace complimented.

"Hey, I'm your office manager. Looking after you bitches is part of my job."

"Ladies! Someone has to take our baby girl into the wild," Jane said looking at Harmony. She scanned her friends and said, "Okay, Supermodel, you're up! And don't come back until you've danced with someone."

"What? No. It's too soon."

"Dag, when I asked if it was too soon to make arrangements for your mother's burial, what did you tell me?"

"Mommy said, 'When I die, plant me in the ground as soon as possible and get back to dancing!'"

Jane nodded. "I think you should take her advice."

Forcing herself to stand and smile, Dagmar said to Harmony, "Let's go. We have hearts to break." As she walked by her office manager, Dagmar took the fedora off her Suzy's head and placed it on her own. The two women walked toward the crowd and Dagmar asked, "See anyone you like?"

"Over there," Harmony said and indicated a young Hispanic man with two friends.

"I'll set you two up."

Harmony smiled and said, "I may live a very God-filled, conservative life... but I AM Latina. I know how to dance... and I know how to flirt."

She walked directly to the young man of her interest and said, "You like this song?"

He smiled and said, "Yeah. Sure."

"Show me," Harmony said, and led him by his shirt collar to the dance floor.

Looking over her shoulder, Dagmar saw her friends clapping from their secluded area. She then walked to a small group of black men. She walked past all of them, ignoring their compliments until she reached the shortest, quietest, and most awkward of the bunch. She placed the fedora on his head and asked, "Wanna dance?" The surprised man choked out a 'yes' and she led him to the dance floor.

Back at the private area, Xian said, "Dagmar has selected someone to dance with. I thought she would've picked one the more traditionally handsome men. It looks like she is speaking during their slow dance. I wonder what they are saying."

"I will try to eavesdrop on their conversation," Talia said.

"How can you possibly hear through this loud music?"

"I have exceptional hearing. It can pick up every little sound. My mind can isolate those sounds."

On the dance floor, the couple held each other during the slow music and rocked back and forth. "What's your name?" Dagmar asked.

"Er... Ronald... Ron."

"You looked like you need a little help, Ron."

"Maybe after this song we could… well… we could…"

Dagmar leaned back, looked him in the eye and said, "I'm flattered, but I'm not here to find a guy tonight. However, I AM going to help you out. Since we started dancing, there are three hot, HOT girls that have been watching you."

"What? Where?"

"They're behind you. Don't turn around. Just trust me. When this dance is over, take my hat off YOUR head and place it back on MY head. I'll look disappointed and walk away… like you rejected me. Then, turn around, go to the three girls behind you and ask one to dance. I guarantee she'll say yes. Be confident!"

"W-Why are you doing this?"

"Because I needed to dance and you needed some help. Remember, don't smile. You're rejecting me!"

When the music changed, Ron took the hat and replaced it on Dagmar's head. As instructed, he did not smile but gave Dagmar the slightest wink. Looking dejected, Dagmar turned and walked away. When she mixed in with the crowd, Dagmar watched as Ron slowly walked to the women and took one to the dance floor. This made Dagmar smile broadly. Harmony joined her and they walked back to their secluded area.

"He didn't seem your type," Harmony observed.

"Looks can deceive. How was your guy?"

"Ugh. He was too grabby and he couldn't dance. You're right. Looks can deceive."

Dagmar placed the fedora back on Suzy's head and returned to her seat where Talia and Xian were wearing big grins. "Why are you smiling? What did I miss?"

"We know how you helped 'Ron'," Xian said. "We are impressed and proud of you!"

"Wha…? How did you know…?"

Talia simply tapped her ear and said, "I think you earned a drink!"

"But, the music is so loud!" Dagmar exclaimed.

Ignoring her query, Talia said, "Harmony, you haven't ordered a drink yet."

Thinking for a second, Harmony said, "How about a Bloody Mary?"

Talia waved for LaLa who came to her table immediately. "Six Bloody Mary's and two Virgin Mary's," Talia ordered.

As LaLa left, Jane asked, "Who's going to dance while we wait for the drinks?"

"You and Candace haven't been on the dance floor yet," Suzy observed.

"My husband is so jealous," Jane said with a smile. "He made me promise that I wouldn't dance tonight."

"Mine, too," Candace added.

Talia stood and announced, "I made no such promise to Richard."

"What? You're going to pick up some guy?" Jane asked with surprise.

"Of course not! But I am going to dance... with my sister."

Talia took Xian by the hand and led her to the dance floor. Looking nervous, Xian said, "Talia, I don't know how to dance."

Talia reached behind Xian's head and pulled it closer until their foreheads touched. "Just follow me."

Xian could swear she felt a tingle of electricity between her and her sister but she dismissed it as she walked into the crowd. Talia began to dance and Xian instinctively copied her. Talia danced faster with more complex moves and Xian kept up easily. People near them stopped to watch the two sisters mirror each other. Xian began dancing on her own as Talia slowed up to allow her sister to be the center of attention.

When the music changed, Talia hugged her sister tightly. Then, she heard something she had never heard before.

Talia heard Xian laugh.

It was a beautiful musical laugh that was infectious. They walked quickly back to their friends and Talia threw herself into Jane's arms. "Listen! Listen to my other sister laugh!"

As they watched Xian run to Dagmar, embracing her with joy, Jane asked Talia, "You've never heard her laugh before?"

"No. Never. Not as a child. Not as an adult. Never. Jane, I am so happy I could burst!"

Xian squeezed Dagmar tightly. No longer the frail woman she first met, Xian's strength was surprising. She kissed Dagmar on the cheek and said, "I want to dance with you, and Jane, and Candace, and Harmony, and... EVERYONE! That is... if you can keep up with me!"

Hugging the deliriously happy woman back, Dagmar said, "I think I created a monster!"

"This is the best night of my life and I owe it all to you! Dagmar, I want you to know, if I could bring back Mommy's life... I would. I would bring her back for you if it were possible."

Dagmar bit her lip to stop it from quivering. Finally she said, "Thank you, Xian, but you can't bring her back. If she were here right now she would tell you to live your life to the fullest." Dagmar looked at the bright beaming face in front of her. "My God... all the wonderful things you're going to do with your life!"

"Yes... I am. But, right now, I want to dance... with you!"

"Baby, it's going to have to wait because... the drinks are here!"

"Yes. YES! The drinks!" Xian raised her voice and announced, "Everyone get their drink because I want to make a toast!" All the women took their Bloody, or Virgin, Marys and Xian lifted her glass high. "To my wonderful sister, Talia, who set the wheels in motion for me to join her here on the east coast. To the practice of Kane & Teasdale and everyone who works there who has contributed to my recovery. And finally, to my doctor. To Dagmar Lamont, who gave me my wonderful life. Thank you!" All sipped their drink and Xian said to Dagmar, "Join me?"

"Jane and Candace haven't danced yet why not..." Before she could finish her sentence, Xian took her hand and led Dagmar to the dance floor.

Xian danced with Dagmar, who was amazed at how nimble her patient had become considering the tightness in her neck and shoulders a few days ago. The combination of massage and meditation had loosened up Xian's muscles considerably. Dagmar was also amazed at how quickly Xian picked up the ability to dance just by watching Talia and the other people in the club.

Laughing, Dagmar and Xian left the dance floor and were about to rejoin their group when a woman walked up to them. Her name was Shana, and Dagmar had met her in several clubs. She was about the same age and height as Dagmar and she had dark brown and blonde streaked hair. Shana was wrapped in a skintight black dress and was adorned with lots of makeup and expensive jewelry. "Dagmar! How wonderful it is to see you!"

"Hi, Shana. I haven't seen you since the last time I was here."

"Well? Aren't you going to introduce me to your friend?"

Knowing what a gossip Shana was, Dagmar did not want to reveal too much about her patient. "Ah… this is Xian. Xian, this is Shana."

Shana shook Xian's hand and said, "Hello, dear. No offense, but I thought you were someone else."

"Oh. Who did you think I was?" Xian asked.

"You seem to fit the description of the elusive Talia Sedgwick."

Before Dagmar could stop her, Xian said, "Talia is my sister!"

With wide eyes, Shana confirmed, "THE Talia Sedgwick?"

"Yes."

"The mysterious moguls that EVERYONE is trying to do business with?! Is she here?!"

"Yes, why?"

Oh… My… GOD! Dagmar, you MUST introduce me!"

"Er… Shana, she likes her privacy. We're here to have fun, not talk business."

"Dagmar, do I look like I want to talk business? I leave that bullshit to my husband. I just want to have the bragging rights to say I met her! Please! I won't stay!"

"I'm sure my sister won't mind."

With a heavy sigh, Dagmar acquiesced.  "You DON'T stay for a drink.  When I say it's time to leave, you leave, okay?"

"Of course.  I can't WAIT to meet her!"

The three women entered their private area and Dagmar said, "Talia, this is an acquaintance of mine, Shana."

Offering her hand, Shana said, "How exciting it is to meet you.  I thought you were your sister when I saw her on the dance floor."

"Thank you, Shana.  That was a nice compliment."

"I was told you have long hair, like your sister."

"I grow it out, cut it, and donate it for children who have cancer.  A charity a brother in-law contributes to."

Shana smiled.  "You're very mysterious; the smart, savvy, and wealthy business woman who appeared out of nowhere.  Some people think you're a myth.  My husband is going to DIE when I tell him I met you!"

"Thank you, but I am no better than anyone else.  By the way, I love your dress."

"Thank you, dear.  May I see your dress?" Shana asked.  Talia stood and spun around.  "Are you… are you…?"

"I am almost six months pregnant."

Relieved, Shana laughed, "Thank God!  Of course, you're pregnant!  I'm not up on my maternity fashion.  Who are you wearing?"

"This is a homemade dress."

Bewildered, Shana said, "A… what?"

"You know.  Sewing machine.  Needle and thread.  Stuff like that," an exasperated Dagmar said.  "We were about to order drinks so…"

"I can only stay for one."

"You're intruding," Dagmar said flatly.  "Let's go."

"Oh, well.  It was a pleasure to meet you, dear."

"Thank you," Talia said, and Dagmar walked Shana out of their private area.

As they left, Shana huffed, "She wasn't at ALL what I expected."

"Why?" Dagmar questioned.

"She certainly didn't get very glammed up for the club. Very light makeup. No designer dress and was that little bobble on her finger supposed to be her engagement ring?" Looking at her own large diamond she repeated, "No. Not what I expected at all. Isn't she supposed to be wealthy? A self made billionaire?"

Remembering everything she read in Talia's psychiatric file, Dagmar smiled and said, "Her dress, like all of her dresses, is either made or altered by a woman who is so close to her that she thinks of her as her mother. Talia would never insult her by not wearing one of her creations, which I think is fantastic!"

"But that ring…"

"That ring was bought with every cent her husband could afford before he became wealthy. He has offered to replace it. With a word from Talia, he would fill the fingers of both hands with diamonds bigger than yours… but she refuses. That ring means more to her than any piece of jewelry in the world because it was the best he could afford to give her. Besides, the diamond is the purest and clearest I've seen. He wanted to give a perfect stone rather than a showy stone."

The story about Talia's diamond started Shana thinking about how little she sees her husband and how emotionally distant they are. Shana's diamond ring did not seem as impressive to her anymore.

"And…" Dagmar continued, "I don't know how much money she has but she has two beautiful children that give her no trouble. Her husband is handsome, charming, and moral. He loves her with all his heart and soul. She loves him with all her heart and soul. Talia could have two cents to her name and she would still be the most wealthy woman I know."

"Oh," Shana said, looking sad.

"You're having problems in your marriage, aren't you Shana? It's written all over your face." Dagmar watched as Shana began to choke up. Taking a card out of her purse and handing it to the heartbroken, superficial woman, Dagmar said, "Call my practice. Tell our office manager you know me and we'll hook you up with someone good."

Shana took the card, looked at it, and took Dagmar's hand for a moment. "Okay," was all she said… and disappeared into the crowd.

When Dagmar rejoined her friends, Candace barked, "Why the HELL did you bring that woman here?!!!"

"It was my fault," Xian admitted. "I thought there would be no harm."

Getting her sister's attention, Talia explained, "I like to limit my exposure to strangers for security reasons. I do not worry about myself, but I have a family and good friends to protect."

"I'm sorry, Talia. I didn't know."

Smiling at her sister, Talia said, "Do not give it another thought. You did nothing wrong."

"Besides," Dagmar added, "I just made lemonade from that lemon. She is going to call Kane & Teasdale for an appointment. Shana has some problems we can help her solve. By the time I finished talking to her, Shana was more focused on herself than Talia."

"You're supposed to be having fun, not scouting for patients!" Jane scolded.

"It's what I do." Changing the subject, Dagmar asked, "Hey, who's going to dance with Xian next?"

Xian danced with each of her newfound friends all night long. When a man approached to cut in, Xian's dance partners instinctively would not allow it. They were all protective of this new, fresh, naive soul that blossomed before their eyes.

After a long night of drinking and laughing, the women all piled into the limousine. When they got to Talia's home, it was obvious that no one was in any condition to drive. The only drinker that was sober was Dagmar. Talia opened the front door allowing Dagmar and Xian to help Jane and Candace into the house. They dropped on the couch in a giggling heap.

The sound of laughter alerted Rich, who was waiting up for his wife. He went into the room wearing shorts and a tank top. He looked at Jane and Candace and said, "I knew this would happen."

160

"I believe we are going to have company tonight," Talia said. "I am going to bring the others inside."

"No you don't!" Rich exclaimed to his pregnant wife. "I'll bring the rest in the house. You just relax." He went to the limo where Dagmar had already returned and was having a hard time getting the other women to exit. She practically pushed Harmony out the door and into Rich's arms. He brought her inside and sat her on the recliner. When he approached the limo again, he saw Dagmar struggling with Suzy. "What's wrong?"

Exasperated, Dagmar said, "She's like goofy, giggly Jell-o."

Rich reached into the limousine, grabbed Suzy's arm, and with one smooth motion, he pulled her out and put her over his shoulder like a sack of flour. Laughing hysterically as Rich brought her in the house, Suzy said, "Rich! I never, EVER thought my ass would get this close to your face!" He placed her in a chair, but Suzy playfully held on to him. He tickled her under her arm and Suzy let go, coiling herself into a giggling ball.

When he went outside, Rich saw Dagmar struggling with the last woman, Anabelle, who was having trouble walking. Taking one arm and putting it over his shoulder, Rich stopped the tall woman from swaying. Dagmar draped Anabelle's other arm over her shoulder and the two of them began walking her to the porch.

Smiling at Dagmar, Rich said, "It looks like everyone had a good time."

"At least Xian won't be crying any more," Dagmar said sarcastically, referencing Rich's little white lie.

"I… ah… guess you found out that Xian wasn't crying all night."

"Yes I did… jerk!"

They walked Anabelle to a loveseat and she was asleep before her rear touched the cushion.

Dagmar, Xian, Talia and Rich looked around the room and saw their friends either sleeping, giggling themselves to sleep, or snoring. After assessing the situation, Talia said, "I think we should leave everyone right here. Xian, will you help me with the comforters?"

When Talia and Xian left the room, Rich apologized. "I'm sorry I told you that one little lie, but look at how much fun everyone had! If you weren't with them, they would have thought about you all night. You know that the evening went better for Xian because you were there." Still seeing anger on Dagmar's face, Rich continued, "If it makes you feel better, the crying thing was the one and only lie I told you."

"So, you really think I'm beautiful?"

"Yes, of course."

Looking satisfied with Rich's admission, she said, "Well I have a confession for you. Everything… EVERYTHING I said about YOU was a lie!"

Not believing Dagmar, Rich played along. "Really? When you said I was 'hot as hell…'"

"Lie."

"When you said if you knew I was stopping by you'd have made yourself, 'luscious' for me."

"Lie."

"And when you said you wanted dibs…"

"Lies, lies, LIES! I lied to you about everything! I might have believed your one 'little' lie but you believed ALL of mine!"

"Even the part about us making beautiful babies?"

"That was a lie, too! Well, my half of the babies would be beautiful. You're half would be ugly!"

Doing his best to suppress his laughter, Rich said, "Okay. I just want you to know, every nice thing I said about you, I meant."

Dagmar, also finding it hard not to laugh, returned, "Well, I just want you to know, every nice thing I said about you was a LIE!"

They both stared at each other withholding laughter. "I'm… going to go out and pay the driver."

As Rich walked out of the room, but was still within ear shot, Dagmar said, "Don't lie to him!"

She then began removing the shoes of her friends and loosened some of their clothes to make sure they were comfortable. Jane was curled in a ball with

162

her feet under her butt so Dagmar smacked her rear. "Jane, move your ass so I can take off your shoes."

Jane smiled with her eyes closed in a drunken haze. "Rich, you're touching my feet! Here comes the sex!"

Dagmar said with surprise, "Woman, we have GOT to have a conversation when you wake up!"

Talia and Xian came into the room with a dozen comforters, quilts, and blankets and placed them over the sleeping guests. Then, they brought in robes and placed them by each of the women.

Rich came back inside and looked around. "Everybody all tucked in?"

Dagmar said, "They're all asleep, so I guess I'll be going."

"No, Dagmar!" Xian said. "Please stay!"

"We have several bedrooms and three guest houses," Talia said. "Besides, even though you appear sober I do not want you to drive."

"But…"

"It's settled," Rich said, and then turned to Xian. "I hope clubbing with the girls wasn't TOO much of a shock."

Xian and Talia looked at each other, smiled, and began dancing to an imaginary tune.

"I didn't know you could dance, Xian!"

"Neither did I!" Xian exclaimed and the two sisters fell into each other's arms laughing.

Rich smiled at the sound of Xian's laughter. He turned to Dagmar and said, "Doctor Miracle Worker."

Talia said, "Dagmar, take the guest room upstairs at the end of the hall. That's the room our sister Rini uses when she visits. There is a large window that faces the forest. You will wake to a lovely view in the morning."

"I don't want to be a bother."

"Then help with breakfast," Talia said, and looked at the women passed out in her living room. "We are going to need a LOT of hot coffee!"

Jane was the first in the living room to wake up. She cracked open her eyes at nine a.m. and said, "What happened?"

"You got drunk off you ass," Dagmar informed as she stood with her hands on her hips. "Don't worry. You aren't alone."

Jane looked around and saw her friends sleeping in chairs and sofas. "Why are we in the living room?"

"Rise and shine, sleepyhead," Talia said cheerfully as she walked up to Jane. "You all were in no condition to move to an upstairs bedroom. All except Dagmar."

Mumbling, Jane asked Dagmar, "Where did you sleep?"

"Where all good non-drunken girls sleep, in a beautiful bedroom with a beautiful view." Dagmar turned to Talia and said, "I'll wake the others while you work on breakfast. I'll be in to help you in a minute." When Talia left the room, Dagmar sat on Jane's couch and said to her, "Notice anything missing?"

Putting her hand over her eyes, Jane said, "I'm too hung over to care."

"Don't worry about it. I'm sure Rich will give you back your shoes."

Jane removed her hand to reveal wide-open eyes. "What?"

"When he thought I wasn't looking, Rich took off your shoes and massaged your feet."

Jane sat up with a start. "What? He… he…"

"I knew it!" Dagmar exclaimed in a loud whisper. "You've had sex with Rich! Just be glad Talia didn't hear you talking about it in your sleep!"

Jane rubbed her face and said, "She knows."

"She knows?!!!"

"Christ, Dag, we were nineteen and it was only once. Well, several times but only one night. It was, what, fourteen years ago? Rich and I are just what

164

we seem, good friends. So don't tell anyone!" Jane looked around and asked, "Where is Xian?"

"Still asleep. She must be tired from dancing up a storm. Let's look in on her."

Jane stumbled to her feet and followed Dagmar to Xian's first floor bedroom. A soft knock got no response and Dagmar opened the door. Xian was sleeping soundly with a smile on her face. As they backed out, Dagmar observed, "That is the most relaxed I've ever seen her."

"She looked so peaceful," Jane said as the two doctors walked back to the living room. The other women began waking up and looking around.

Harmony held her head in her hands and moaned, "Madre de Dios!"

"It's called a hangover, darling. Get used to it," Candace informed as she forced her eyes open.

"Now I remember why I don't hang out with you," Anabelle hoarsely groaned to Candace.

Suzy fell out of her chair as she was waking. She shook her head, jumped up, and said, "G'morning everyone. Awesome night!"

"Shut up!" Anabelle, Candace, and Harmony demanded in unison.

"What a pathetic bunch!" Dagmar snickered as Talia entered the room.

"Come," Talia said. "Have a light breakfast. It will make you feel better."

The women put on their robes, trudged into the kitchen, and plopped down in chairs while Dagmar, Rich and Talia served them toast, cereal, and coffee. With every bite, Harmony adjusted her robe to make sure it was closed until it got Suzy's attention.

"Something wrong with your robe?" Suzy asked.

"I don't want it to open too much," Harmony replied.

"Why?"

"There IS a man at the table," Harmony answered, indicating Rich. "I don't want him to see my underwear. Don't you worry about it?"

"Rich isn't going to see my underwear. I'm not wearing any."

"Suzy!"

"Hey, I'm not the only one!" Suzy said, pointing her fork at Candace.

Shrugging, Candace said, "How could I possibly wear a bra and panties with last night's gown? By the way, Harmony, you weren't wearing a bra last night. How do you have one now?"

"I keep an extra in my bag," Harmony said casually.

Jane stopped in mid bite and asked, "You carry a backup bra?"

"Doesn't everyone?"

"That explains why you never have a clutch purse."

Talia blurted out, "Richard likes two cups in the morning! Coffee, that is!"

Smiling, Candace said, "Darling, did you just make your first boob joke? I'm so proud!"

"Do you all talk this way in front of your boyfriends and husbands?" Rich sighed.

As Jane was about to sip her coffee she gasped. "Husband! I didn't call home last night!"

"Relax," Rich assured. "When the limo didn't bring everyone home at midnight, I called all of your families to tell them you were staying the night. Then, I had our nanny, Delmare, bring the kids to one of the guest houses so they wouldn't see their hung over aunts in the morning."

"So, Nick is all right with me not coming home?" Jane asked.

Rich snickered. "Of course he's not all right with it! But at least he knows you're safe. He sounded angry; your husband too, Candace."

Candace sneered at Rich. "Oh… Bite Me! Say, where's Xian?"

"Xian gets to sleep in," Dagmar informed. "She danced all night long so she's tired from physical activity. The only physical activity YOU did was to lift your glass to your mouth."

166

Glaring at Dagmar. "You can Bite Me, too!"

Then, they heard it. And, they will remember the sound for the rest of their lives.

A blistering screech rang out through the house. It was so loud it seemed to shoot through everyone's head. "Good GOD!" Suzy exclaimed. "What's that?!"

Dagmar's eyes widened. "It's Xian!!!" she shouted as she bolted from the kitchen with everyone following.

She pushed open the bedroom door and saw Xian pounding her fists against her head. Her body was jerking so hard she fell off her bed. When Xian hit the floor she began withering and screaming as if she were clawing her way out of hell. Dagmar dropped to her knees and took Xian's head in her hands. "Xian! XIAN!! CAN YOU HEAR ME?!!!" Xian's eyes had rolled in the back of her head and she was gnashing her teeth.

"What's happening?!!!" Talia panicked.

"Oh, SHIT!" Jane exclaimed. "She's seizing!"

Pointing to Suzy, Dagmar said, "Get the doctor's bag from my car! HURRY!!!" Without word or thought, Suzy shot out of the room. Then pointing to Rich, Dagmar said, "Get me her toothbrush and facecloth. NOW!" Rich ran to Xian's bathroom and returned with the objects. Dagmar wrapped the facecloth around the toothbrush and said to Xian, "Open your mouth." Xian continued to gnash her teeth. "XIAN!" she repeated to no avail. Dagmar braced herself and gave Xian a backhanded slap that was so hard, everyone in the room jumped. Xian relaxed her jaw for just a moment, which was barely enough time for Dagmar to push the facecloth wrapped toothbrush sideways into her mouth. Immediately Xian clamped down on the makeshift bit and began whipping her head back and forth. Screaming at some unseen terror, Xian continued hitting herself in the head. "Rich, Talia, hold down her arms!" Dagmar demanded. It took all of their strength, but the husband and wife team were able to keep Xian from hitting herself.

As Suzy entered the room with the doctor's bag, Dagmar shouted, "Jane! Twenty of Lorazepam!"

Jane dug into the bag and filled a syringe with the drug. "That's an awfully big dose!"

Dagmar took the syringe from Jane and jabbed it into Xian's taught arm. "Prepare another!" Dagmar ordered.

"Dag! That's too much!" Jane shouted.

"Do it! I want another dose ready to go!"

Hesitantly, Jane filled another syringe. Dagmar snatched it from Jane and watched her patient carefully. "C'mon, Xian," Dagmar whispered. "Come back to us."

As Dagmar was thinking she might have to use a second dose, Xian shut her eyes tight for several seconds, then snapped them open. Her iris and pupils were now visible and the shaking began to subside. "Let go of her arms and help her sit up," Dagmar said. Rich and Talia helped the tortured woman to a seated position on the floor. Xian took the wrapped toothbrush from her mouth and placed her hands on her head as if it was falling apart and she was trying to hold it together. "Okay," Dagmar said with some relief. "Now that she's stable, let's get her to the hospital."

"No," came a hoarse voice. "No more hospitals," Xian croaked.

"What happened to you?" Dagmar asked. "Do you remember?"

Xian raised her head to look at Dagmar. Her body was drenched with sweat, which also was dripping from matted hair. Bloodshot eyes rested in hollow sockets framed by a bruised face. "Remember? Yes. I remember."

"What?" Dagmar questioned. "What do you remember?"

Xian answered the question with one word.

"Everything."

# Chapter Twenty-Four

# Recollections

Talia, who was sitting on the floor next to her sister, reached to Xian and held her. The woman that danced so gleefully, and laughed so melodically last night, felt like a corpse in Talia's arms. "My dear sister, please tell me you are all right!" Talia pleaded as hot tears rolled down her cheeks. She took Xian's battered face in her hands and looked into her eyes. "You… you have changed! Inside… you have changed!"

"Yes," Xian said with a voice raspy from screaming. "What I've lived through… what I remember… it has changed me." As Talia started to cry, Xian pushed back her sister's hair with a shaky hand and kissed her cheek in a soothing and reassuring way. "I am not the frail and broken woman that was at your wedding. I am not the standoffish snob that arrived here in Connecticut. And I am not the wide-eyed innocent of the last few weeks. First and foremost, I am your eldest sister… and I love you. That will never change." Turning to Dagmar, Xian continued. "And, Doctor Lamont… Dagmar… thank you. You never gave up on me. I hope I can continue to call you my doctor… and my friend."

"Of course," Dagmar said. "But Xian, we have to talk about what you remember… now." Turning to Talia, "Please bring a pan of warm water and some soap so I can clean up your sister."

"It's all right," Xian interrupted. "I can take a shower."

"Are you sure? You look unsteady."

Xian stood and took a couple steps. "I seem sound. I shall wash quickly."

"We'll go to the living room to give you privacy."

Xian nodded. "I will join you there."

Everyone left the bedroom and filed into the living room. Dagmar stood by the entrance to listen in case her patient called. "Talia," she spoke up, "Would you get a protein drink and a glass of ice water for your sister?" As Talia left the room, each person settled into chairs and looked at each other for several awkward moments.

Jane broke the silence. "I guess we should leave to allow Dagmar to talk to Xian."

"I guess," Candace echoed. "We have a of couple pissed off husbands waiting for us at home."

"So... I guess we should go home..."

"I guess."

"... but..."

"But?"

"I want to hear what Xian has to say."

"Thank God you said that. I want to hear, too!" Candace admitted.

"Just a minute," Anabelle interrupted. "When have either of you had a session where the rest of us sat in? Have you thought Xian may not want us gawking at her as she pours her heart out?"

"Let's wait and ask her," Dagmar said. "I hear Xian drying her hair."

Talia entered the living room, placed the drinks on an end table and sat down, nervous and shaking. Her husband sat beside her and gave Talia a playful poke in the ribs. She looked at Rich's face and could not help but return his infectious and assuring smile. Closing her eyes, Talia rested her head on Rich's chest as he wrapped a comforting and supportive arm around her.

170

Xian appeared in the living room entry and Dagmar went to help her. A raised hand stopped Dagmar as the freshly showered woman walked slowly, white bathrobe wrapped tightly around her. Harmony stood, offering Xian her chair.

As Xian sat, Dagmar said, "Everyone here wants to listen to our session but that is completely up to you. Personally, I think it should be private but I will respect any decision you make."

Xian thought for a second and then said, "I have nothing to hide… however, what I have to say is… horrific. I have no objection to anyone listening to our therapy… I have spent time with all of you and I can sense you are all good people… but be warned. There are some things that cannot be… unheard."

"Well, I want to hear everything first hand. Everything!" Jane said.

"As do I," Candace added.

"Yes, me too," Anabelle said.

Dagmar smiled. "I knew the shrinks would stay, but Suzy and Harmony…"

"You're going to need dynamite to get me out of here!" Suzy declared.

Looking at Harmony, Dagmar said, "How about you, young blood? I think you should leave."

"I don't run when things get tough," Harmony replied. "I want to stay."

Rich looked at Talia, "Maybe we should go."

Talia turned to her husband and said, "Richard, I love you and trust your opinion, but I must… MUST hear this!"

Rich sighed and said, "I guess we're all in."

"Sister," Xian said to Talia, "This is not something you are going to want to hear. As you notice, remembering it all… changed me. I don't want it to change you."

With intensity, Talia returned, "Do not worry about me being 'changed.' I have been through quite a bit in my life and I will be good as long as I have my husband… my rock." Talia grasped Rich's hand, then continued, "I do not ask to hear what happened to you… I demand it!"

Dagmar brought the protein drink and water to Xian and turned to everyone in the room. "Remember, you are all observers. No comments or questions until we are through." Reaching into her doctor's bag, Dagmar took out a small notepad and a pen. She waited until Xian finished some of the protein drink, then pointed to everyone else in the room and said to Xian, "Speak to me and me alone. They are not here, understood?"

"Yes, I understand. Dagmar, do you know why I regained my memory at this time?"

"I can't be sure, but you WERE very tense. The therapeutic massage, my music therapy, and the distraction of the club, may have allowed your constrained memories to surface." Dagmar sat on a chair directly in front of her. "I want you to think back to your earliest memories. How far back do you remember?"

Xian looked through Dagmar as if she were looking into the past. "As a child, the world was very confusing, chaotic… a living nightmare. This could have been the beginning of my 'second sight' that Talia recently restored."

Everyone except Xian turned and looked at Talia. "You never told me about a 'second sight'!" Jane announced.

"Me neither… and I'm your therapist," Candace added. "We have a lot to talk about."

With a hint of anger in her voice Dagmar said to Talia, "No more tricks on my patient!" Turning back to Xian, Dagmar said, "Continue."

"I saw so much… ugliness in everyone around me."

"Everyone?" Dagmar questioned.

"Everyone. The butlers and maids secretly loathed us. In my father's mind, he was still an aggressive boy trying to please my long dead grandfather. My mother has never gotten past having to prove her worth to her in-laws."

"And, your sisters?"

"Valentina and Aiko were two sides of the same coin. They both had a strong desire to prove themselves to the family. Valentina had Father's strength and Aiko had his anger. Rini was just a baby with the same raw character of any infant. Her undeveloped personality hurt my mind."

172

"And… Talia?"

Xian closed her eyes for a moment to consider what to say and then opened them. "Talia was the most frightening of them all. She was like the others… only worse. I felt anger from her… much more than my father. She was cold… calculating like mother… only more so. She was like everyone… only smarter. Talia was not competitive, because she knew instinctively she was better than everyone in our household… and perhaps, the world."

"Why was Talia so angry?" Dagmar asked.

"Talia was strong and brilliant, but there was one thing she missed… love. Our home was bereft of love and that drove her a little mad. She was also suffering from our 'second sight,' where she knew everyone and everything at a glance. Between that and the speed at which her mind works, I would imagine the world was very slow and boring to her."

"How did you get along with Talia?"

"We would look at each other with a sympathetic understanding… but we mostly avoided each other. I could see her psychosis and she could see mine. We sympathized but could not help each other."

"Your parents tried to help you and Talia, right?"

"An aristocratic couple with two daughters who screamed and cried or spend hours staring at a spot on the wall was an embarrassment. I don't know what they did to Talia but I know what they did to me. First were the therapists. They tried to engage me in conversation but I could not understand them, and they could not understand me. Then, came the psychiatrists with their drugs. My father demanded immediate results so I received injections daily, sometimes from multiple doctors. Nothing seemed to work until the day I received a particularly strong injection. It may have been that concoction or it's interaction with other drugs still in my body, but this injection created a fog. It dulled everyone and everything around me. My 'second sight' was diluted to nonexistence. The world was held at bay by the fog."

"Talia said you were unresponsive and unable to speak."

Xian smiled. "My other sisters avoided me. Looking back, I probably frightened them. Only Talia approached me. With my mind hazed, she was able to interact with me without causing herself pain. I was deeply immersed in my own mind but Talia would come to my room and read to me. Her visits were enough to get me to speak and read again. Her emotions were so strong I could feel them through my fog. She pitied my dullness and was envious at the same time, but mostly… she wanted to help. She understood me and wanted to help. To this day,

Talia does not know the bond I feel for her… the love.  The love I could never express through my fog.”

“Did your ‘fog’ ever completely go away?”

“During my courtship, it lessened to the point where I could interact with people.  It remained… until Mommy’s wake.”

Continuing, Dagmar asked, “And your ‘second sight’…?”

“That was lost to me when I was eleven years old and my protective fog took over.  It was gone until Talia returned it to me.  Now that I think of it, my mind had two weapons to protect itself: A fog which dulled my world and my second sight which heightened it.”

“I want to know about the man who became your husband.”

“His name is Masaru Kami which means ‘victorious God.’  He was enamored with me.  He loved my face, which was unique with mixed ethnicities yet distinctly Asian.  He mistook my ‘fog’ as a demureness that was missing from the other women in his life.  After a discussion with my parents I was whisked away in the dead of night to his beautiful complex in Japan.  I had access to the entire estate.  The grounds were filled with paths that led through breathtaking gardens.  He had a stable with thoroughbred horses.  And I had my own spacious room.  Mister Kami would send me fresh flowers twice a day with a complimentary note.  He would never come to my door, but would join me as I walked through the gardens or sit with me on a bench by the fountain.  With much humility, he would ask me to join him for dinner, or to see a play in the city or visit a museum.  One evening, he arranged a fireworks display… just for me.  He always walked me to my room but never asked to come inside.  For that month, I immersed myself in Japanese culture and… my fog was starting to clear.  Mister Kami was so smart and charming that, despite the difference in our ages, I was beginning to… care for him.  He was attentive and engaging, yet the perfect gentleman.  I could not ask for a more loving and caring suitor.”

Nodding, Dagmar said, “And, how long did your courtship last?”

“About a month.  One evening, Mister Kami brought me to one of the gardens where a string quartet played romantic music.  On bended knee, he proposed marriage to me and I accepted.  As usual, he walked me to my door.  This evening, I invited him inside but he refused.  He said that he made a promise to my mother that my virginity would remain intact until my wedding day.  My new fiancé sounded so noble, so gallant.”

“How long did your engagement last?” Dagmar asked.

"A week. We returned to California where I met with my parents in their home. I confirmed Mister Kami had been a perfect gentleman and I told them of the luxury and culture that surrounded me. My wedding was scheduled for the day after next at a grand hall of my father's choosing. All arrangements were paid by Mister Kami. While I was being fitted for my gown, Talia entered the room to talk to me. She ordered the seamstresses to wait outside and implored me not to marry Mister Kami."

"And you ignored her warning."

Xian looked across the room to Talia and said, "I did not... ignore her. My sister is brilliant and I listened to every word. But she had no knowledge of how kind he was... how intelligent he was... how warm he had been to me. I tried to allay her fears, but she could not be persuaded. In frustration, Talia ran out of my dressing room, crying. Crying as she is now."

All in the room looked at Talia to see tears streaming down her face. Rich held her tightly as her body shook from the spasms of her silent cry.

Xian continued, "I was so under Mister Kami's spell I forgot how my younger sister could see through pretense as if it were glass. Talia, I apologize for not taking your advice. The most important decision of my life became the biggest mistake of my life."

Getting her patient back on topic, Dagmar asked, "Did your wedding proceed as scheduled?"

"Yes."

"And when did the abuse start?"

Xian paused, then looked Dagmar in the eye and said, "That night."

# Chapter Twenty-Five

# Honeymoon

"Your abuse started on your honeymoon?  So soon?" Dagmar asked. "Are you sure?"

"Yes… I am sure," Xian said.

Xian began her story (all dialogue is translated from Japanese):

After their wedding reception, Mister Kami and his new bride, Xian, were hustled into a waiting limousine by his security forces.  She looked at her husband and said, "We left in such a hurry I was barely able to change out of my gown.  Do you like my dress?"

Glancing at her, Mister Kami said, "No, but it will do until you can change into a proper kimono."

"The wedding happened so quickly that I do not know where we are going."

"We are going home."

"We are not going to travel? We are not going away for a honeymoon?"

Mister Kami opened his briefcase and began sorting through some papers. "There will be a honeymoon but it will be at home. You will be traveling with me for business as the need arises."

Pausing a moment then Xian continued, "How do you wish me to address you? Masaru? Husband?"

"Mister Kami will suffice. If I need you to call me something less formal in front of business clientele, I will let you know in advance."

"So you wish…"

Mister Kami shot her a mean look. "Silence! Your prattling questions are disturbing my work."

Xian withdrew and said nothing for the rest of the limousine ride.

When they arrived at the airport the married couple and their entourage boarded a large corporate jet. As they walked through the huge aircraft, Mister Kami stopped suddenly, turned to one of his female aides, and nodding toward Xian said, "Keep her occupied." He then continued to the back half of the plane and closed the door, isolating himself from his new wife and aide. The aide placed several magazines on the table in front of Xian, took a notebook computer from her carryon bag, and wordlessly, began working. Xian did not touch the magazines.

When the plane landed, Mister Kami emerged from the secluded section followed by his aides and advisers. He had changed out of his tuxedo into lavish red and gold robes. Mister Kami walked by Xian without a look and, when the last of his entourage passed, the aide assigned to stay with Xian stood. She walked a few steps, turned, and gave Xian a what-are-you-waiting-for look. Xian stood and followed everyone off the plane to two waiting limousines. The car she entered was second in line. Her husband was in the first car. When they arrived at Mister Kami's compound, everyone poured out of the vehicles. As Xian exited, she saw her husband waiting for her. "Go to your room and change out of that… dress. I shall attend to you later," Mister Kami said and walked away with aides following.

Xian sat on her bed for hours, completely confused. The man who was so respectful and attentive had become distant and cool. She racked her brain questioning every word she said, every movement she made, for a clue as to why this warm man turned icy cold. There was a knock on the door and Xian answered it to find one of the servants beckoning her into the hall. He walked and she followed until they were at Mister Kami's bedroom. The servant knocked twice and Mister Kami said, "Send her in." With eyes lowered, the servant opened one of the double doors allowing Xian to step into the room.

Her new husband was standing in front of his bed wearing a powder blue silk robe. "It is time to begin the honeymoon," Mister Kami said. Pointing to a settee against the wall facing the bed he said, "Sit." As Xian walked to the small sofa she heard the sound of a flushing toilet from Mister Kami's private bathroom. He smiled as a Japanese woman entered the room. She wore a sheer yellow and orange robe completely open in the front. The woman was almost three times heavier than Xian and walked with a hint of a swagger. Large breasts overflowed her leather bra and a prominent belly somewhat covered matching panties. Straight hair, partially pulled into a bun, was streaked very black and very blonde. The woman was heavily made up with black, thick lashes and bright blue eye shadow. Her lips were thick and bright red, as were her cheeks. Mister Kami beckoned the woman to his side and she smiled as he slipped his arm around her ample waist.

"Who is this?" Xian asked.

Looking at the woman beside him, Mister Kami asked, "What shall your name be tonight?"

"In honor of our American guest, call me Cindy."

Xian said tightly, "And what is 'Cindy' doing in your bedroom?"

Ignoring the question, Mister Kami said to Cindy, "Did you know my new bride is a virgin?"

A broad smile filled Cindy's face. "Really? Mister Kami, I'm impressed! How did you find one?"

Xian stood. "This is outrageous! If you have an interest in such… women, why did you marry me and why do you want me in this room?!!"

Mister Kami nodded to the bed. Cindy walked to it and laid down. He then approached Xian and slapped her so hard she fell back on the settee. Leaning over her with a smile on his face, he said, "You are… window dressing. When I go to business meetings and civic functions, I can't bring 'Cindy' with me. You shall be my proper wife." Walking to the bed he said, "As my wife you are expected to perform wifely functions. You are here to observe 'Cindy' so you will know… what I like."

Xian stood and announced, "I'm leaving!"

Mister Kami ran back to Xian and kicked her in the stomach so hard she doubled over. After pushing her back on the couch, he went to his nightstand and retrieved two sets of handcuffs. Mister Kami roughly took one arm and handcuffed it to the arm of the settee. "I have power of your life and death. As far as you are concerned, I am God! You do what I say, when I say it!"

As he handcuffed her other arm to the sofa, Xian choked, "But… why… why…?"

"Why have I changed? Why was I so caring and romantic?" Mister Kami said, anticipating her questions. He grabbed her chin and lifted her head until they were face to face. "I enjoy… no, I LOVE the chase! It was so much fun manipulating you… making you fall in love with me. Such a beautiful, pure, innocent soul you are. Now, it's time to blacken that soul, which will also bring me great pleasure! It's time you received your first lesson in sex. Watch carefully as your God satisfies his earthly needs!"

"I will not watch!" she said with defiance.

Releasing her chin and slapping her, Mister Kami said, "These handcuffs are my kindness. I have other ways of making you watch. I have chairs that were used as ancient torture devices. I can seat you in one that will lock your body in place and hold your head stock-still. If you close your eyes, I have medical implements that will keep them open. Your vision may be damaged in the process, but you WILL watch me tonight!"

"I'm getting cold," Cindy complained.

Mister Kami returned to the nightstand and removed a syringe from the drawer. He plunged the needle into his arm, closed his eyes and smiled. As he climbed into bed he said to Cindy, "We have an obligation to educate my new bride. Let's make sure we do our job well!"


Xian ended her story:

Looking away from her therapist, Xian began to choke from the lump in her throat. Dagmar handed her a glass of water and she took a sip. Xian paused for the water to go down and for her emotions to settle. Taking her hand, Dagmar said, "We can take a break if you'd like. Or we can stop…"

"No," Xian said hoarsely. "Mister Kami and the woman proceeded to perform various sex acts and made sure I was watching. Must… must I tell you everything that happened?"

"I think I get the idea."

Staring into space, Xian said, "No… you probably don't. Let me just say that I saw every bodily function and fluid, 'Cindy' and Mister Kami could excrete… and they relished every moment."

There was absolute silence in the room.

Finally, Dagmar asked, "You said Mister Kami injected himself before getting into bed. Do you know what it was?"

"No, but more drugs were taken by both of them during the night. The sex lasted until about four in the morning. The air stunk of sweat and various… bodily functions. Mister Kami woke first and lightly slapped the woman to awaken her. He then went into the bathroom and 'Cindy' wrapped her filthy body in a robe. As she left the bedroom she winked and blew me a kiss. When Mister Kami returned, he picked up the telephone, mumbled a few words and left the bedroom without looking at me. Moments later, two woman entered the room. They unfastened the handcuffs and pulled me to my feet by my stiff, aching arms. I was dragged to my room, brought inside and the women slammed the door behind me. That was my honeymoon night."

After taking a second to absorb what she heard, Dagmar asked, "What were you thinking when you were finally alone?"

"I didn't know what to think. I fell into a fitful sleep interrupted by servants bringing my meals. That night, Mister Kami entered my room and did the same things to me he did to 'Cindy'. The fog that helped me through so much had mostly left me when I thought my future with Mister Kami was bright. Now that I needed it, the full force of the fog that obscured my world did not come back. I was fully aware of every vile thing he did to me."

"Did you resist?"

"I fought him bitterly. However my resistance seemed to add to his enjoyment."

"So, you're saying he raped you?"

Xian thought for a moment to formulate her words. "Despite being married six years, I have never made love. Any sexual contact I ever had… has been rape."

If there was anyone in the living room who thought, even a little bit, that it would be fascinating to listen to the salacious details of a failed marriage, that person got far more than bargained for.

And Xian's story was about to get worse.

# Chapter Twenty-Six

# Rules

Doing her best to keep her composure and to ignore the unsettling movement of listeners who have become uncomfortable with what they were hearing, Dagmar continued with her questions. "You've never been a willing participant in sexual activities?"

"Never."

"How did you... endure?"

"My husband would enter my room unannounced. He would revile me and then try to 'cleanse' me with intercourse. After noticing how much he enjoyed forcing himself on me, I became more docile. I would no longer fight him. Mister Kami said he wanted me as 'window dressing,' so that is what I gave him. I exhibited all the passion of a mannequin... a doll. During sex, I made myself as dull and uninteresting to him as possible. It... shortened our encounters since he lost interest in me sooner, however it did not stop him from coming to my room. I was never sure if that course of action was correct."

Dagmar gave a very faint smile. "Xian, you survived. You're here with us today. Whatever you did to keep alive was the right course of action. I assume your lack of resistance also lessened other physical abuse."

"No. Mister Kami believed a wife should be beaten on random occasions whether she deserved it or not. Having formulated a rule for his forced sex, I developed another rule for my physical abuse."

"What KIND of rule?"

"Since I was so distant during forced sex… or to be more precise… during rape, he relished striking me. At first, I would cower and cover my head, which would delight my sadistic husband. So, I made a rule. No matter what he did, I would not hide. I would not make noise. I would not complain. No matter how hard he hit me, I would not react. If he were screaming and about to slap me, I would offer him my cheek."

Dagmar gasped, "Oh, Jesus! Your wedding band… when I saw it, I jumped and screamed. You must have pushed your cheek toward me, offering it to be struck, as a reflex!" Dagmar opened her mouth to say more, but the words were stuck. The psychiatrist was visibly shaken and buried her face in her hands. She tried to wrap her brain around the fact that, due to her reaction to the ring burned into her patient's finger, Xian offered herself up to her for abuse.

Then, Dagmar heard someone approaching her from behind. Without looking, she pointed in the direction of the sound and commanded, "SIT! I HAVE THIS!" After a moment she looked around and saw her friend and colleague, Anabelle returning to her seat. Then, softer, "I have this under control… but thank you."

"Are you all right?" Xian asked her doctor.

"I've seen battered women, before but none who have been so entrenched that they make themselves an easy and willing target; not like that. Was there no way you could call your parents?"

"No. All the telephones required access codes that I didn't have, and cellular telephones were not allowed on the property. Besides, Mister Kami told me that if our marriage failed, or even faltered, it would result in an enormous loss of business for my father."

"So you thought you were protecting your father's business?" Dagmar questioned.

Xian nodded. "Mister Kami said that my father had much of his corporate wealth tied up in his business contacts. A word from my husband and contracts would be canceled, deals broken and shipments rerouted to other partners. Mister Kami assured me that Father's business would suffer irreparable harm. I was protecting my father's business, and by extension, my family."

"Your father still has a thriving business today." Dagmar turned to Talia and asked, "Is this true? Did your father have an large amount of his business tied up in Japan?"

Talia replied, "Father had less than one quarter of his funds going through Mister Kami's business contacts. He did not suffer an 'enormous' loss of business and I was able to replace Father's investments with better opportunities in China."

For the first time since she regained her memory, Xian had the hint of a smile on her face. "Mister Kami hates the Chinese. He called them dirty, rutting pigs with no self-control. He thought of the Chinese as the gutter people of all the Asian races."

Dagmar turned back to Xian, "Yet, he married a woman who was part Chinese."

"At first, he thought of me as exotic. Eventually, Mister Kami began to hate my one-quarter Chinese heritage and my name, which is Chinese."

"So, on top of being a sadist and a misogynist, Mister Kami was also a racist?"

Xian nodded. "He believed in maintaining the pureness of the Japanese bloodline. He said during World War II the Japanese people were aggressive warriors since they attacked Pearl Harbor. The Kamikazes and their suicide runs made the biggest sacrifices for the Axis. My husband was a student of World War II and would go on for hours about the mistakes Adolf Hitler made and the way he would've done things differently."

Under her breath, Suzy hissed, "Monster!"

Xian continued, "Mister Kami feels the Japanese were a race superior to their former allies the Italians and Germans. He also believes this holds true today, and that the 'Land of the Rising Sun' could rule the world with the right leadership."

"Don't tell me he's planning on running for political office!"

"No. My former husband feels being a wealthy businessman is the best way to control the destiny of the world. All the fascist philosophy was part of my indoctrination into Mister Kami's life. His real life. Not the fairytale life he used as a lure. I listened to his words and pretended they did not revolt me. Then on the fourth day…"

"Wait," Dagmar interrupted. "'Fourth day?'"

"Yes. The humiliation, multiple rapes, and classes in his philosophy took place in the first three days of my honeymoon.

# Chapter Twenty-Seven

# In-laws

       Xian sat quietly for a moment, bracing herself. Opening her blackened eyes she said, "On day four, my… sister-in-law arrived. Kamiko Kami had been away traveling for two months so this was the first time we met."

       Making a note, Dagmar repeated, "Kamiko?"

       "Kamiko means 'Superior Child'," Xian explained and began her story.

       Xian was awakened early one morning by one of the maids rushing into her room. "Mistress! Master Kami needs you awake and dressed now! Mistress Kamiko is back and we must all greet her!"

       "Who?" Xian questioned.

       "Your sister-in-law!"

       Xian rushed to dress with the help of the maid. "Your name?"

"Atsuko."

"Thank you for your help."

Atsuko's face lit up. "You are very welcome Mistress! Thank you for your kind words!"

Xian was fitted in a festive blue kimono with a yellow, orange and red floral pattern. The young maid led Xian outside to a carport where much of the staff was standing. Mister Kami was in front of the crowd with his back to his employees waiting patiently. Moments later, a large limousine drove into the carport and two butlers scrambled to remove the luggage from the trunk. A third butler opened the door and helped Kamiko from the car. She was an inch taller than Mister Kami with long streaked black and gray hair piled high on her head. She did not look at any of the staff and barely looked at Mister Kami as she swept by in her black, purple and gold kimono. As the staff went back to their duties, Xian followed her husband and sister-in-law several steps behind.

"How was your trip, sister?" Mister Kami asked.

"Boring."

"And, how was the 'traveling companion' I arranged for you?"

"Also boring. You note, I returned alone."

Mister Kami looked at her with steely eyes. "Nothing makes you happy anymore!"

"I will be happy when there a reason to be happy. Masaru, who is the person following us?"

They stopped walking to allow Xian to join them. "This is my wife Xian," Mister Kami introduced.

"Another?" Kamiko asked flatly. Turning to Xian she asked, "Why are you following us?"

"I am now family. I thought we should meet," Xian said.

"You wanted to meet… me?"

"I thought it was appropriate."

188

Kamiko's hardened face showed the hint of a smile. "I shall send for you once I'm settled."

Two hours later, as Xian was walking through one of the lavish gardens, a maid came to her with a folded piece of paper. Xian opened the parchment that simply said to follow the maid and was signed by Kamiko. The maid bowed politely and began walking toward the main house. Xian followed her inside until they came to a set of double doors with extravagant carvings. Using the door's knocker twice, the maid opened the large wooden slabs and backed away while indicating to Xian to go inside. As Xian entered the darkened room the doors closed behind her. A large regal canopy bed streamed with veils was in the center of the room.

From a dim corner, Xian heard Kamiko's voice. "Join me." Kamiko was sitting at a table with two cups and a teapot. As Xian sat, Kamiko poured her a cup of hot tea. "You have a dreadful American accent. You will have to refine your Japanese. I will tell my brother to arrange for a language tutor." Pouring tea in her own cup she asked, "Your first marriage?"

"Yes."

Sipping her tea, Kamiko asked, "How do you like the life of a married woman?"

"It's different," Xian answered. Not knowing how much she should trust Kamiko, Xian tried to keep her answers vague.

The sister-in-law's hard face softened with a hint of a smile. "He is not what you expected." Glancing at Xian's cup, Kamiko observed, "Your tea is getting cold." As Xian drank her tea, Kamiko continued. "You seem a delicate woman and you strike me as weak of mind. Little wonder my brother was attracted to you. He hates smart people… especially women. What do you think about smart women?"

"I don't know what you mean?"

"Are YOU attracted to smart women?"

"In what way?"

"Maternal? Friendship? Sexual?"

Puzzled, Xian answered, "I think of other women in no special way… especially sexually."

Sitting back in her chair with a smirk on her face, Kamiko asked, "How do you like your tea?"

Xian looked at her cup, but it was out of focus. "My head… it's swimming."

Kamiko walked to Xian and helped her stand. Leading her to the bed, Kamiko said, "Rest. You'll feel better."

Xian felt herself being gently pushed on the bed as she drifted into unconsciousness.

The smoke from a non-tobacco cigarette greeted Xian as she woke. Through bleary eyes, she saw Kamiko sitting on a chair with a hand rolled cigarette in one hand and a martini glass in the other. Finishing the drink, Xian's sister-in-law stood to refill her glass. She had changed into a thin unfastened white robe that opened revealing her unattractive nude body. Kamiko poured vodka into the glass and turned to see Xian's half opened eyes. With no attempt to close her robe she said, "If you can walk, you should leave."

Struggling as if a heavy weight were on her back, Xian crawled off the bed and limped her way into the hall. She staggered until she came to her room and fell through the door.

After a half hour, the room stopped swirling enough to stand. The drug that was in Xian's tea began to wear off and she became aware of the pain between her legs. Clutching at her crotch, she noticed her underwear was missing. As the realization of her situation began to sink in, tears began to flow and the pain between her legs became more severe, Xian started to cry; a few tears at first until she broke out into an uncontrollable crying jag. Running into the bathroom, she turned on the shower full blast and started washing herself and shrieking. The soap slipped out of Xian's hands but she continued to rub her hand on her body as if she were still clutching it. The damaged woman stumbled out of the shower and onto the bathroom floor while the water continued to flow.

Xian did not know how long she was unconscious on the floor but woke to a gentle hand shaking her shoulder. Opening her eyes, she saw Atsuko looking concerned as she covered her body with a large bath towel.

"Mistress! Mistress! Are you not well? I came to get you for dinner but…"

Xian tried to put on a stoic face as she attempted, but failed, to stand. "Do not look at me. Please leave."

"Yes, Mistress. I shall tell the Master you've taken ill. Is there nothing I can do for you?" Atsuko asked. She saw Xian trying to focus her eyes and recognized the look on her face. Atsuko gasped, "You, too? I did not think Mistress Kamiko had the nerve!" Taking Xian's face in her hands, Atsuko said. "Do not drink or eat anything Mistress Kamiko gives you! Take NOTHING from her! Mistress Xian, you have ordered me away and I will go… unless you change your mind and wish for me to help you." Xian nodded her agreement and the young thin maid shut off the shower and assisted her out of the bathroom and into a chair in the sitting area of her room. Atsuko placed a comforter around Xian. "I find it best to become invisible here. Don't stand out. Everyone has an agenda. No one can be trusted. If something is done to you, don't retaliate. It could mean your life."

"Why do you work here?"

"Master Kami pays well and my family needs money."

"You know about Kamiko. Did she…?"

Atsuko went to the bathroom. She returned with a glass of water and handed it to Xian. "Drinking water will help your body recover. There is aloe in your medicine cabinet that will help to soothe any soreness you may have. It is best if you don't ask for anything. Try to block out the pain."

"Thank you for your kindness."

Smiling, Atsuko said, "I must go to excuse you for dinner. I will return later if my duties permit." The young maid slipped out of Xian's room, but did not return that night.

Xian paused her story and Dagmar asked, "Did your husband know his sister was a lesbian rapist?"

"I… am sure he knows, however Kamiko is not a lesbian. Nor is she bisexual. In fact, I think of her as asexual… if I understand the term correctly. What she did to me she has done to men as well. Her molestation is not for sexual gratification. She enjoys control and humiliation. I avoided her as much as possible, but she would occasionally find a way to get me alone to torture and assault me. Most times, without sedation."

"Did you tell your husband?"

"I made that mistake… once. He called me a liar and beat me."

Dagmar was quiet for a moment trying to push the revulsion from her mind and then said, "So, in the six years you were married…"

"Kamiko assaulted me twenty-three times. Sometimes rendering me unconscious with drugs and sometimes by overpowering me," Xian explained.

"Sweet Jesus," Dagmar whispered.

Trembling, Xian asked, "Do you want to hear each… encounter?"

"No. Not right now. Between your Mister Kami and Kamiko, your life was a living hell!"

"Yes… and there was one more. Mister Kami's son, Kichirou."

"Does that name have a meaning?"

"Kichirou means lucky son."

Jotting down more notes, Dagmar asked, "Which wife was his mother?"

"Neither. Kichirou was the love child… more accurately the lust child… of my former husband and one of the servants. I don't know what happened to the woman, but she is no longer employed by Mister Kami. Like his aunt, Kichirou was away on his own adventure for several months and came back to the compound two days after Kamiko returned."


Xian began her story:

All the staff was gathered in an open area near the main house to welcome the arrival of Mister Kami's son. As with his sister, Kami waited with nervous anticipation until he heard the sound of a distant engine. Dramatically, a helicopter appeared over the tree line causing a terrific wind to whip around the waiting staff. As the helicopter gently landed on the grass, Xian looked around for Atsuko. This time, a different maid had come to her room to summon her for a family arrival. As the swirling blades slowed, a tall, striking, energetic Japanese man came bounding from the helicopter with a duffel bag slung over one shoulder. He ran to the master of the house and dropped his bag as father and son embraced in a show of affection Xian rarely saw in the compound. Next, the young man hugged

192

his aunt as she smiled broadly. After releasing Kamiko, he waved and bowed theatrically to the unsmiling staff. Mister Kami made a dismissive jester to his employees and they began to disperse. As Xian walked away, she heard her name being called. Turning, she saw Mister Kami wave to her to join his son and sister.

When Xian approached, Mister Kami said, "Son, this is my new wife, The Lady Xian. Xian, this is my son Kichirou."

"An honor to meet you, Kichirou," Xian said.

Bowing deeply he said, "The honor is mine." Then, as if to indicate the formality had been fulfilled, Kichirou gave her a large smile as he put his hands on his hips and looked her up and down. "Father, I had no idea you remarried. You still have an eye for exquisite beauty! I notice some Chinese and a little Mediterranean in you. Am I correct?"

Xian nodded, "Yes. Greek and Russian."

"Russian too?" He cocked his head and smiled. "Yes... I see it now. Amazing people, the Russians. Great vodka too! And you have Greek ancestry. The very cradle of civilization. The blood of the world's greatest philosophers courses through your veins!"

Sighing, Kamiko said, "She's a mutt, but we will mold her into a suitable Japanese wife."

"Aunt Kamiko, please!" Kichirou scolded. Turning back to Xian, he said, "I think your mixed heritage is fantastic!"

"My boy is quite the traveler," Mister Kami said with pride. "He is well educated and experienced in world affairs. He shall be a perfect successor as soon as his wanderlust diminishes."

"Father, no matter where I go, the sun rises on no finer land than Japan."

"Come," Mister Kami said. "A feast has been prepared for your return!"

Kamiko led the way back to the main house followed by Mister Kami and Kichirou. Xian followed behind them but felt eyes on her. Looking over her shoulder, she saw Atsuko from a distance looking grim and shaking her head "no" as if to offer a silent warning.

They entered a large formal dining room adorned with handmade tapestries. Butlers held the chairs out for the family members around a big table covered with silk. Meticulously prepared food was arranged around each place setting, and as they ate, Kichirou regaled everyone with stories of his travels.

"The difference in social classes in India was stunning!" Kichirou exclaimed. "There are the abject poor and the abundantly wealthy throughout the country. The wealthy really know how to live! They are friendly but have strict customs. Have you been to India, Father?"

"Yes, but only on business," Mister Kami said with a hint of disdain. "Their food is retched. I have no desire to return unless I have a business reason." Then, smiling, he said, "It is good that you have an understanding of the people in the lands you visit. Knowing local mores will make it easier for you to do business once I retire."

"Come now, Father! You are never going to retire! You love the art of the deal too much."

"I will not be alive forever. You know I want you to continue my work."

Nodding, Kichirou said, "Of course, Father. Whenever you wish."

Studying his son for a second, he smiled and said, "Enjoy your youth. Learn and absorb as much as you can. There will be time for business later. So… where else did you travel?"

"Oh, so many places! In Europe I visited France, Germany, and Switzerland. Then I went to South America and saw Venezuela and Columbia."

Anger shot across Mister Kami's face. "I warned you that our family is to avoid Columbia!"

"I was careful, Father! I went incognito. It was a short visit and I paid cash for everything." Turning to Xian, Kichirou explained, "My first step mother was the sister of a wealthy Columbian. Her death in our country created some hard feelings."

"Not her concern!" Mister Kami barked as he looked at his son but nodded toward Xian. "Are those the only places you went?"

"My favorite place was Amsterdam. Amazingly free spirited country. The morals and rules are delightfully loose!"

194

Mister Kami sniffed, "One of the reasons they were never a conquering nation."

"It's a big world, Father. There's room for sheep as well as lions."

Mister Kami tapped his fingertips together as he considered Kichirou's words. A small smile crossed his face. "The son teaches the father. A proud day for us both."

"Thank you, Father," Kichirou said and then turned to Kamiko. "So, Aunt Kamiko how was your trip?"

"Dull," Kamiko droned. "I wish I could see the world through your young eyes."

"And your 'traveling companion'…?" Kichirou questioned.

"Disappointing. I left him in Saragossa…"

"There are worse places to be left than Spain."

"…without money. He can find his own way home… or not."

"Well, Aunt Kamiko, I may be able to lift your spirits. I have gifts for you and Father. I will present them to you once I've unpacked."

Kamiko's frozen face cracked a smile. "Thank you, my dear. You know how your 'gifts' make me happy."

Turning to Xian he said, "If I knew I had a new step-mother, I would've brought something for you as well." Looking around the table, Kichirou continued, "While I like to travel I love coming home. Father, I wish to reacquaint myself with the grounds. Would you mind if I went for a walk with The Lady Xian?"

"I have no need for her right now. You may do as you wish."

Turning to Xian, Kichirou asked, "Would you honor me with your company?"

"Of course," Xian answered.

Kichirou leaped to his feet and pulled out Xian's chair as she stood. While the pair walked from the table, Kichirou asked, "Is there any part of the grounds you haven't seen?"

"I have been given free access. I mainly walk through the gardens."

"Yes. They are very lovely. Hm. Where might you have missed? The stables?"

"No, I have not seen the stables."

"Then, that is where we shall go."

Kichirou kept a respectful distance from Xian and engaged her in light and enchanting conversation. His quips and stories were so charming that Xian found herself beginning to smile.

The stable area was large and well kept. There were several employees grooming the dozen or so horses kept on the grounds. Xian was fascinated because she had never seen a horse in person. Kichirou motioned for her to come closer and pet one of the horses. She found the hair above his nose smooth and silky.

"Isn't he magnificent?" Kichirou said as he picked up a two-by-four piece of wood being used by some of the workmen to repair one of the stalls.

"Yes," Xian answered as Kichirou took a small stone and batted it with the wood into the field as a baseball player would strike a ball.

Making a few practice swings with the makeshift bat, Kichirou said, "Would you like to ride him?"

"Oh no, thank you."

"Well, whenever you want to ride, let me know."

Xian was focused on the horse but saw a quick movement out of the corner of her eye. Kichirou had swung the two-by-four directly at Xian's head. A dull thud was all she heard as she hit the ground. Before losing consciousness, Xian saw the stable hands running to help her as Kichirou laughed hysterically.

The first thing Xian saw when opening her eyes was a man in a suit inspecting her head with his hand. Mister Kami and Kichirou were also in the room looking grim. "She should get an x-ray," the man said.

Mister Kami looked at Xian and said, "She'll be all right, doctor. That will be all."

As the doctor left the room, Kichirou walked up to her. "I guess no one told you that I have a small problem with self control." Smiling, he said, "Sometimes, I just can't help myself. You won't hold it against me, will you? I suppose I should do something about the problem… but I actually like it."

Dagmar interrupted Xian's story. "You're saying Kichirou was engaging, and charming, and then out of the blue, he clubbed you?"

"Yes."

Dagmar exchanged glances with the other psychiatrists and explained, "It sounds like he has an Impulse Control disorder. Impulsive violence is one way the problem can express itself."

"He enjoys his mental disease… if he truly HAS a mental disease. If he is not simply an unthinking, uncaring, mean, spoiled child. He was only a few years younger than I, but he never grew up."

"What about your husband? He could see the damage his son caused. Did he do something about it?"

Looking even grimmer, Xian said, "Yes, he did something for me. He inflicted me with… the twins."

Xian continued her story:

Xian was lying in her bed recovering from her attack when her door swung open without a knock. Mister Kami and two women entered the room.

Her husband walked up to Xian and said, "I concluded a meeting with a businessman a few minutes ago. He asked to be introduced to my new wife. I had to make excuses for you. Attending formal functions and meeting guests as my proper wife is your reason for being." Mister Kami made a motion with his hand and the two women stepped forward. To Xian, they looked like twins. Their facial features were different, they were obviously not related, but their height, hair and their stoic demeanor were mirror images of each other. "These women are your handmaidens. Their main purpose is to keep you out of trouble. Their names… are not important. Nor is their voice. They are to remain silent and nearly invisible. They will watch you close and from afar. Any of your carelessness or foolishness will be reported directly to me." Turning to the twins, Mister Kami said, "See to her wound." The two women went to Xian. One held her head while the other ripped off the dressing. As if the two women had the same brain, they worked together to reapply fresh gauze and tape. They were not gentle but they were efficient.

Xian concluded her story.

"Those were the people most involved in my life while I lived in Japan," Xian said as her voice trailed off. Looking in the distance, she shuttered as she relived more memories. Her shaky hand reached to the end table. Water danced in the glass as she tried to bring it to her lips. Dagmar put her hands over Xian's hand to steady the drink. She took a sip of water, and as Dagmar began to take it away, Xian quietly said, "No." She held the glass in her trembling hand and focused her gaze on it. Through force of will, Xian steadied her hand and returned the glass to the end table. Looking at her stilled hand, Xian said, "My mind seems to be stronger. I have a sense of self control and clarity I've never felt." Xian's face expressed a small amount of happiness and surprise at this newly discovered ability.

"Maybe we should stop for today," Dagmar suggested.

"No. There is more to tell and I do not want to bring back these harsh memories after today."

"I thought The Twins would protect you."

Xian shook her head. "No."

Xian continued her story:

While walking through one of the gardens with The Twins respectfully behind her, Kichirou came jogging beside Xian. "Hello, Lady Xian. Isn't it a beautiful day today?" Xian simply nodded. "Say, come to my room. I have something fantastic to show you."

"No thank you," Xian said immediately.

"Please. I want to apologize for the incident at the stables when I first arrived. I've settled down and I'm under control now. Your handmaidens may come along if you wish.  In fact, I insist on it."  Kichirou saw the hesitation on Xian's face and put on his most charming smile.  "Please?  It would mean so much to me."

"Very well," Xian said reluctantly.

"Splendid!" Kichirou exclaimed and led Xian and her handmaidens to his room.

He held the door open for the women to enter.  Kichirou's room was neat but filled with reminders of his various travels.  Pointing to a rug on the floor he said, "This is a tiger I shot while on safari.  Over here is a vase I brought back from India."  They walked deeper into the room and Kichirou pointed to a large tapestry covering most of one wall.  "This is something I know you will like.  It's a wall hanging from ancient China.  Note the intricacies of the hand woven cloth."  As Xian stepped closer, Kichirou said to The Twins, "You may go."  Xian turned around to watch her handmaidens walk out of the room.  When she began to follow, Xian felt Kichirou grab her from behind.  As a wet rag was pushed against her nose and mouth, the last thing Xian heard before she lost consciousness was, "Does this smell like chloroform?"

When she woke up, Xian found herself lying face down on Kichirou's bed with a ball gag in her mouth.  When she tried to move, she realized her wrists and ankles were tied to the four corners of the bed with silk scarves.  Xian picked her head up enough to realize she was lying backwards on the bed.  She watched as Kichirou walked back and forth wearing nothing but black leggings.  He was pouring and mixing something the way a child would play with a chemistry set.  Then, Xian noticed him filling syringes.  She tried to scream.  He turned and smiled at her.

"Ah!  There you are!  You woke up quickly," Kichirou complimented.  As Xian struggled with the scarves binding her limbs, Kichirou said, "I'm sure you have a question or two.  You want to know why your handmaidens left you, right?  All the servants must obey my father, my aunt, and… me.  While protecting you is important, it's not as important as our wishes."  Kichirou sat on the bed and pulled Xian's kimono up, exposing one leg.  As she struggled, he continued, "I'm not going you harm you.  Actually, we're going to have a lot of fun."  He held the exposed limb still as he injected something in a vein on the back of her leg, behind her knee.  As Xian slumped into a state of twilight consciousnesses, Kichirou laughed.  "That would've knocked out a large man.  You're made of sterner stuff than you appear!  This is going to be MOST enjoyable!  I like you.  I want to keep you around for a long time.  Your predecessors were no fun!  My first stepmother was Columbian.  She was looking out of the observation tower window when I entered her room.  I was so quiet as I walked behind her and gave her the smallest push.  Poor thing fell through the casement and broke her neck.  My second stepmother was from Sicily, and after some fun and games, she went a little insane.  I think Aunt Kamiko had a bit more to do with that than I did.  Anyway, she hanged herself just to spite us. Not fair at all! They were both such strong women from powerful families, but they made horrible stepmothers. Well, all things happen for a reason. They had to go so that YOU could come into my life. We are going to have such a good time. Too bad you won't remember any of this."

There was another needle prick on the back of her leg. She felt Kichirou lift her kimono higher and she then saw his black leggings being flung across the room. Dramatically, Kichirou said, "Lady Xian! What a beautiful and shapely rear you have!"

Xian concluded her story:

"Kichirou then raped and sodomized me. He would inject me with more drugs and the cycle would continue. I did not acquiesce, but I did not fight. I tried to turn off my brain and become as lifeless as possible. When Kichirou was… finished, he gave me a strong tranquilizer to render me unconscious. The next thing I knew, The Twins were helping me back to my room and I had no memory of what happened to me."

Dagmar looked perplexed. "If you didn't remember anything, how can you tell me what happened?"

"I didn't remember anything then. I remember everything now. I remember every insult, every attack, every violation… everything."

## Chapter Twenty-Eight

# Life Lesson

Dagmar busily made notes as Xian looked around the room at everyone staring at her. Xian almost smiled as she said, "You are all hanging on my every word. I have never had a captive audience."

When Dagmar caught up with her notes, she observed, "Between the three of them, I don't know which one was worst."

"Mister Kami had the run of the house and had more access to me, providing more opportunities for abuse."

"Just to be clear," Dagmar questioned, "every time you were alone with Mister Kami, you were abused?"

"No. Not every time. It sounds odd but he liked me in the room with him when he worked. I was present when he made business calls, did paperwork…."

"It sounds like he wanted to show off in front of you."

Xian thought for a second, then nodded. "Yes. Looking back, I believe you're correct. It was another way of showing me his dominance. He would explain his business dealings as he worked on them and brag about how he was a

201

superior negotiator. Mister Kami would lie to, and cheat, his business partners. He was so good at manipulating funds that his associates perceived him as an honest, hard working, and intelligent man."

"But, why would his partners do business with him if they didn't make money?"

"Oh, they would make money, but Mister Kami would siphon off just enough from their deals where his duplicity would not be detected. He said the one thing that separated him from his business partners was that he was not greedy. Mister Kami laughed at the Americans that put together simplistic 'ponzi schemes' which could only fail miserably. His building trust, having his organization do all the complicated paperwork, and working hard at putting together convoluted deals, reaped big rewards. Even my father, an extremely smart and savvy businessman, was fooled by him. I'm sure he researched Mister Kami, and I'm sure he received glowing praise from everyone he did business with."

"He did not fool ME!" Talia hissed quietly from the back of the room.

"When he was done with work, his desk was usually a mess. One day, in frustration with his own disorder, he said, 'Make yourself useful and clean this up!' and stormed from the room. When he returned minutes later with a glass of saké, he was surprised to find that I had cleared his desk by filing his papers. My husband said, 'At least you're good for something.' After that, he would routinely have me file his papers and even organize his computer. I would also assist by sitting in on meetings as his 'proper wife' when his more family orientated business partners would visit. One such meeting was particularly poignant."

Xian began her story:

The Twins primped and polished Xian by giving her a manicure, a pedicure, and styling her hair. They selected a cream and white kimono for her to wear for her meeting with the Australian businessman coming to visit Mister Kami. Wordlessly, The Twins led Xian to Mister Kami's office where she sat and waited. Five minutes later, her husband entered and sat behind his desk. Turning to his wife he said, "This potential partner holds fidelity to his family in high regard. You are to be my proper wife. We will be speaking English during this meeting. You may speak when spoken to, but do not elaborate."

Mister Kami worked at his desk until he received a phone call. He mumbled a few words into the phone and walked to his wife. Beckoning Xian to stand, they waited until a butler ushered in a tall man with an angular, attractive face. The dynamic gentleman shook Mister Kami's hand vigorously.

202

"Masaru Kami?  I'm Alexis Simms.  Pleasure to meet you!"

Disguising his revulsion of being touched by someone he just met, Mister Kami returned the vigorous handshake and smiled.  "Welcome to my home. May I introduce you to my wife, The Lady Xian?"

The Australian businessman looked at Xian and instead of a handshake, he humbly bowed.  "An honor, Lady Xian."

Xian nodded and Mister Kami offered Alex Simms a seat.  He waited until Xian returned to her chair before he sat down.  "So, Mister Simms, how was your flight?"

"Smooth as glass… and call me Alex."

Nodding, Mister Kami returned, "And please call me Masaru."  He expertly hid his distaste of anyone aside from a blood relative using his first name.

"Beautiful home you have!  Flippin' Shangri La it is!"

"Thank you.  Would you like something to drink?  I believe we have some beer from Australia."

"Naw!  I can drink that swill any time.  What's YOUR favorite poison?"

"I prefer saké."

"Right, right!  I've heard of it.  If that's what you drink, I'm game."

Mister Kami picked up his phone and said, "A bottle of my finest saké and two glasses."

When Mister Kami hung up the phone, Alex Simms said, "Have to hand it to you, mate.  You impress me by involving your lady in your business transactions!  My sheila would be here if she weren't in a family way.  Eight months, she is, and scrappy as ever!"

Smiling, Mister Kami said, "Please give my regards to your wife, Sheila."

Alex Simms burst out laughing.  "No, mate.  My wife's name is Adaline!  'Sheila' is another name for a girlfriend or for a wife.  For example, The Lady Xian is your sheila," and turning to Xian he added, "If you don't mind me saying so."

Nodding her acceptance, Xian said, "I find your phrasing… refreshing, Mister Simms."

Turning to Mister Kami, Alex Simms said, "She's a keeper, that one!" indicating Xian.

A maid entered the office with the saké and placed it on an end table. "Pour for us," Mister Kami said. Xian dutifully stood and poured two glasses of saké.

"Shows how different our cultures are. If I told Adaline to pour my drink, she'd punch me in the eye!"

"How sad for you," Mister Kami consoled.

"No… I like her that way."

"Well, my wife likes to serve me."

Looking at Xian for a sign of agreement and finding none, Alex Simms said, "Right. Well, as I said, different cultures and all that."

Xian gave her husband and guest their drinks and returned to her seat. Mister Kami rose and said, "A toast to a lucrative business deal."

"Excuse me, Lady Xian. You won't be joining us for a pop?"

"I'm afraid my wife doesn't drink."

Snickering, Alex Simms said, "If I were to leave Adaline out of a round, she'd punch me in the other eye!" Raising his glass, he said, "To lots of money!" He drank the saké straight down and said, "Smooth! No kick, but I bet it sneaks up on you, eh?"

They sat and Mister Kami began business. "I assume you looked over my business proposal. I noticed you have no briefcase. If you need a copy…"

"Naw! I know what's in it. It looks good. Real good. Actually… too good!"

"What are your fears?"

"Well, Masaru, you say you'll back up and guarantee the deal. I've done some research. You're a wealthy man, but even YOU don't have that kind of money. I don't want to insult you, but the figures just don't add up. Sorry, mate. I came here hoping there was something I overlooked. If there is, I'll reconsider. I know you have a good rep an' all, but I can't see how you'd make good if the deal doesn't bring in the money you say."

Mister Kami was quiet for a moment as he played different scenarios in his mind. Finally, he said, "Come with me." He stood and walked to the door.

Alex Simms stood and turned to Xian. "You're not coming?"

Xian looked at her husband and Mister Kami answered for her, "Yes, of course. Come along, Xian!"

The trio walked downstairs to a vault with a very large door and electronic lock. Mister Kami placed his body between the touch pad and Alex Simms to hide the combination. When he finished the input, latches on the vault snapped and the door slowly opened.

"A moment, Alex. I want to make sure the room is presentable," Mister Kami said and slipped inside the vault.

Alex Simms turned to Xian and quietly said, "Are you all right? Pardon me for saying, but you look scared out of your mind! If there is anything I can do, you just say the word!"

Xian trembled as her mind sought an answer to his query. "It is best that you don't concern yourself with my problems."

Mister Kami came out of the vault and said, "All… in order. Did I hear you two talking?"

"Yes, sir! I told her that I'm sorry she didn't get to meet Adaline. I think they'd hit it off."

"Yes, perhaps," Mister Kami said skeptically. "Alex, would you join me? We will be right back, Xian."

Alex Simms and Mister Kami entered the vault as Xian waited at the door. Moments later, the men walked out and Alex Simms had a big smile on his face.

"As long as my partners agree, we can do business Masaru! In fact, I'm getting a taste for more of that saké!"

Mister Kami closed the vault door and all three went back to the office. As they entered he looked at Xian and pointed to the saké. Xian poured two glasses and delivered them to her husband and Alex Simms.

"I only have time for one drink. If you would, I'd like to be taken back to my hotel."

Mister Kami picked up his phone and made arrangements as Xian placed the saké in front of him. "Are you sure you don't want to spend the night here?" Mister Kami asked.

"Thanks, mate, but I've got some business calls to make and some partners to soothe." He smiled as Xian gave him his drink, then she placed the bottle back on the table. As Xian lowered her arms, her wedding ring slipped off her finger and bounced on the floor near Alex Simms. He retrieved the ring and handed it to her saying, "Here ya go."

"Thank you, Mister Simms."

"Lost a little weight since the wedding, did you Lady Xian?"

"It… seems so."

When they finished their drink, Mister Kami said to his guest, "I will send a car for you tomorrow afternoon." They shook hands, Alex Simms bowed to Xian, and was escorted to the carport by one of the butlers.

When Mister Kami was certain his guest was gone, he grabbed Xian by her hand and dragged her out of the house to the stables. "Leave!" he shouted, and everyone working in the stables left the area. He pulled Xian to the blacksmith area where the horseshoes were made. Mister Kami put her hand on the anvil palm side up, and then put his foot on it so it would not move. He took a glowing hot poker and placed it on the wedding ring. The hot ring sizzled as it burned its way into Xian's finger. She opened her mouth to scream but nothing came out as the smell of burned flesh filled her lungs. He then put her hand in a water bucket to quickly cool the ring. Xian fell to the ground withering in agony. Mister Kami proceeded to kick her in the ribs. "Next time you are asked if you are all right, you say, 'I'm fine.' Do you understand? YOU… ARE… FINE!" Mister Kami left her rolling on the ground sounding more like an animal than a human. Minutes later, The Twins came for her. They helped Xian to her feet and took her back to her room. They applied salve to her injuries. Then, they bandaged her hand, bound her ribs and gave her a sedative to allow her to sleep through the night.

The next afternoon, Alex Simms arrived at the Kami home and was brought to the office. Once again, he was greeted by Mister Kami but Xian seemed different somehow.  Her smile was a little fuller.  She stood a little straighter.  "G'day Masaru.  G'day Lady Xian."

"Welcome, Alex," Mister Kami said and shook hands.  "Please sit."  Again, Alex Simms waited for Xian to be seated before he sat.  "Do you have good news for me?"

"I talked to my partners last night and they gave me a thumbs up.  I'm ready to sign on the dotted line."

"Excellent!" Mister Kami exclaimed and picked up his phone.  He mumbled a few words and a butler came into the room with a small table, the contract, and an expensive pen.  Placing everything in front of Alex Simms he quickly scrawled his signature.  The butler handed the papers to Mister Kami who smiled and placed them in his drawer.  "Would you like another saké to celebrate?"

"Yeah!  Don't mind if I do!"

The butler brought in the saké and poured two glasses.  Handing a glass to Alex Simms he turned to Xian and said, "Not pouring the drinks today?"

"Unfortunately," Mister Kami interrupted, "The Lady Xian injured her hand yesterday."

Alex Simms noticed her hands were tucked into opposing sleeves of her kimono.  "I used to be a field medic in the core.  If you'd like me to look at it…"

"A very gracious offer, Mister Simms," Xian said.  There was a flatness in her voice and a rehearsed sound to her speech.  "However, my hand has been treated by our doctor.  He does not want to risk infection."

Now Alex Simms realized what seemed wrong with Xian.  She did not look at him.  When she spoke, she looked through him, as if he were a ghost.  "Lady Xian… are you sure there isn't something I can do for you?  Anything?"

"No thank you, Mister Simms.  I am… fine."

Xian ended her story:

"Mister Kami said I learned a lesson about staying alive."

"Why didn't you say something to Alex Simms?" Dagmar asked.

"I didn't know if I could trust him.  Would he ruin a very profitable business deal for me?  Besides, what could he have done?  No.  It was better to obey Mister Kami."

"This has nothing to do with you, but I'm curious.  Did you ever find out what was in the vault?"

"I was curious as well.  The day after Alex Simms left, I sneaked down to the vault at 2 a.m.  While Mister Kami did an excellent job of shielding his button presses from Alex Simms, I saw them out of the corner of my eye.  When I went inside the vault I saw a tarp covering a four-foot mound.  I lifted the tarp and saw it covered a large pile of gold bars.  It seems he had been using the gold as collateral for his deals.  The top bars were upside down.  When I turned over one of the heavy bars, I saw a strange marking on it.  I am not sure what it was… a symbol and a bird… but it was nothing I'd seen in Japan.  I would guess the gold bars were stolen but I'm not sure."

"So," Dagmar said, "We can add theft to Mister Kami's sins: theft from his partners and possibly theft of his gold reserve.  And now we know how your wedding ring was burned into your finger.  There are… other things we found when doing your physical that I have a question about."

Nodding, Xian said, "I think I know what you are referring to."

# Chapter Twenty-Nine

# Death Lesson

Xian began her story:

One morning The Twins brought breakfast to Xian's room. She took one look at the food and ran to the bathroom to vomit. The Twins waited patiently for Xian to come out of the bathroom. When Xian returned, the handmaidens went into the bathroom to clean it. When they were done, The Twins tried to present the tray to Xian again. She waved off the food saying, "I'm not hungry. Please take that away." The Twins left with the tray.

Two hours later, one of the maids came to Xian's room. "Mister Kami requests your presence. Please follow me."

Dutifully, Xian followed the maid to a room she had never seen. It was a clean white room with an examination table and a desk. Mister Kami's doctor was behind the desk and he stood as Xian entered the room. "Please come in, Lady Xian. I hear you were sick this morning. I haven't given you a full examination since you came to Japan, so at your husband's request, I'd like to perform one now." Pointing to a door, the doctor continued. "There is a hospital gown in that room for you and a cup for you to leave a urine sample. When you are finished, leave the cup on the sink and come back here."

Seventy-five minutes later, Mister Kami walked into the doctor's office and saw his wife on the exam table with an IV in each arm.  As the doctor finished his very invasive examination, Mister Kami asked, "How is she?"

"Pregnant," was the doctor's only reply.

Mister Kami nodded his head, and the doctor injected something into the intervenes.  Before she could say anything, Xian felt her head swirl as she lapsed into unconsciousness.

Xian woke in her room, tucked comfortably in her bed and observed by The Twins.  As she tried to sit up, Xian was surprised by a sharp pain in her abdomen.  She fell back on the bed and one of The Twins stood and left the room.

A few minutes later, The Twin returned behind Mister Kami.  He walked to her bed and said, "You are to rest until you are healed from your procedure.  Your handmaidens will be here until you can manage on your own."

"Mister Kami… Masaru… did I hear the doctor say that I am pregnant?"

Looking down at her, he said, "Yes, that is what you heard."

"Then… I am to become a mother?"

Forcefully, he replied, "I have no interest in children.  I have ONE son.  ONE!  His status in my dynasty will not be compromised by a mixed breed child.  No, Xian, you are not to become a mother… ever!"

As Xian ended her story, the room fell silent.

The quiet was broken by Talia whispering, "He… he aborted the child who would be my niece or nephew.  He made sure there would be no others.  That… that… bastard!  That cur!"  Trembling, Talia turned to her husband and said, "I want to hunt him down like the dog he is, and kill him with my bare hands!"

Rich wiped the hot tears from his wife's eyes and said, "He WILL be punished."

"But…"

"We'll talk about it later… after Xian's session."

Xian looked down and saw she had subconsciously placed her hands on her abdomen. Touching her patient to get her attention, Dagmar asked, "I hate to sound like a typical psychiatrist, but what are you feeling?"

"So much," Xian said. "I feel sad because I will never give birth. I am furious that the choice was taken from me. I feel rage toward Mister Kami, and I am angry with myself that I allowed this abomination."

"It sounds to me like you had no choice."

"I could have taken my life."

Dagmar closed her eyes for a second as she thought and then said, "I'm not supposed to interject. I'm supposed to guide you to your own conclusions. However, I'm compelled to point out that you are here right now, and you are safe. You couldn't say that if you killed yourself."

From behind Dagmar, Jane added, "Xian, your best days are ahead of you. Do you remember the party at the club last night? Remember how much fun you had?"

Smiling, Xian said, "Yes, of course."

Returning the smile, Jane continued, "Woman, that's just the beginning! Everyone in this room is behind you and will support your return to a normal, productive, and happy life."

"Amen," Harmony added.

Dagmar turned around and gave Jane and Harmony a stern look. When they were properly contrite for speaking when they should have been listening, Dagmar turned back to Xian and asked, "I can't imagine what it was like to have this happen and have nowhere to turn... no one to talk to."

Hesitantly, Xian said, "There was... one."

Xian began her story:

For two days, Xian healed and said nothing. She ate when The Twins brought food. She stood and walked to build her strength. After the second day, The Twins stopped their visual, and at one a.m. Xian left her room. Being careful to make sure she was not followed, she made her way to the servants' quarters and searched until she saw Atsuko's familiar sandals outside her door. Xian knocked quietly but rapidly on the door. Atsuko's sleepy eyes burst wide open when she saw her visitor. She looked around and pulled Xian into her room.

"Mistress! This is a most unexpected and dangerous surprise!"

The room was barely large enough for Atsuko's cot and hot plate. Xian looked at her and saw her bare feet. "I… I am rude." Xian began taking off her sandals but Atsuko stopped her. "No. Please. You are my Mistress. It is an honor to have you here."

Atsuko watched as Xian began to emotionally fall apart. "They… they…" was all Xian could say, and Atsuko caught her as she fell to her knees.

The young maid held her Mistress in her arms as Xian cried and rocked back and forth. Trying to soothe her, Atsuko stroked Xian's hair with her hand and spoke comfortingly to her. When Xian began to regain her composure, Atsuko asked, "Is my Mistress able to tell her humble maid what happened?"

Choking out the words, Xian said, "I thought I would tell you… but it is too terrible. I can only say that I am no longer the woman I was when I came here."

"What can I do to help you? Say the words and I will do whatever you ask, my Mistress!"

Looking into Atsuko's earnest eyes, Xian said, "You have been a good and loyal friend. Please use my name and not my title. Please call me Xian."

Smiling, she replied, "Using your name instead of your title will be a difficult habit to break and impossible outside this room, but I am deeply honored. Again, is there something I can do for you? Anything?"

"Yes. You can protect yourself! I am going to give you a telephone number. Do not write it down. Memorize it. It may save your life someday!" Xian made Atsuko repeat the number over and over. When she was sure she knew it by heart, Xian asked, "When do you go home?"

"Every third weekend. I am just coming back from a visit with my family. They gave me something to make my stay more bearable. Would you like to see it?" Xian nodded, and Atsuko went to a corner of the room and reached inside a box. She took out a purring ball of fur and handed it to Xian. Looking up from her cupped hands was a newborn kitten. "Would you like to feed her?" Atsuko asked, handing Xian a small baby's bottle filled with milk. Xian put the bottle near the kitten's mouth and watched it lick and bite the nipple.

Xian's maternal instincts were beginning to assert themselves. "She… she is so precious. What is her name?"

"I have not selected one for her yet. I want to take the time to pick a good name. Of course, it's against the rules to have a pet. I have to keep her well hidden."

Xian was so intriguing with the animal in her hands, she became relaxed until she remembered the time. "I am keeping you awake when you have a full day's work ahead of you."

"It is all right."

"No," Xian said as she returned the kitten. "I must go. Thank you for listening to me and sharing your pet."

It was three a.m. when Xian left Atsuko's room. She thought she felt someone watching her but saw no one. Xian carefully made her way back to her room.

The next day Xian was summoned to Mister Kami's study. When she entered, he was hard at work. As Xian walked to his desk, Mister Kami did something he had not done for a long time, he smiled at her. "Please, take a seat," he offered. When she was settled in one of the large chairs, he asked, "How are you feeling?"

"I am still a little sore," was the answer that met with a disapproving look from her husband. Xian quickly added, "But, I am fine."

Now with a more satisfied look, Mister Kami said, "Good. You had no problem walking here?"

"No."

"I would think not. I am told you went for a walk last night."

Xian's heart froze. Did she somehow endanger Atsuko? "I… could not sleep."

"And you decided to visit one of the maids?" Mister Kami added. "Atsuko, was it not? Do you like her?"

Xian tried to hide her friendship while explaining her visit. "She is one of the few servants I have spoken to, or even seen, on more than one occasion. I thought it better to disturb her sleep than yours."

Nodding, Mister Kami said, "Good, as long as you weren't friendly with her. You see, I was told we have too many maids on staff and I had to dismiss her. It was a shame, too. Her family needed money desperately. However, my sadness is tempered by the fact that she DID break one of the rules." He reached into his drawer and brought out her small purring kitten. "I do not allow the staff to have pets. Atsuko left so quickly, she forgot to take this kitten with her."

Xian knew Atsuko would never willingly leave her kitten behind.

"What should I do with it?" Mister Kami asked.

"Since she has been through the disappointment of a lost job, I would think she would wish to have her pet back."

Smiling once more, Mister Kami said, "I agree." The kitten made a gurgling sound as Mister Kami closed his hand into a fist. He squeezed it so tightly his arm shook, and when he opened his hand, all that was left was a furry, bloody pulp.

Xian tried to remain stoic. Her face portrayed no emotion, but as hard as she tried, her body did tremble. Mister Kami took the bloody mess, flung it in the trash can, and wiped his hand on a towel. He pressed his intercom and one of the butlers walked into the room. Handing him the trash can, he said, "See that this is returned to Atsuko." When the butler left, Mister Kami turned his attention to Xian. "I hope you remember this the next time you befriend one of the staff. Now leave! I have wasted enough of my valuable time dealing with you!"

Xian ended her story.

Still trembling at the memory, Xian said, "Something inside me died that day. It was the day I knew I had to withdraw into myself to protect my loved ones. Also, that was the moment the cloud returned to haze my mind. It distanced me from the world. It numbed me. It protected me. The cloud stayed with me until Mommy's wake."

Looking down at her pad, Dagmar paused to write something else, then placed her hand across her face to mask her emotions. She then looked up and said, "Why did he have to kill the kitten? Wasn't firing her enough? Did he HAVE to kill it and return the corpse to her?!"

214

"Squeezing the life out of the kitten was done to punish and horrify me."

Still emotionally distraught, "Yes, of course I know that but… it seems so extreme… so completely heartless… so…"

"Evil?" Xian added.

# Chapter Thirty

# Wheels in Motion

Dagmar closed her eyes for a moment then snapped them open to refocus. She looked over her notes and asked, "Whose phone number did you give Atsuko?"

"Mine," said a voice from the back of the room. Talia continued, "She called my cell phone to tell me that my sister was alive but not well. Atsuko told me Xian was being abused, but assured me there was nothing that could be done about it. I told Father immediately."

All eyes turned to Talia as Dagmar asked, "What did your father do?"

"Nothing," Talia said flatly. "He believes no one should interfere with a marriage… or so he says. He has little problem commenting on mine. He needed more proof than a fired employee. I knew something was seriously wrong with their marriage from the start, but Father and Mother NEVER trusted my intuition even though I have never been wrong."

"But, your father DID initiate a divorce, returned Xian home, and had her citizenship restored," Dagmar clarified.

"Yes… eventually," Talia relinquished. "I pressed the issue when I saw Xian at my wedding with her handmaidens… but without her husband. I convinced Father to have Mother check for signs of abuse."

Dagmar asked Xian, "Did your Mother talk to you at Talia and Rich's wedding?"

Xian nodded, "Yes, at the reception."

Xian began her story:

Xian sat at the head table with The Twins sitting close by keeping an eye on her. When the main meal was over and before the cake was served, Mrs. Tamislav stood and walked to Xian. "Come. We must talk."

Dutifully, Xian rose and walked with her mother. They went to the bathroom where a woman was reapplying her lipstick. The stately Athena Tamislav glared at her and commanded, "Leave!" As the shocked woman opened the bathroom door, The Twins began to enter. Mrs. Tamislav blocked the door with her body and said, "I am having a private conversation with my daughter!" The Twins were stunned as Xian's mother slammed the door in their faces and locked it. "Show me your arms!" Athena Tamislav demanded.

"Mother, it is better not to…"

"I won't ask you again… show me your arms!"

Slowly, very slowly, Xian began lifting the right sleeve of her kimono. Mrs. Tamislav's patience was at an end. She took the sleeve and jerked it up to Xian's shoulder. Her eyes widened as she saw deep bruises on her daughter's arm. Hiking the left sleeve up, she saw the entire arm was black and blue with abrasions. Trembling with anger, Mrs. Tamislav began unlacing the intricately layered kimono until it dropped in a coil around Xian's feet. She took her cell phone from her clutch and began photographing the immense bruising on her daughter's back, sides, and stomach. Not wishing to take the time to redress her daughter in the complex garment, Mrs. Tamislav said, "I have to show these to your father… right now!" She partially opened the door, looked around, and then said, "Those two hags are nowhere to be found. As soon as I leave, lock the door and get dressed. Open the door to no one but me, understand?"

"But, Mother, what of Father's business arrangement? Mister Kami would not look kindly on…"

Interrupting her, Mrs. Tamislav said, "I'd rather be penniless than see one of my children go through such abuse! Do as I said!"

Mrs. Tamislav stormed out of the bathroom. Xian took the time to raise the kimono to cover herself and then went to the door. In that split second, The Twins rushed in and dragged Xian from the bathroom, and pushed her into a waiting limousine. The car sped to an airfield and Xian was hustled into a private jet. Once the jet took off, The Twins finished dressing Xian and settled in for the long flight from Connecticut back to Japan.

When the plane returned home, a car took them to Mister Kami's compound where Xian was brought to her room. Minutes later, Mister Kami entered with a smile on his face.

"You're father called me. He is furious with the way I treat you. He wants me to divorce you and return you to the United States of America. Did you tell him you were being mistreated?" Xian remained mute. "Hmm. No, I don't believe you said anything. It must have been that devil-sister of yours, Talia, that figured it out. Unfortunately for your father, I have no intention of returning you to him. Also, I have no intention of breaking my business contracts. I'm cheating him out of much too much money for that! My father in-law will have to live with the fact that I am in control. I should be angry… but I'm not. I like that Mister Yuri Tamislav is impotently screaming on the other side of the ocean while I do as I wish with his money… and his first-born.

Xian finished her story.

"Mister Kami and his family continued to abuse me. I withdrew even more. I let the cloud keep all the monsters at bay. I did as I was told but nothing else. Even servants who were kind to me I deflected for fear they would be fired like Atsuko. I had to accept that this was my life until I died."

"You didn't know your family was working to get you away from Mister Kami?" Dagmar asked.

Talia spoke up. "I harassed Father for almost five years to bring my sister home. We got both governments involved and there was much political arm-twisting. Even when the Japanese government appealed to Mister Kami to let Xian go… he refused. However… the wheels were in motion. My father used every political connection he had to force the Japanese government to send Xian back to us."

"Yes," Xian added. "I was in Mister Kami's office when he received a visitor from the government.


Xian began her story:

One day while Mister Kami was in his office, gloating to his wife about a business deal, he received a phone call saying he had an important visitor. Mister Kami stepped from behind his desk to greet the government official.

"Welcome to my home. To what do I owe the honor of a visit from the Minister for Foreign Affairs?"

The Minister took an offered seat and said, "I am here to ask why you have not honored your government's request to divorce your wife and return her to the United States?"

Feigning shock, Mister Kami said, "Because… I love her! Is the government in the habit of invading the sanctity of a marriage?"

The Minister looked at Xian, who had been staring off into the distance the entire time. Turning back to Mister Kami, he said, "Allow me to be direct. The United States government is making this a very big issue. They are demanding a full investigation of this woman's abuse. We feel it would be best for all involved to divorce your wife and return her to her homeland. I have brought all the papers with me."

Mister Kami shouted, "I don't recognize your authority in family matters, Minister!"

"This isn't coming from me!" the Minister for Foreign Affairs said with anger. "This comes from The Emperor…"

"Bah! Who cares about that figurehead?!"

"…and the Prime Minister!"

The Minister's words quieted Mister Kami. "I see."

"You have always had a polite relationship with the government. However… we do not like you! Many feel the taxes you pay are not in line with your lavish life. There are many who would love to inspect your finances more closely. There are many who would love to have the military raid your home. We have not done so because we have not had a reason for looking at you closely. The

Secretary of State from The United States will be here tomorrow and will personally bring Xian Tamislav back. It is an unofficial promise our government has made." The Minister opened his briefcase and placed documents on Mister Kami's desk. "I would NOT want to make an enemy of The Prime Minister. Sign!"

Reluctantly, Mister Kami took The Minister for Foreign Affair's pen and signed the divorce documents. He turned to Xian, laid out the documents, and repeated, "Sign!"

Xian dutifully did as she was told and The Minister put the documents back in his briefcase. Without thanking Mister Kami, The Minister turned to leave, but stopped in the doorway. "The Emperor and Prime Minister have guaranteed Xian Tamislav's safe return. Should this woman die, or be injured when The Secretary of State comes to get her, the full weight of the government will be brought to bear on you. Do NOT embarrass your government!" The Minister for Foreign Affairs left without another word.

Mister Kami sat motionless for several minutes and then directed his gaze toward Xian. He picked up his telephone, mumbled a few words, and stood. "Come with me," he said evenly to Xian. She followed him to the courtyard where the entire staff had been assembled. When he was sure he had everyone's attention, Mister Kami announced, "It is my sad duty to inform you that my wife and I signed divorce papers. She is no longer your Mistress. Tomorrow, she will be leaving forever. You are all dismissed except for the guards and her handmaidens." When the others left, Mister Kami said to The Twins, "You will see to my former wife's needs until she leaves tomorrow. You may go." When The Twins walked away, Mister Kami sighed as he looked at his guards. "Nothing on the hands, feet, or the face."

Two guards took Xian by her arms as Mister Kami walked away. The security staff was made up of very large and imposing former mercenaries. They took Xian to a secluded area of the property and began beating her until she lost consciousness. She woke to find her hands tied to a wooden board as her former son in-law, Kichirou was injecting her with a drug in his favorite place, behind her knee.

"Now, now, ex-mommy," Kichirou laughed, "You don't want to fall asleep and miss the fun!"

The guards took turns whipping Xian until her red back had several long splits. Kichirou stopped the guards and told them to back away. As the guards watched, Kichirou raped Xian unmercifully. When he finished, he stepped away, pulled up his pants and said to the guards, "She is all yours." Kichirou smiled as he left, not looking back as the guards brutalized Xian. They violated her using bottles and shovel handles.

When the guards finished raping and sodomizing Xian, they tied the makeshift yoke to one of the horses and slowly dragged her body around the property. Finally, at the end of the day, a battered and half naked Xian was thrown into her room where she fell into unconsciousness on the floor.

The next morning, The Twins entered Xian's room. As if nothing had happened, they stripped off her tattered kimono and fitted her with a new one without dressing the numerous wounds on her body. They packed her belongings in two suitcases, made up her hair and applied her makeup. They brought Xian to a formal living room where Mister Kami was drinking tea and reading a book. They placed Xian in a chair and turned to the Master of the House.

Mister Kami closed his book and said, "Your duty to this person is over. She will be leaving in a few minutes. You may say good-bye."

The Twins walked to Xian, and one at a time, spit in her face. As they walked away, Mister Kami smiled and returned to his book.

Xian ended her story:

"About ten minutes later, The Secretary of State arrived and took me to a car which went directly to the airport. I sat silent for the entire trip. The government jet landed at a Connecticut airport where my sister and brother in-law picked me up. I greeted them and said little else. Talia was heartbroken to see how I was more withdrawn than ever. Rich visited the psychiatric practice of Kane & Teasdale who promised they would help me." Looking at Dagmar directly, Xian added, "And… you did. You did help me. You never gave up, no matter how rude I was to you. And… I now remember… you saved my life when Mister Kami sent the letter, the letter that convinced my submissive mind into attempting suicide. As the Japanese call it… Seppuku!"

# Chapter Thirty-One

# Decisions

Dagmar reached to Xian and took her hand. She looked at the scared ring finger still healing from the removal of her wedding band. Looking Xian in the eye, Dagmar said quietly, "I'm sorry."

Confused, Xian asked, "You have no need to apologize to me."

"I feel that someone should. Healing begins with someone saying, 'I'm sorry'. I'm so deeply sorry for all that has happened to you."

"Thank you," Xian said, and looked at the tear stained faces in the room.

Harmony stood first. She walked to Xian, who rose from her seat as she approached. The young woman wrapped her arms around Xian and squeezed her tightly. When they separated, Harmony asked, "Have you ever had beans and rice with a Puerto Rican family?"

Smiling, Xian said, "No, I haven't."

"You haven't lived until you've had my mother's beans and rice. I want you to come to my house for dinner! Soon!"

"Thank you, Harmony. I would be honored."

Suzy jumped to her feet, went to Xian and practically pulled Harmony from her. She held Xian and said, "I'd like to invite you over to eat but... I can't cook for shit!" Pulling back and looking at Xian, Suzy said, "But I know the best restaurants and bars in the tri-state area! And, I want to take you to dinner!"

"Suzy, I would love to go to dinner with you."

Anabelle walked to Xian, hugged her, and said, "Normally, I'm pretty humble, but in all honestly, I'm the best cook here! I want you to come to my home for dinner. I would love to introduce my daughter to such a strong role model."

"Thank you, Anabelle. I look forward to meeting your daughter."

Candace stood, embraced Xian and said, "You've met my husband briefly at the wake. What you don't know is that he's an amazing chief... but if you tell him I said that, I'll deny it. I'm going to have him create an Italian meal for you that will make you swoon! AND, I have a seven month old child that you can't help but love!"

Jane stepped up to Xian, held her tightly, and kissed her on the cheek. She took Xian's face in her hands and said; "You've seen the rest, now here's the best! MY husband taught Candace's husband to cook so you know you're going to have the best Italian food you've EVER tasted. I have a one month old I'm dying to introduce you to. Most important, since Talia and I are sisters..."

"...which you must explain to me," Xian interrupted.

"That makes us family," Jane continued. "I'll be there whenever you need me. No matter what."

Talia ran to Xian, wrapped her arms around her, and cried. Rich put his arms around both women and said to Xian, "Welcome to your new home."

As Talia and her sister rocked back and forth, Xian looked at the tear filled eyes of her doctor. "These are your friends?"

"Yes," Dagmar choked.

Tears streaming from her eyes, Xian said, "You have... good friends."

"WE have good friends. We have the BEST of friends."

224

Looking around the room, Xian said, "I thank all of you. I would like to speak privately to Talia, my brother in-law, and my doctor."

The women went off to shed their robes and put on last night's clothes. One by one they said their good-byes and left the house.

"You have a lot of dinner invitations," Dagmar observed with a smile.

Nodding, Xian responded, "Yes. The one I'm looking forward to the most is having a piece of Red Velvet cake with my best friend and her father."

"Anytime, Xian."

As the friends left the Sedgwick home, the nanny, Delmar, and Talia's two children left the guesthouse and walked back to their home. The children heard the sound of their mother sobbing and the oldest, Jaynette, practically dragged her nanny to investigate. They stood in the doorway of the living room and saw Xian, Talia, and Rich embracing.

"Mommy, why are you crying?" Jaynette asked.

Rich answered. "Something… sad happened, but it's over. Everything is okay now."

Jaynette looked at Xian and said to her mother, "Something bad happened, didn't it?"

Before Talia could speak, Xian said, "Yes."

"Something bad happened… to you, Aunt Xian?"

Smiling at her niece's empathic nature, she said, "Yes."

"You're different today."

"Yes, I am."

"I liked you better yesterday."

Leaving Talia's embrace, Xian walked to Jaynette and sat on the floor in front of her. "I liked myself better yesterday, too. I am going to work very hard to be the happy and bright spirit you favored. It will take a lot of time but with the help of my new friends, your parents, and my doctor, I will be as I was."

Jaynette looked deeply into her aunt's eyes as if trying to read her thoughts. "What happened to you was really, REALLY bad, wasn't it?"

"It's in the past."

"Why won't you tell me about it?"

"Some day... I will."

"Can I help? Would a hug help?"

Smiling broadly, Xian said, "A hug from you is exactly what I need!"

Aunt and niece hugged tightly, and when they separated, Jaynette saw tears on Xian's cheeks. "You're crying."

"Yes, but from now on, only tears of happiness."

"Mommy says those are the best tears."

"Mommy's right. Jaynette, would you please go to my room and bring my laptop computer to me?"

"Sure!" she said and ran from the living room.

Jaynette's infant brother George began twisting, signaling his nanny to place him on the floor. He took a few staggering steps to Xian. She scooped George up in her arms and kissed the top of his head. Aunt and nephew looked into each other's eyes deeply. He reached forward and touched the tears on her face. Perhaps it was a coincidence but George nodded as if he understood everything about Xian his young mind could. He then left Xian, went to Dagmar and raised his arms. She lifted the baby and he cooed contently in her arms.

In spite of the emotional grief Talia had been through, she wiped the tears from her eyes and laughed. "Dagmar, George wants to let you know he still loves you."

Smiling at George, Dagmar said, "It's okay, Baby. I know you still love me. And I still love YOU!" Dagmar handed George back to Delmar and said, "Would you please take the children in another room? We have a few things to talk about."

Jaynette came back into the living room and handed the computer to Xian.

"Come, Jaynette," Delmar said. "I'll make breakfast for you."

Jaynette took Delmar's hand and walked with her and George into the kitchen.

After watching the children disappear from sight, Xian said, "Talia, I am going to impose on you for some important matters."

"Of course, Xian. Whatever you wish."

"First, when Atsuko called you, did she mention her family was desperate for money?"

"No. She was only concerned with you."

"That is the first order of business. Sister, I wish to track down their family and take care of their financial needs… immediately!"

Talia nodded. "Consider it done."

"Good. I would now like to hear what each of you think I should do about Mister Kami."

Talia quickly spoke up. "He should die a slow and horrible death for what he did to you! Ideally, I would love to capture him and torture him for weeks or months! If that is not possible, I would hire mercenaries to assassinate him or… do it myself!"

"Just a second," Rich interrupted. "I'm not going to risk my wife being caught up in a murder. I think we should continue to work on the Japanese government to press charges. Xian could testify against him and see that he is brought to justice."

"But, Richard, our lawyers said there is little hope of Mister Kami being prosecuted."

"Then, we'll hire new lawyers! I won't give up!"

"That could take forever!"

"Tally, the best way to do this is through safe, legal channels!"

Xian turned to Dagmar and said, "You disapprove of both solutions, don't you?"

"It's… really not my place to say."

"Please. I want your opinion."

Dagmar spoke slowly, "In my religion, we are taught to forgive. Sometimes, it isn't easy. Sometimes… it's impossible, but we try. Xian, you are back in the United States. You're here in Connecticut away from your dysfunctional family in California. You're away from the hell you went through in Japan. Can't you just put it behind you and move forward with the wonderful family and friends you have?"

Xian closed her eyes for a moment. When she opened them she said, "Dagmar, you are a good woman and I respect your opinion. I would prefer to follow your advice except that there is one thing I didn't tell you about Mister Kami. During his humiliation of me, on many occasions, he assured to me that if I was to leave or die, he would simply find another wife to take my place. If I do nothing, I will be subjecting another woman to what I, and his first two wives, went through. Whether I want to forgive him or not… he must be stopped."

Nodding grimly, Dagmar said, "I understand… but I have no solution."

"A moment," Xian said and opened up her laptop computer. She began searching the Internet. "That symbol and bird looked so familiar," Xian whispered to herself. She found what she was looking for.

Xian closed her computer, smiled an evil smile, and said, "What if I could make ALL of you happy?"

## Chapter Thirty-Two

# Reunion

For the next couple of weeks, Xian was a very busy woman. She spent her days learning investment strategies from Talia, exercising, playing with her niece and nephew, and building on her friendships. She was also the guest of honor at many sumptuous meals. Dagmar would observe Xian and spend hours with her in therapy. Xian had "sugar coated" much of what happened to her. She had only scratched the surface of the depravity and abuse she endured.

One very special day, Dagmar was called into the office to attend a meeting. She was at her desk early to finish some paperwork when her cell phone rang. Glancing at the caller ID, Dagmar sighed and brought the phone to her ear. "Hello Bryce."

"Hi Dagmar. Er... I guess it's my turn to try to get back with you."

"What do you mean, 'Your turn'?"

"Well, you DID come visit me at work."

"You mean with my battered patient? You think I beat her up just to see you again?"

Grumbling on the other end of the phone, Bryce said, "I'm trying to save face here."

"The only reason I went to your ER is because I thought you were a good doctor and a friend."

"I AM a good doctor… and friend."

"You took advantage of my mommy's death to drug me and you tried to bring me back to your place!"

"Be fair! You were a little crazy that day."

"A GOOD doctor would've used a tranquilizer instead of an antipsychotic… and you know it!"

"I had the best intentions!"

"You did? So, do you drug all your patients and take them home?"

Disgruntled, Bryce said, "I thought we were special."

Laughing, Dagmar said, "I'm not special to you! Why didn't you come to Mommy's wake or funeral?"

"I didn't know when it was."

"It's been over a month. You couldn't have sent flowers? Or given me a call? Or sent a card? Or a text?"

"I thought you were a forgiving woman."

"I AM a forgiving woman… but I'm not a doormat! To show you how forgiving I am, I talked Jane out of trying to go after your medical license."

"Yeah? Well, I'm still going to get her permissions revoked at my hospital!"

Angrily, Dagmar shot back, "If you do that, I'll go after your medical license myself! And, after you're fired, I'll get Jane's permissions reinstated! Either way is fine with me!"

"Whoa! Slow down! Can't we just talk face to face? Meet me for breakf…"

Dagmar hung up her phone.

230

Just as she was about to continue her paperwork, the intercom buzzed. "Doctor Lamont, Doctors Kane and Teasdale need you in the conference room."

As Dagmar went to the conference room, she saw Anabelle coming her way. "You're in early today, too? What's this about?"

"No idea," Anabelle shrugged.

They entered and sat in two chairs opposite Candace and Jane. A second later, Suzy and Harmony came into the room and placed contracts and packets of information in front of Dagmar and Anabelle. When they finished passing out the documents, Suzy and Harmony stepped to the side and smiled.

"What's all this?" Anabelle asked.

"Doctor Anabelle Virginia Loomis," Candace announced formally, "You took over this practice while the named partners were absent for medical reasons. We never lost a patient and never received a complaint. You did this while being a single mother to a teenage girl. In light of your hard work and dedication, the psychiatric practice of Kane & Teasdale would like to formally invite you to become a full partner."

"Are... are you serious?" Anabelle asked, still replaying the words in her head.

"Doctor Dagmar Rochelle Lamont," Jane announced formally, "You are responsible for bringing in the majority of our patients. Approximately seventy-five percent of our income has been generated by you. As our office manager has said, for many, you have been the face of this practice and you have represented us well. The psychiatric practice of Kane & Teasdale would like to formally invite you to become a full partner." Jane paused, and thinking about Xian, she continued, "And when you take a patient, you do a motherfucker of a good job!"

Stunned, Dagmar said, "This is the last thing I expected, and a big honor... but I know there's a 'buy in' to enter an established practice. And... I just don't have the money."

"Neither do I," Anabelle echoed.

"It's okay," Candace said. "The 'buy in' for you both has been taken care of by someone who wants to encourage the good work Kane & Teasdale does."

"But, who...?" Anabelle asked.

"Your benefactor wishes to remain anonymous," Jane answered.

Dagmar and Anabelle looked at each other, then recognition flashed across their faces. "Rich and Talia," Dagmar whispered.

"As I said… anonymous," Jane reiterated. However, the smile on her face confirmed Dagmar's guess.

"So, we'll be earning more money?" Anabelle asked. "I can use it to pay down my student loans."

"Me too," Dagmar added.

"Included with the 'buy in', there are funds earmarked to pay off your student loans," Candace added.

"Is… is this a joke?" Dagmar asked.

"Darling, I NEVER joke about money!" Candace said with a smile. "Normally, we'd toast with champagne, but Jane and Dagmar have someplace to be. So, sign the damn contracts and get out of here!"

Scribbling her name on the documents, Dagmar asked, "Are our names going to be on the letterhead?"

"No!" Candace answered immediately. "The founding partners have to have SOMETHING of their own. And, no matter what, I am, and will always be, head bitch!"

"No argument," Dagmar and Anabelle said together as they handed Candace their signed contracts.

"Congratulations, Doctors," Harmony said. "We'll see you after your meeting. This is a big day for Xian."

"It's going to be big for lots of people," Jane countered.

"By the way, how did Xian like dinner at your place?" Dagmar asked.

Laughing loudly, Harmony said, "Xian is very quiet compared to my family, but she loved my mother's cooking. And all my brothers want to marry her! Don't worry, Doctor Lamont. I'll keep my dogs leashed."

As Dagmar and Jane began leaving, Suzy said meekly, "Good luck… and… tell Rich I said hi."

They stopped in mid-stride. "Don't tell me you STILL have a crush on Rich?" Jane asked exasperated. "For God's sake, Suzy, he's married with two kids and two more on the way!"

"I know, I know!!! But it's just… I mean he's… the man is just such a… oh, you know what I mean!"

Dagmar and Jane looked at each other, not wanting to agree out loud. Candace noticed they were stuck for words and said, "We ALL know what you mean, darling."

As Dagmar and Jane began to leave the conference room Suzy piped up again, "Don't forget to tell him 'hi'!"

As Jane rolled her eyes Dagmar winked at her and went back into the conference room. "Suzy," Dagmar said, "You don't remember the limo dropping us off from our night out in New York, do you?" Suzy shook her head. "To get you inside his house, Rich had to carry you."

"He… He did?"

Smirking, Dagmar said, "He threw you over his shoulder. It was very masterful… like a caveman bringing his woman home! You said to Rich that you never thought your ass would get so close to his face!"

Suzy slumped in a chair and took the first thing she could reach, the contracts, and began fanning herself.

Candace slammed her hand on the table and said, "Put those contracts down and get back to work, or the thing that will come in contact with that ass of yours will be my Jimmy Choo's!"

Helping Suzy out of the chair, Harmony said, "C'mon, Blondie."

As Dagmar and Jane left the room they laughed upon hearing Suzy say, with complete seriousness, "I've got to start putting perfume on my ass!"

Dagmar's Porsche turned down the private road, Love Lane, and stopped front of the main house. Dagmar and Jane were still laughing at Suzy.

"The expression on her face was priceless," Jane said as she laughed. "Dag, you're an evil bitch!"

"I have my moments," Dagmar admitted as she nonchalantly inspected her nails. "Although…"

"Although… what?"

"I can't blame her too much. We've all fallen for Rich at least a little."

"Not me."

Dagmar shot Jane a look. "You forget what I do for a living. You may fool your other friends but you don't fool me."

"Naw… I can't even fool them. Look, even though Rich is fantastic, I wouldn't trade my hubby for any other man in the world. My lust for Rich is sort of in the past. The love I have for him will always be there, but the lust is gone."

"He seems so available while unavailable. Rich is always so sweet and charming, and just when you start to fall under his spell, he'll let you know how much he loves his wife. Somehow, it makes you love him MORE! It makes a woman feel… itchy."

Nodding in agreement, Jane said, "I couldn't have said it better myself. Dag, you really know people and you're such a good psychiatrist."

"Thanks, Jane."

Noticing Dagmar lost her smile a little too soon, Jane said, "You seem different somehow."

"Probably the scars from Mommy's death."

"Please don't take this the wrong way, Dag, but sometimes it takes a loss to help you advance as a person."

"Mommy once told me you become a woman when you face real adversity and survive it. I've been a baby, a girl, and a lady, but never a woman… until now. For the first time in my life I know… really know, what it is to be a woman. It isn't fun, but it's… solid. Am I making sense?"

"Perfect sense," Jane said and looked at her watch. "C'mon, Supermodel, we have an appointment to keep."

As Dagmar and Jane got out of the car, they heard a strange noise from the patio. The doctors walked to the back of the house and saw Jaynette roller-skating. She was gliding on the patio with her eyes closed, chanting.

234

"Jaynette?" Dagmar said. The young girl snapped open her eyes, smiled, and skated to meet her guests. "Why were you skating with your eyes closed?"

"I know my patio. I don't need to have my eyes open. I'm trying to skate by feeling the way the wind blows."

"Air currents?" Dagmar asked. "Jaynette, that's dangerous."

"Not for me! Besides, my chant calms me down when there's danger. I say, 'Shala Shalay.' That's one of my chants. I learned it from Aunt Jane."

Looking at Jane, Dagmar said to Jaynette, "So that's what you say when you're in… Dire Straits?"

"C'mon," Jane interrupted. "We have to get inside. See, you later, Jaynette!"

As they knocked on the back door, Dagmar said, "I've been thinking about chanting. How does, 'Shoo-be Do-be Do-be Do-Da-Day' sound?"

"As I said, you're an evil bitch."

Rich opened the patio door and beckoned them to come inside. Dagmar stopped in her tracks, wide-eyed. Mister Lamont, her father, was sitting at the kitchen table with Xian and Talia. He was wearing clean, crisp blue dress pants and a blue work shirt. There was something different about him. He looked trimmer and he had his confident smile back.

"Daddy? What are you doing here?"

"I'm having a meeting with my new boss, Talia," Mister Lamont said with a big smile on his face. "I'm the Maintenance Manager for her coffee shops."

"But, Daddy, what happened to your job with the general contractor?"

Mister Lamont admitted, "I was ashamed to tell you, but I was fired from my old job. I'd lost my wife. I'd lost my job. I didn't think I could get any lower. Then, I started talking to Candace. No therapy. We're just talkin' like folks. She's been helping' me through things. She even helped me get my new job."

"Daddy, why didn't you tell me you got fired?"

"Pride," Mister Lamont said. "Just pride. I'm not supposed to burden you with my problems. I knew you were comin' here today, and since I had to have a meeting with Talia, I decided to stick around and see you… tell you about talkin' to Candace and my job."

"But, Daddy, you're working for Talia?"

"Yes," Talia confirmed. "My managers have been doing general repairs at my coffee shops. It has been taking up too much of their time doing a job that is not part of their expertise. Your father has been fixing all the things that break from wear and tear… molding, chairs, even broken espresso machines. He is quite handy! If a project is too big, he will take bids from contractors. Your father is management in my organization. Along with his salary, that includes a retirement and savings program as well as medical benefits."

"This is a lot to take in," Dagmar said shaking her head. "Talia, thank you for helping my Daddy."

Smiling, Talia said, "He has been a great help… a blessing to me. One more thing, Dagmar. Xian and I have need of your opinion. I mentioned it to your father and I now want to know what you think. We have been so fortunate that we feel it is time to give something back. Richard and I want to start a scholarship to help underprivileged young men and women go to college."

Dagmar nodded and said, "It sounds like a great idea."

"I am glad you approve!" Talia exclaimed. "We will need someone to head the Board of Directors. Can you think of someone who would like to preside over the Jennifer Lamont Academic Fund?"

Dagmar was so surprised she literally shook. "Talia? Rich? What…?"

"It was Xian's idea. You may use any criteria you wish to distribute the scholarships. We have placed a large amount of money in some high-yield accounts. All you have to do is pass out the funds."

Softly, Xian said, "We can't bring Mommy back for you, but we can keep her memory alive."

Dagmar walked to Xian and gave her a bear hug. "What a beautiful thing to do. I love you," she said and kissed Xian's cheek. Then, Dagmar went to Talia. She hugged her tightly and said, "I love you," as she kissed her on the cheek. "I love this whole family!" Turning to her father, she said, "Daddy, you knew about this?!"

"I found out just before you got here. I know your Mama is watching from heaven, and she's real happy to have her name on something as important as a scholarship," Mister Lamont said.

"Daddy, I have a meeting in a few minutes. Can you stay?"

"Sorry, Baby. I have to get back to work! Mysty says she has a broken coffee maker in her Westport store," Mister Lamont said as he stood. "The manager… That Mysty Moore… is a real task master!"

"Daddy, I didn't see your truck outside."

"That's 'cause I got a new one. You probably walked right by it. Baby, I want to take you to dinner tomorrow. I'll pick you up in my shinny new truck." He got as far as the door and then turned around. "I thought I lost your mama, but I got her. She's here," Mister Lamont said and placed his hand over his heart. "I take her with me everywhere I go." He paused and smiled as he thought about his wife. Then, Mister Lamont sighed and said, "I better get to Westport. Bye."

Dagmar watched her father leave. "Jesus love me! I can't believe the change!"

"And… working with Candace?" Jane said in disbelief.

Rich smiled. "It seems like you two aren't the only miracle workers at Kane & Teasdale."

"Talia, I appreciate you hiring Daddy, but I can't allow you to support him. He's my responsibility," Dagmar said.

"This is not charity. Your father is earning his salary, and his job provides him with a sense of accomplishment. You may be pleased to know all of our employees like your father very much."

"Okay," Dagmar said, "But I insist on paying for his healthcare."

Interrupting, Xian said, "Your family is under the protection of my family. There will be no negation about that!"

"But, Xian," Dagmar continued, "I know that Rich and Talia paid for my 'buy in' at my practice. It's too much…"

"Is it?" Xian asked Dagmar. "I started life as a screaming mad child. Since I was eleven, I've been little more than a vegetable. In a few months, you've given me a life worth living. How much is that worth? I can NEVER repay you the debt I owe. Dagmar, I've thought about hiring you to be my personal therapist... no other patients. While my sister liked the idea, Rich did not. He felt it would be selfish to keep your talents all to myself."

"I never used the word 'selfish'," Rich corrected.

"No, Rich. You were more polite with your language." Turning back to Dagmar, she continued. "He also likened such a business arrangement as 'buying a friend'. While that is not my intent... it could be the result. I want you as my friend... but of your own volition."

Dagmar thought for a second and said, "Therapists aren't supposed to be friends with their patients... but after what we've been through, I can't think of you any other way. I really should pass you off to one of the other therapists."

"If you must, then do so. However, I would not prefer it."

"Okay, we'll keep things as they are for now. We'll see how it goes."

"And," Jane added, "You can come to me, Candace, or Anabelle if there's something you don't want to bring up to Dagmar or if she's unavailable."

"Thank you, Jane."

"Speaking of patients," Dagmar said to Jane, "I'd like to be more hands on when it comes to helping people... more involved."

"I guess my brother-in-law is right," Xian sighed. "I'll have to share your medical expertise with the world." Looking at the clock on the wall, Xian continued. "It's almost time. Are we ready?"

"I installed everything and tested it last night. We're ready," Rich said.

The media room at the Sedgwick house was a large, open space where their big screen television could be watched in comfort. Today, the television was going to watch back. The furniture had been pushed against the walls and only a small end table remained, which held the tablet style remote control. Rich and Talia stood facing the television while the others waited just outside the room.

Looking at the tablet, Rich said, "We have all four signals. Are you ready?"

238

"Very ready," Talia said.

Rich touched a section of the tablet and the television came to life with four live video feeds. Mr. and Mrs. Tamislav, Talia's parents, were in the upper left corner of the screen. To the right, was Talia's older sister Valentina. Below her was Talia's younger sister Aiko, and to the left of Aiko, beneath her parents, was Talia's youngest sister Rini. The entire family shared Xian's deep, black hair with only her parents showing the beginnings of some gray. Newly installed cameras allowed Rich and Talia to see everyone perfectly while all saw them on their own computers.

"Good morning everyone," Rich began. "We have something very important to discuss and we felt this would be the best way to do it."

"Make it quick, Richard," Mister Tamislav demanded. "My business day has already started."

With an angry tone, Talia said, "You will have to MAKE time for this. You may want to clear your day."

"Impossible!" Yuri Tamislav shot back.

"We shall see."

"I guarantee we won't waste your time," Rich said then called out, "Jane!"

Jane Teasdale entered the room and stood in front of the big television. "Mister Tamislav, I know you wanted me to talk to Valentina and Aiko about working together, but…"

"Father!" Aiko interrupted, "What is this?"

"Aiko! Just listen!" Talia demanded.

Jane continued, "We have a better idea. I have two people to introduce you to." Jane waved toward the door and Dagmar, wearing her most professional looking business suit, entered the room. "First, I want you to meet Doctor Dagmar Rochelle Lamont. She is one of the psychiatrists at my practice and is now a partner."

"So?" Mister Tamislav said rudely.

"So," Jane said, "I would like to show you a sample of Doctor Lamont's work," and waved at the door.

Confidently, Xian walked into the room wearing a new, black, woman's business suit with a teal blouse. She stood for several seconds while the viewers said nothing… because they did not recognize her.

Rini figured it out first. "Yeeeeeeeee! Xian?!!! Is that you?!!!"

A smile from Xian was her answer. "Hello, Rini."

"My daughter," Mrs. Tamislav whispered as shocked faces spread across all four quadrants of the television.

Talia stepped forward. "To appreciate Doctor Lamont's work, I want to show you how Xian arrived to us. A half an hour ago, a special courier dropped off a large envelope to each of you. The outside of the packet says 'Do Not Open Until Meeting.' You may open your informational packs now."

Xian watched as each family member opened the envelopes that contained photographs of scuffed skin with gravel, wood, and glass from being dragged around the compound behind a horse on the day before she returned home. They gasped at pictures of Xian's back streaked with blistering whip marks and confirmation of broken bones and long-term abuse. The family read in horror of the evidence of multiple rapes and the sexually transmitted disease she received from at least one abuser.

Valentina, normally the strongest and most stable in the family, spoke with a quivering voice. "Father… are you reading this? Are you seeing the atrocity I'm seeing?!!!"

Yuri Tamislav literally shook with anger as the words stuck in his throat. His wife managed to choke out, "We see."

Through clenched teeth, Aiko hissed, "This man must die… horribly!"

Intensely, Talia said, "For once, Aiko, you and I agree!"

"But, sister," Rini said haltingly, "How can this be? You have gone through so much in the past few years, yet you look and sound better than you EVER have!"

"There are many I have to thank. I have to thank Atsuko for telling Talia of my plight. I have Talia to thank for telling Father all I was going through when I didn't have the will or courage to speak. I have Father to thank for using his political connections to force my divorce and regain my citizenship." Xian took Dagmar's arm and brought her upfront where her family could see her. "However, I would still be as lifeless as a broken doll if it were not for Doctor Lamont."

240

All were quiet. They did not know what to say. Finally, Rini spoke up. "If no one is going to say anything, then I will. Doctor Lamont, thank…"

"No!" came the loud voice of Yuri Tamislav. Then softer, "No, my youngest. I must say this. Doctor Lamont, I don't know what you did or how you did it, but you managed to take my oldest daughter and undo the mistakes I made. I wish to formally thank you on behalf of my family, my wife Athena, and my daughters Xian, Valentina, Talia, Aiko, and Rini. And I want to give you my personal thanks."

"No thanks necessary," Dagmar said.

"Dagmar is more than my doctor," Xian added. "She is also my trusted friend. I have many more, but none as special and gifted as she."

Xian folded her hands and stepped closer to the television. "Father, I now remember my youth very clearly. I realize how difficult I was. I know you and Mother did what you thought was best for me… and later, Talia. She still holds some anger for you both… but I do not." Xian took a deep breath and said, "This family has been working at cross purposes for too long. I need the help of my family to… deal with Mister Kami for what he did to me."

"What he did to US," Aiko corrected.

"Thank you, Aiko. Do you all feel this way?" All nodded their approval. "Good," Xian said with a slight smile. "We shall all work together for this common purpose."

"Then, come back home," Mister Tamislav said. "I shall make plans to deal with Mister Kami."

"No, Father. This is now my home. My strength is here. I have met some amazing people and rediscovered an amazing sister. I wish to unify us by building trust with my family. I will hide nothing. And, in the spirit of full disclosure, I would like to tell you all that Jane has become Talia's sister."

"Xian!" Talia exclaimed.

"No, Talia. They should all know." Turning back to the video feeds, "The story is long and complex. Suffice it to say, I also consider Jane MY sister… our sister." Xian walked to Jane and embraced her. "Where once there were five, there is now six. In the coming weeks, I will explain how Jane saved Talia's life. Jane had no family… now she has us." Xian walked to Dagmar and hugged her. "Dagmar has a family which she shared with me. I feel closer to her Daddy than I do to you, Father. In that same spirit of honesty, it's something I thought you should know.  It is also important that you all know, in her capacity as a medical doctor, Dagmar saved my life.  As a psychiatrist, she gave me a life worth living.  She is a brilliant and capable woman, but if she ever needs help, my family WILL be there for her.”

Shaking her head, Dagmar said, “That’s not necessary.”

Turning back to the television, Xian added, “Her humility shames us all.  I want you ALL to meet her… soon.”  Then, Xian went to Talia.  “Look carefully at our sisters.  Do you see it?”

Through the images on the television, Talia saw very faint sparkles around them.  “When I concentrate hard… yes.  I see what you mean.”

Turning her attention to her sisters, Xian said, “Talia has a… gift for Valentina, Aiko, and Rini.

With a puzzled look on her face, Valentina asked, “What kind of gift?”

“That is all I wish to say for now.  An explanation won’t mean much.  When you come to Connecticut…”

“Just a minute,” Mister Tamislav interrupted Xian.  “We are not going to the East Coast.  I must orchestrate a response to Mister Kami!”

“Father, I have a plan.  With Talia’s help, everything is ready to implement.”

“Plan?  What plan?”

“It’s a simple concept, but complex to execute.  Father, I have discussed my idea with the three people who have the strongest and most diverse opinions; Talia, Rich, and Dagmar.  They all are in agreement with me.  This plan will ‘pay back’ Mister Kami for all he has done, prevent him from doing this to another woman, and working together, unite our family into one strong unit.”

Yuri Tamislav thought for a moment and then spoke to his middle daughter, “Talia, you would agree to work with me?  You agreed with this plan?”

Intensely, Talia said, “MY original idea was to kidnap Mister Kami and torture him to death!  Slowly.  Over several months.  However, Xian’s plan is more… practical.  It is acceptable to me.  And yes Father, I will work with you.  Will you work with me?”

“Yes… if your ideas are sound.”

Before Talia could protest, Xian spoke, "Father! That attitude is not conducive to a good working, or family, relationship! You know that Talia has been a successful businesswoman while barely trying! To be blunt, it's your rigid and predictable ways of doing business which allowed Mister Kami to cheat you!"

Mister Tamislav looked stunned. "He... cheated me?"

"Yes, and he bragged about it! I'll make a report about exactly how much you lost and email it to you."

"How can you do this?"

"I would clear the desk for my former husband, file his papers, and organize his computer. I remember all of his business information and passwords. Talia and I have remotely logged into his computers and verified his claims."

Through clenched teeth, Yuri Tamislav said, "How do you propose we crush this man?"

Xian nodded. "Very well. First, I need to dismiss all who will not be directly involved. That includes, Jane, Rich, Dagmar, and my youngest sister, Rini."

"I WANT to be involved," Rini demanded.

"I know you do," Talia said smiling. "I have a very important way that you can help. Xian's body has extensive scarring. Since you are a doctor, I want you to use your contacts and find the best plastic surgeons in the world to fix that scarring."

"Talia, I told you, that is not important!" Xian exclaimed.

"Sister, I have done everything you have asked without question. Allow me to do this one thing."

Xian sighed, "If you must..."

Talia turned to the television and said, "Rini, you will coordinate with Doctor Lamont. I will send you her cell number."

"I shall get it myself. I am only forty-five miles away and I am leaving now. Xian... I can't wait to see you!" Rini's image on the television winked out.

Xian turned to Rich and said, "Would you excuse us, please?"

Nodding, Rich said, "We'll let you know when Rini arrives." Rich, Jane, and Dagmar left the room.

Xian turned back to the screen showing her parents and siblings. "There is much to do. Talia has updated me on your organization, Father. Valentina, you travel for the company and you're currently in Paris, are you not?"

"That's correct."

"I'm recalling you." Turning to Aiko, Xian continued, "Aiko, I need you to legally change your name and procure a new passport. You will be given a traditional Japanese surname and a nom de plume as well. Not to worry. You will change your name back when we are finished."

Mister Tamislav looked angry. "And what is to happen to MY business while you co-opt my other daughters?"

"Aiko and Valentina will continue to work for you as well. However, their primary focus will be on my project. Talia and I will pick up any work they are too busy for."

"Given Talia's animosity toward me, I don't want her to know the details of my business."

With some annoyance, Talia said, "Oh, Father, PLEASE! I have been hacking your servers since I moved to Connecticut! I know your company at least as well as you do. If I wanted to do harm, I would have done it years ago."

Trying to calm her increasingly angering father, Xian said, "Allow me to give you the details of my plan to set your mind at ease."

For an hour, Xian explained what she wanted to do and all listened closely. Any concern raised was quickly quelled. All contingencies were accounted for by Xian.

As the proposal was finishing, Dagmar poked her head in the room and said, "Excuse me, but your sister Rini has just arrived."

Xian motioned Dagmar to enter, then turned to her family on the television screen. "I must see my youngest. You all have enough to do to get started."

Grumbling, Mister Tamislav said, "I am still uncomfortable about giving up so much control over my company."

His wife, Athena, who had been listening by her husband's side and rereading Xian's medical records, spoke up. "Yuri! Hush! Xian, you will receive your father's full cooperation."

"Thank you, Mother. Thank you all. We shall set up another meeting tomorrow." Xian shut off the television and the images went away.

"Sounds like you had an intensive meeting," Dagmar observed. "I hope you'll have time to continue our sessions."

Xian smiled, "Our sessions are very important. However, it's more important that I have you as my friend… and my confidant."

Talia said, "Would you tell Rini we'll be out shortly? There is one quick thing I must cover with my sister."

As Dagmar left, Talia said, "Xian, you now share my ability to 'read' people. The one person I cannot read is my husband. It is actually exciting and elating because he surprises me constantly, however… he IS a man, and he seems to enjoy the attention of other women…"

Xian smiled, "And you want me to tell you how Rich feels about you? He has seen the dark side of you lately. I know you try to suppress it, but you haven't been doing a good job. I would forego any more talk of revenge and torture in his presence. By the time you reach your eighth month of pregnancy I will easily be able to carry out our plan alone. You have a far more important job. You are to bring two more beautiful children into the world. Assure me you will place all your focus on that task."

"I shall," Talia replied. "But, sister, you have not answered the question that you know is in my heart."

"My dearest Talia, your husband is a natural 'flirt' as is his friend Jane. But when I look at them both, I see a rich core of loyalty. Yes, his ego likes the attention of other woman, but he doesn't take it seriously. The most important things in his life are you and his children. Talia, he is yours, and only yours… forever."

"Thank you, my eldest."

"You should feel a little ego boost yourself! This man who is attractive to so many women is only interested in you!"

"Yes, Jane has told me that, but I feel better hearing it from you."

Xian opened her arms and Talia walked into her embrace. She kissed Talia on the cheek and said, "Now come! I am anxious to see our youngest sibling!"

As the two sisters left the media room they walked to the foyer and stood for a minute. They watched as Jane, Rich, and Rini played with the delighted baby George being held by Dagmar. George reached for Rini who pushed her face toward his hand. He touched his aunt's cheek lightly, then leaned back, looked at Dagmar, and waved his arms. She hugged him as George wrapped his arms around her neck.

Xian whispered to Talia, "Your son doesn't just love Dagmar; he trusts her. Despite the difference in their ages, they will be good and true friends." Talia could not suppress a tear rolling down her cheek. "Talia, you're upset?" Xian stared at Talia and read her emotions. "Talia! First you doubt your husband's feelings for you. Now you doubt your child's feelings?" Taking Talia's face in her hands, Xian placed her forehead against her sister's forehead. "Talia, feel what I feel."

It was all there for Talia to see.

The deep, unflagging love Rich has for her and her alone.

The love Jaynette has for Talia and the childhood similarities they share that strengthens their bond.

George's absolute joy at seeing all of his uncles and aunts. His feeling of love and trust for Dagmar. But there is a special place in his heart for his father, who provides strength and security... and mother, who provides him with love and serenity. The fact that Talia had such a chaotic mind for most of her life and now is a source of peace for her son, fills her heart with joy.

Then, Talia feels the love Xian has for her. She feels Xian's eagerness to put her ex-husband behind her so that she can become the daughter, the sister, the aunt, the sister in-law, the friend, and the woman, she was meant to be.

246

Talia leaned back from Xian. There was now a clearness in her eyes and a confidence in her smile. "Thank you," Talia whispered. The two sisters stood side by side with their arms around each other's waist as they watched everyone play with George.

Out of the corner of her eye, Rini caught a glimpse of her two sisters smiling at her. She took three slow steps and bolted to Xian with a force that almost knocked her over. Rini pushed the hair from her sister's face. "I can't believe it," she whispered to her older sister.

"It's me, Rini… the REAL me."

"All those things… did they really happen to you?"

"Yes, but I'd rather think about the future with my family and friends."

Nodding, Rini said, "Of course. Xian, you know that I'm a surgeon. Later, I'd like to see your scarring."

"Rini…"

"Xian will cooperate," Talia interrupted. "I won't rest until every sign of that man is gone from this world… especially the marks he left on our sister."

"Xian, it IS a way I can help. And I want very much to help," Rini said compassionately.

Sighing, "You're both right. But it can wait for now. I want to spend time with my baby sister."

"Xian," Talia said, "Maybe we can give her the gift now."

"I need no present. Having my eldest sister whole is gift enough."

"May I?" Xian asked Talia.

Talia nodded and Xian began threading her fingers through Rini's jet-black hair. Motioning for Dagmar to join them, Talia said to Rini, "I have this 'second sight' and as I was hugging my daughter, I accidentally unlocked it in her. Then, I unlocked it in Xian."

Xian finally worked her hand to touch Rini's scalp. Rini felt a tingle in her brain and a moment of dizziness. As Dagmar approached them, Xian said, "Now, Rini, concentrate. Meet the REAL Dagmar Lamont."

Rini gasped as she looked at the images overlaid on top of Dagmar. The words of a thousand books hovered over her head, belying her intelligence. The armor she wore showed she was a warrior. The wings behind her showed she was an angel. And, on top of it all, a warm red glow made her seem that she was all heart. There was a seam… a scar on her heart. Dagmar had suffered a big loss recently that she is trying to heal. In a moment, Rini knew everything important about Dagmar."

"Glorious!" Rini whispered.

# *Chapter Thirty-Three*

# Phoenix

Eleven months and an odd number of days have passed since Xian's first video meeting with her parents and sisters.

Much has happened in those months.

In Japan, everything was quiet in Mister Kami's compound. The gardens, which had been so beautifully tended, were now overgrown. The only sound in the stables was the occasional banging of a wooden pen door. The horses and stable hands were gone along with the gardeners. None of the expensive security guards were on the property. The staff had been reduced to less than one quarter of its size from just a year ago.

The halls of the great house seemed desolate due to the absence of most of the maids and the presence of a fine layer of dust. As Mister Kami walked through one of the barren corridors, he passed by his sister's room and noticed the door was open. He saw Kamiko lying half naked on the floor mumbling to herself as her cheek rested in a puddle of her own vomit. Mister Kami paused to look at his sister. He had seen her like this often of late. Cleaning up Kamiko had become a nauseating, exhausting, and fruitless task that he could no longer stomach.

To clear the stench of his sister's room from his nose, Mister Kami walked outside to the weed filled gardens. All was quiet except for the faint sound of giggling. Following the sound, he discovered his son, Kichirou lying in the garden with a silly grin on his face. His sleeves were rolled up exposing numerous track marks on each arm. A small stream of blood was drying from a fresh injection site. The father spoke his son's name but the only response he got was more giggling.

Sighing, Mister Kami went to his office. He called his remaining accountant and financial adviser, but slammed the phone on the desk as they gave him more bad news. His partners were breaking deals with him, reneging on payments, and letting contracts lapse without renewal.

All of the familiar staff was gone to be replaced by fewer and newer, less expensive employees. Even his doctor and The Twins were gone due to late and partial paychecks.

A young man, part of the new and unfamiliar staff, knocked on the office door.

"Excuse me, Mister Kami, you have a visitor who wishes to talk to you."

Mister Kami looked at the servant with tired eyes and said, "Tell him to make an appointment."

"It is a woman with two aides. She says she has a solution to all of your problems. The woman wanted me to tell you that she is… Black Lotus."

Kami's eyes widened. He had heard of a mysterious and talented Japanese-based businesswoman who was buying and selling companies worldwide at a rapid pace. "Black Lotus," he whispered. "Send her in, but keep her 'aides' outside."

The young man bowed and left the room. Moments later, two large and imposing men wearing dark suits walked into the office dragging the young servant with them. "I'm sorry, Mister Kami! I could not stop them!"

A woman appeared in the doorway wearing a black hooded kimono and black leather gloves. She had a messenger bag over one shoulder and a black veil obscured her face. It looked like death itself just walked into the room. Speaking in English, the woman said, "My guards do not leave my side. If you don't wish to speak to me, I will gladly leave and watch your business, and your life, crumble.”

Mister Kami motioned for his servant to leave. When the guards released him, the young man ran out of the office. “Have a seat… Black Lotus,” Mister Kami offered in English.

“No,” she said succinctly as she walked to his desk. Slowly, she raised her veil and pulled back her hood. The woman seemed familiar to Mister Kami, but he did not recognize her. Smirking, she said, “I want an unobstructed view of your face. In case you’re too dim to figure it out, I and my associates are responsible for your problems.”

With a questioning look on his face, Mister Kami asked, “Do I know you?”

“We met long ago, but you don’t know me.”

“Who… are you?!”

“My nom de plume is Black Lotus. My legal name is… unimportant. But, my birth name is… Aiko Tamislav! There is someone who wants to speak to you.” Taking a tablet computer from her messenger bag, Aiko tapped a few virtual buttons and turned the screen around to show Xian looking calm, rested and healthy, sitting behind a desk.

“Hello, my former husband,” Xian said with a smile.

Raising his eyebrows, Mister Kami said, “Xian! I almost didn’t recognize you.”

“How have you been, Masaru?”

“You know that I hate being called Masaru.”

Still smiling, Xian said, “I will call you whatever I please… and my question was rhetorical. I know how you’ve been… exactly how you’ve been. You look surprised.”

“I am. You look very different. What happened?”

“My sister Talia and her husband found a talented psychiatrist who helped me with the trauma I suffered during our marriage.”

Now smiling, Mister Kami said, “And, you expect me to believe that YOU orchestrated the decline in business I’ve had?”

"My sisters all have amazing gifts. I never had a gift until now. It seems I am a natural leader with an excellent memory. I'm also a quick study. My father and sisters have all complimented me on how easily I've learned the workings of the business world. I want you to know that it is the business I set up in Japan, with my own money, that is ruining your life."

"You mean money you took from your family."

Xian laughed. "My family became partners after I started my business. However, you are right. I did not have cash to start my company. However, I did have collateral." She took an item off of her desk and held it between her thumb and forefinger close to the camera. Mister Kami recognized it as the large and expensive gold wedding band that he had burned into her finger. "I wanted the one thing of monetary value I got from you to be instrumental in your downfall."

"So, this is some sort of revenge?"

"Revenge?" Xian repeated. "No. What Talia wanted to do to you was revenge. Be glad I interceded. What she would have done to your ears alone…" Xian said and shivered. "Let's just call this… payback. How are Kamiko and Kichirou doing?"

Now visibly angry, "What have you done to them?!!!" Mister Kami demanded.

"I have done nothing to them. However, I might have an idea as to why they are little more than lifeless corpses. You see, I went to pay my respects to the families your former wives. You know them, the wealthy families who make their money trafficking drugs… allegedly. I told them the truth about how their Columbian sister and Sicilian daughter lived their life in your house, how they died, and who was responsible. Naturally, they wanted to do some horrible things to Kamiko, Kichirou, and you… however, I was able to talk them out of such a barbaric revenge that could eventually be traced back to them. I don't know exactly what they did but I might have let it slip that Kamiko and Kichirou are recreational drug users. My guess is that your son and sister found a very cheap supply of drugs. Very cheap. Very powerful. Highly concentrated to make them very addictive. I would assume that even the more benign drugs would be spiked with opiates. Again, I did not do any of this myself. I merely showed the still grieving families an Achilles heel. Of course, you weren't affected by allegedly adulterated drugs because you had your own personal supplier… your family doctor. You remember him. He's the one who gave me my unwanted tubal ligation. My company hired him away from you. We set him up to dole out prescription drugs, for recreation, to a detective. He is now in prison. How is life without your stamina enhancing drugs, Masaru?"

"You BITCH! How could you have done all this?!!!"

"Easier than I thought it would be. Even though you change your passwords regularly, Talia and I installed 'backdoors' and hacked your computers. We have all the records of all the businessmen you've cheated. They were more than happy to do business with ME as long as it would hurt YOU! You might be interested to know that many of the smaller businesses you sold to raise capital were bought by me and sold at a huge profit to companies in the People's Republic of China. I know how much you hate the Chinese. They now have a bigger foothold in Japan... thanks to you."

Xian paused for a moment and said, "Masaru, where are your manners? You haven't asked about me and my loved ones yet! Well, Talia had twins; a boy and a girl. They are delightful and I am a very proud aunt! As you know, I can't have children, but I'm having a wonderful time spoiling my nieces and nephews. My father is pretty much retired. For all intents and purposes, I own and run his company. Two of my beautiful and talented sisters, including the one in front of you, are making more money than ever and having a great time while two others are doctors... a surgeon and a psychiatrist. Talia has her own business and we work together as much as possible. I now have many new friends including the therapist who chased away the cloud I used to protect my sanity from you and your retched family."

Baring his teeth in a sadistic smile, Mister Kami spoke with venom in every word. "You think you are clever! Had you not thought that I might have secret resources that are not recorded in my computer? Now that I know who has been attacking me, and how you've done it, I'll be able to use my hidden reserves to rebuild my empire. Once I'm strong again, I'll go after you, your family, your friends, and especially that therapist you like so much!"

Mister Kami was distracted by Aiko, who failed to suppress her laughter. "You shouldn't have said that," Aiko chuckled.

Looking back at the tablet screen Aiko was holding, Mister Kami saw Xian smiling, too.

"Your 'secret resources'? You mean the gold in your vault?" Xian asked as the blood drained from Mister Kami's face. "I know you've been using it to make some bold, if unsuccessful, business moves. I calculate you have about one third of your reserve left. It is still enough to mount a successful comeback. I would imagine you might be able to scrounge up some unsuspecting people to do business with... but you aren't going to get the chance. I have alerted the police and the military. They are on their way to raid your home as we speak. They were very interested when I told them earlier today about your gold... your Nazi gold! Gold stolen from Jews all over the world, melted into bars embossed with an eagle and Swastika. My dear ex-husband… you've just become a war criminal!"

"Xian, you have to stop this! I'll do anything… ANYTHING if you stop all this!!!"

Xian snapped her fingers as if she just remembered something. "Masaru, I forgot to tell you one other thing about me. I never had a middle name. In the year I've been away from you, I've given myself one. I am now, Xian Phoenix Tamislav. Like the Phoenix, I have risen from the ashes to be born anew! I am the Phoenix… and you are a toothless old dog."

Tears were now in Mister Kami's eyes. "P… Please, Xian! I'm begging you! Have mercy!"

After a second or two, Xian called to her sister, "Aiko." Aiko turned the tablet so the camera was facing her. "You may give him the package." Aiko took a box out of her messenger bag and placed it on the edge of Mister Kami's desk, just out of easy reach. She turned the tablet back toward him and Xian spoke to Mister Kami for the last time. "Inside that gift wrapped box is the key to ending your problems. If you use it, you will not be arrested. I will stop my attack on your company and your family. If you do NOT use what I gave you, you be arrested in minutes and I will go after what's left of your family and turn that wretched home of yours into rubble! The choice is yours. Aiko!" Aiko looked at Xian's image on the tablet. "You've done an excellent job. I'm very proud of you. Come home, my dear sister. Destroy the tablet and leave immediately!"

Mister Kami jumped as Aiko smashed the tablet computer on the corner of his desk. She turned to leave, paused, then turned back and spit in Mister Kami's face. She then signaled her guards and all left the office.

Mister Kami sat alone in shock for several minutes trying to absorb the nightmare he just experienced. The only thing that snapped him out of his haze was the sounds of sirens from outside. True to her word, Xian had told the local police and the military exactly where to find his illegal gold reserve. He looked at the gift-wrapped present. Mister Kami leaned over his desk, grabbed the package, and began ripping off the paper exposing a beautiful leather covered box. He had no idea what could possibly be in this box that would keep him from being arrested. He snapped open the clasp and opened the lid to see a gleaming, expensive ceremonial knife with one word emblazoned on the inside cover of the box. "Seppuku"!

Thank you for reading

## Broken Dolls

For more about the past of these characters see

## Confidant Trilogy